Billions Fueling Chaos

"The only thing necessary for the triumph of evil is for good men to do nothing."

— Edmund

Table of Contents

The Secret Hand

Chapter 1: Shadows of the Past

1. The Mysterious Letter

The rain drummed steadily against the windowpane as Alex Reed sat hunched over his desk, the dim light casting shadows across a cluttered expanse of papers. It was the kind of night that encouraged reflection, and the weight of his recent investigation hung heavy in the air. He had always been drawn to mysteries, the thrill of unraveling tangled threads of deception. But tonight felt different. Tonight, something was waiting to be uncovered.

He had received the letter a few days earlier, slipped under his office door in an unmarked envelope. Its contents were unsettling—typed, with no return address, yet the words resonated with an eerie familiarity. "They are watching you," it read, followed by a cryptic phrase: "The past holds the key." Alex's mind raced, connecting dots he had yet to see. Who sent this? And what did it mean?

The note gnawed at him, invading his thoughts like an uninvited guest. He picked it up again, the paper cool between his fingers, and scrutinized every word. There was no signature, no clue to the identity of the sender, but the urgency pulsed beneath the surface. Whoever it was clearly knew more than they let on.

His instincts urged him to dig deeper. The "they" in the letter could refer to the very organization he had been investigating—a powerful syndicate known for its ruthless tactics and iron grip on the city's underbelly. Could they be aware of his probing? A chill ran down his spine. If they were, he needed to tread carefully. He couldn't let them anticipate his next move.

In the hours that followed, he combed through old case files, searching for anything that might connect to the ominous message. Names and dates blurred together in a haze of frustration until one name stood out: Isabelle Hart. A former journalist who had gone missing under suspicious circumstances a year ago, her story echoed in the minds of many, a haunting reminder of the dangers lurking in their world.

Alex's instincts told him that Isabelle might have stumbled onto something significant before her disappearance. A hasty decision led him to her last known location, a small café on the outskirts of town where she had often met informants. The air was thick with anticipation as he walked through the door, the bell chiming lightly above him. He scanned the room, searching for a hint, a whisper of her presence.

The barista, a woman in her thirties with tired eyes, recognized him. "You're looking for Isabelle, aren't you?" she asked, her voice low. It was more a statement than a question, and Alex felt the weight of her gaze.

"Yes," he replied, trying to mask his urgency. "I need to know what happened to her. Did she mention anything... unusual?"

The barista hesitated, glancing around as if checking for eavesdroppers. "She was nervous. Kept talking about a big story she was chasing. Something about a connection between the syndicate and a high-ranking official. She believed she was onto something huge."

"Did she say who her sources were?" Alex pressed, his pulse quickening.

"Only that she had a meeting lined up. Then, she vanished." The barista's expression shifted to one of concern. "You need to be careful. If you're looking into this, you could be in danger too."

Alex nodded, the gravity of her words sinking in. "I appreciate the warning. I just— I need to find out what happened."

As he left the café, the rain had turned to a drizzle, and the streets glistened under the soft glow of streetlights. The letter weighed heavily in his pocket, an ever-present reminder of the lurking threat. It was clear that someone didn't want him digging too deep, but he couldn't turn back now. He had to follow this lead, no matter where it might take him.

The days that followed were a blur of interviews, late nights, and clandestine meetings. Each piece of information felt like a breadcrumb leading him deeper into a dark forest of conspiracy. He learned that Isabelle had indeed been close to revealing something monumental, but her investigation had drawn too much attention.

In his pursuit of the truth, Alex began receiving strange phone calls—static-filled voices warning him to stop. He ignored them, fueled by a mix of fear and determination. The deeper he delved, the more he felt the shadows closing in. He had to be smart; he had to play the game.

Then, one fateful evening, he received a tip-off. An anonymous source claimed to have information on Isabelle's last moments. "Meet me at the old pier, midnight. Bring no one." The message sent a shiver down his spine. It was exactly the kind of dangerous encounter he had been anticipating.

As he approached the pier, the moon hung low, casting an ethereal glow over the water. Each step felt weighted with the significance of the moment. Would he finally uncover the truth? Or would this meeting seal his fate?

A figure emerged from the shadows, cloaked in darkness. Alex's heart raced as he prepared himself for whatever revelation lay ahead. The mysterious letter and Isabelle's fate intertwined, leading him to a confrontation that would change everything.

"Who are you?" he demanded, the tension palpable.

The figure stepped closer, a glint of recognition in their eyes. "I'm someone who knows what really happened."

And just like that, the game changed. The pieces were in motion, and Alex was about to find out how deep the rabbit hole really went.

2. Echoes of a Forgotten Life

The rain fell softly against the windowpane, creating a rhythm that echoed the memories swirling in Alex's mind. He stared blankly at the faded photographs scattered across his desk, each one a portal to a past he had tried to forget. A mix of nostalgia and pain washed over him as he picked up a picture of his childhood home—a quaint little house on the outskirts of the city. It looked so different now, abandoned and overrun with weeds, just like the memories he had buried deep within himself.

Growing up, Alex had always known his family carried secrets. Whispers followed them, cloaked in shadows and half-truths. His father, a once-respected lawyer, had fallen from grace, ensnared in a web of corruption that would eventually lead to his downfall. Alex could still recall the hushed conversations between his parents late at night, their voices tense and worried. They never told him what was happening, but the fear in their eyes spoke volumes.

Years passed, and the echoes of those days lingered in his mind. As he delved deeper into his father's past, he discovered a world filled with deceit and power struggles. His father had become embroiled in a case that spiraled out of control, a high-profile trial that exposed the dark underbelly of their city. With each revelation, Alex felt the weight of his lineage pressing down on him, a burden he could neither escape nor embrace.

He spent countless nights at the local library, pouring over old newspaper articles, desperately piecing together the fragments of a life that had been torn apart. Each article told a story of greed, betrayal, and broken promises. The powerful figures involved were untouchable, their names synonymous with success, while his father was left as the scapegoat, a cautionary tale of what could happen when one dared to challenge the status quo.

As Alex navigated through this labyrinth of information, he found himself drawn to a particular name that kept resurfacing: Veronica Sterling. She was a formidable attorney, known for her ruthless tactics and unyielding ambition. Reports suggested she had orchestrated the downfall of many, leaving a trail of ruined lives in her wake. The more he read about her, the more Alex felt a strange kinship. She had been a driving force in the very case that had shattered his family. But why had she done it? What had motivated her to destroy his father?

Determined to find answers, Alex began to dig deeper. He reached out to former colleagues of his father, hoping to uncover the truth behind their shared history. Each conversation revealed new layers of complexity. Some spoke of a rivalry, a feud that had simmered beneath the surface, while others hinted at a more sinister connection—one that suggested his father had been privy to secrets that were never meant to see the light of day.

The deeper he delved, the more he uncovered the undercurrents of corruption that flowed through the city like a poison. Powerful men and women were willing to go to great lengths to protect their interests, and in that world, loyalty was a currency that could be bought and sold. Alex began to realize that he was not just a passive observer; he was part of this narrative, a player in a game that had long since left the confines of his father's life.

It was a rainy evening when he finally found himself standing before the dilapidated remains of his childhood home. The once vibrant walls now loomed like ghosts, whispering secrets he had yet to uncover. With a heavy heart, he pushed open the creaking door and stepped inside, the familiar scent of damp wood and dust wrapping around him. Each step echoed through the empty halls, a reminder of laughter and love that had once filled the space.

As he explored the remnants of his past, he stumbled upon a hidden compartment in the floorboards. Inside, he found a collection of letters, meticulously preserved but yellowed with age. They were addressed to his father, penned by Veronica Sterling herself. His hands trembled as he unfolded the first letter, the elegant script revealing a complex dance of admiration and manipulation.

Each letter detailed their tumultuous relationship, a blend of professional rivalry and personal intrigue. Veronica had once seen potential in his father, a brilliance that she wanted to harness. But as ambition clouded her judgment, the line between ally and enemy blurred, leading to a catastrophic fallout. Alex felt a mixture of anger and sadness as he realized the extent of the betrayal—a betrayal that had not only cost his father his career but had also shattered their family.

Days turned into weeks as Alex grappled with the revelations. He found himself haunted by the echoes of a forgotten life, the choices made by those before him reverberating through his own existence. But with each new discovery, he felt a growing resolve. The time had come to confront the shadows of the past, to challenge the powerful forces that had dictated his family's fate.

He reached out to those who had known Veronica, gathering information and seeking to understand her motivations. It became clear that she was not merely a villain in his father's story; she was a product of a system that rewarded ruthlessness. The more he learned, the more he recognized the cyclical nature of power and corruption.

One evening, as he sat alone in his apartment, Alex made a decision. He would confront Veronica Sterling, not just for his father, but for himself. He needed to understand why the echoes of the past continued to shape his present. The journey ahead would not be easy, but he felt a stirring within—a desire to reclaim his narrative, to rewrite the story that had been handed down to him.

With newfound determination, Alex began crafting a plan. He would gather evidence, compile testimonies, and prepare himself for the confrontation that awaited him. He understood the risks involved; powerful individuals were not accustomed to being challenged, especially by someone with his history. Yet, the pull of justice was too strong to ignore.

As the date of the meeting approached, Alex felt a mixture of apprehension and excitement. He had spent countless hours preparing for this moment, and yet, doubt crept in. What if Veronica was more formidable than he anticipated? What if she dismissed him as just another pawn in her elaborate game?

But deep down, he knew he had to face her. The shadows of the past could no longer dictate his future. With each passing moment, he felt the weight of his family's legacy resting on his shoulders. He was no longer just Alex, the son of a fallen lawyer. He was determined to become a force of change, a voice for those who had been silenced.

The night before their meeting, he reflected on everything he had uncovered—the secrets, the betrayals, the echoes that had haunted him for so long. He felt a sense of clarity wash over him. The truth was messy, complicated, and often painful, but it was also liberating. He was ready to face Veronica Sterling and, in doing so, confront the ghosts of his past.

When the day finally arrived, Alex stood outside her office, the towering glass building a stark contrast to the memories he carried with him. Taking a deep breath, he stepped inside, determined to reclaim his narrative and seek the answers he had longed for. The echoes of a forgotten life had brought him here, and he was ready to confront them head-on.

3. A Case Reopened

The office was dimly lit, with shadows creeping across the walls like whispered secrets. Detective Clara Evans leaned back in her chair, staring at the case file spread out before her. Dust motes danced in the single beam of light filtering through the grimy window, illuminating the faded photographs and yellowed documents that spoke of a life once vibrant but now reduced to a mere collection of memories and unsolved mysteries.

It had been nearly a decade since the infamous Wren murder case had gone cold, leaving a trail of unanswered questions and a community on edge. Clara had been a rookie back then, eager to prove herself in the gritty world of criminal investigations. The case had gripped the city, but ultimately, it had slipped through her fingers like sand. Now, with a new piece of evidence surfacing, the case had unexpectedly been reopened, reigniting old wounds and sparking curiosity in a town desperate for closure.

She picked up a photograph of the victim, Anna Wren, a bright-eyed journalist with dreams of changing the world through her words. Clara had followed Anna's story closely, having admired her tenacity and passion. Anna's life had been cut tragically short, her body discovered in a rundown motel on the outskirts of town, a place that seemed to have been forgotten by time. The circumstances surrounding her death were murky at best. Clara remembered the whispers in the precinct—theories about her involvement in something far bigger than a simple murder, something that might have put her in the crosshairs of those with power.

Clara's fingers traced the outline of the photograph. There was something unsettling about the way Anna looked, frozen in time. Her smile seemed to hide secrets, and Clara couldn't shake the feeling that there was more to the story than anyone had uncovered. It was as if Anna had been warning them, urging them to dig deeper, to unravel the tangled threads of deceit that bound her life and death together.

The call from her superior had come as a surprise. "Clara, we need you back on this," he had said, his voice grave. "We've received new evidence—an anonymous tip pointing to a witness who claims to have seen something the night Anna died."

Clara had felt a surge of adrenaline as she grabbed her coat, determination coursing through her veins. It was time to revisit the past, to confront the demons that had haunted her since that fateful day. She gathered the case files, her heart racing as she thought about what she might uncover. Would this new lead bring justice for Anna, or would it open a Pandora's box of danger and betrayal?

The witness, a man named Tom, was a local bartender who claimed to have seen Anna arguing with a stranger outside the motel. Clara had a gut feeling about him—his disheveled appearance and the haunted look in his eyes spoke of a man who had seen too much and was ready to speak. As she entered the dimly lit bar, the familiar smell of stale beer and regret hit her, and she approached the counter where Tom was polishing glasses.

"Detective Evans," she introduced herself, and Tom looked up, his expression a mix of recognition and apprehension. "I'm here to talk about Anna Wren."

Tom's face fell, and Clara noticed his hands tremble slightly. "I didn't mean to get involved," he stammered. "I just want to forget what I saw."

"Tom," Clara urged gently, "what you know could help solve this case. Anna deserves justice."

He sighed, the weight of his decision evident. "Fine. I'll tell you what I saw, but you need to understand—I didn't want to get dragged into this."

As Tom recounted his account of that night, Clara felt the familiar rush of adrenaline. The pieces of the puzzle were starting to fit together, but with each detail, a dark cloud of danger loomed overhead. Tom spoke of a tall man, well-dressed, who had been shouting at Anna, his voice rising above the distant sounds of the city. Clara listened intently, her mind racing with possibilities. Who was this man? Why had he confronted Anna?

But as Tom spoke, Clara noticed something else in his eyes—fear. The kind of fear that gnawed at a person's soul, that made them look over their shoulder even in the safety of daylight. "I saw him leave with her," Tom admitted, his voice barely above a whisper. "But I didn't know who he was. I didn't think it was serious. It was just an argument."

Clara's heart pounded in her chest. "Do you remember anything else? A name? A car?"

Tom shook his head, visibly agitated. "No, but I heard them mention a company. Something about funding. It didn't make sense then, but now... I can't help but wonder."

"Funding?" Clara repeated, jotting down notes furiously. "What kind of funding?"

"Something big," he replied, his brow furrowing. "I overheard them talking about a project, something that had a lot of money behind it. That's all I know."

As she left the bar, Clara felt a sense of urgency. The more she dug into Anna's life, the more she realized that the murder might have been linked to something much larger than a simple crime of passion. She had to find out what Anna was involved in. Who was this man Tom had seen? And what was this mysterious project that seemed to hover like a specter over Anna's final days?

Returning to her office, Clara pored over Anna's articles, looking for clues. She discovered a series of investigative pieces on corporate corruption, environmental violations, and a potential scandal involving a powerful local businessman named Victor Hargrove. Hargrove's name had been mentioned in the context of several unsolved cases, a shadowy figure who seemed untouchable, protected by his wealth and influence.

Could Anna have been on the brink of exposing something that Hargrove was desperate to keep hidden? The thought sent chills down Clara's spine. She had always suspected that Anna's murder was not just a random act of violence but a deliberate attempt to silence her. Now, with this new evidence, Clara felt the stakes rising.

As she began to piece together the connections, the telephone rang, jolting her from her thoughts. It was her partner, Jake. "Clara, you're not going to believe this," he said, urgency lacing his voice. "We've got another lead. A connection between Hargrove and the funding Tom mentioned."

"Tell me everything," Clara demanded, her heart racing once more.

As Jake delved into the details, Clara's mind raced with the possibilities. This was more than a simple murder case; it was the beginning of a complex web of deception, greed, and power. With every layer they peeled back, the darkness loomed larger, and Clara knew she was venturing into dangerous territory.

But Anna had been a fighter, and Clara was determined to honor her memory. It was time to confront the shadows, to seek justice not only for Anna but for all those who had been silenced by the machinations of those in power. The case was reopened, and with it, a chance to uncover the truth—no matter the cost.

4. The First Clue

In the dim light of his cluttered office, Prosecutor Alex Reeve sat hunched over a stack of case files, the scent of old paper mingling with the bitterness of cold coffee. The clock ticked softly, each second echoing the mounting pressure he felt. The recent spike in organized crime had rattled the city, leaving a trail of fear and chaos. As the lead prosecutor, Alex knew it was his responsibility to bring the perpetrators to justice, but the deeper he delved into the cases, the more he realized that the truth was buried beneath layers of deception.

His gaze fell on a particular file that had been gathering dust in the corner of his desk. It contained details about a series of unsolved murders that had occurred over the past year, all linked to a shadowy figure known only as "The Benefactor." Rumors swirled about this person—some said they were a philanthropic millionaire, while others whispered of a ruthless crime lord pulling strings from the shadows. What intrigued Alex most was the suggestion that these murders were not random acts of violence but rather deliberate messages meant to send a chilling warning.

As he flipped through the file, a newspaper clipping caught his eye. It featured a wealthy businessman who had been found dead in his penthouse, a high-profile figure with ties to both legitimate enterprises and the underworld. The article mentioned an anonymous tip received by the police, hinting at a connection to The Benefactor. Curiosity piqued, Alex decided to dig deeper. He felt a spark of intuition—this might be the first clue that would lead him to the heart of the mystery.

With a renewed sense of purpose, Alex spent the next few days tracking down leads. He interviewed witnesses, sifted through financial records, and examined connections between the victims. Each discovery only fueled his determination to uncover the truth.

However, the deeper he went, the more obstacles he faced. It seemed as if someone was deliberately trying to obscure the path.

One evening, while poring over financial statements in the dim glow of his desk lamp, he stumbled upon a series of transactions that stood out. They were unusually large sums of money, transferred to various shell companies with no clear purpose. One name kept reappearing: Victor Kline, a notorious figure in the city's underbelly, known for his ruthless business tactics. Alex felt a chill run down his spine. Could Kline be connected to The Benefactor?

Feeling the urgency of his findings, Alex arranged a meeting with his trusted partner, Detective Sarah Miles. He respected her instinct and sharp mind, and they had successfully cracked numerous cases together. As they sat in a small café, the atmosphere buzzed with the chatter of patrons, but Alex was oblivious to it all, his mind racing with possibilities.

"Sarah," he said, leaning forward, "I think I've found something significant. It revolves around Kline and a series of suspicious transactions linked to The Benefactor."

She raised an eyebrow, intrigued. "What do you have?"

Alex explained the connections he had unearthed, outlining the money trails and the victims who had crossed paths with Kline. Sarah listened intently, her expression shifting from curiosity to concern as he spoke.

"Be careful, Alex. Kline isn't just a businessman; he's dangerous. If he catches wind of your investigation, it could get ugly," she warned, her voice low.

"I know," he replied, determination lacing his tone. "But if we don't act now, we may lose our chance to catch whoever is behind this. I need to confront Kline and see what he knows."

Sarah hesitated. "We should gather more evidence first. Let's not tip him off until we're ready."

Alex nodded reluctantly, understanding her caution but feeling the urgency pressing down on him. They decided to watch Kline's movements, hoping to find more leads. As the days turned into weeks, they gathered intelligence, all while navigating the labyrinth of deceit surrounding them.

One fateful night, their efforts paid off. An informant, a small-time criminal with connections to Kline, agreed to meet them in a secluded alley. As they waited, tension hung in the air, thick enough to cut with a knife. The city felt alive around them, yet they were ensconced in their bubble of anticipation and dread.

The informant, a scrappy man with a shifty demeanor, arrived moments later. He glanced around nervously before leaning closer. "I've got information about Kline and The Benefactor," he whispered, glancing over his shoulder.

"What do you know?" Alex pressed, heart racing.

"Kline's been moving money for someone big—someone who's been pulling strings behind the scenes. They're planning something massive, and it involves wiping out anyone who stands in their way," the informant said, his voice trembling.

"Wiping out? What do you mean?" Sarah interjected, sensing the gravity of the situation.

"The Benefactor isn't just a name; it's a code. They're setting up a major operation, and Kline's in deep. If you want to stop this, you need to act fast. There's a shipment coming in next week that could change everything," he explained, eyes wide with fear.

Alex exchanged glances with Sarah, the weight of the informant's words sinking in. "Where's it coming from?" he demanded.

"From overseas. I don't know the details, but I heard it's tied to Kline's connections in Europe. They're making a move that could shake the city to its core," the informant replied, his voice barely above a whisper.

As the informant shared more details, Alex felt a sense of urgency wash over him. They had a lead—something tangible to follow. But as he prepared to ask for more information, the sound of approaching footsteps interrupted their conversation. Alex's instincts kicked in, and he grabbed Sarah's arm, pulling her back into the shadows just as two figures emerged from the alley.

"Did you see him?" one man said, voice low and menacing.

"Yeah, he was here. Let's find him," the other replied, a hint of impatience in his tone.

Alex's heart raced as he realized they were Kline's men. Their informant's face paled as he realized the danger he was in. Without thinking, Alex pulled Sarah away, leading them through the maze of alleyways, their hearts pounding in unison.

Once they reached the safety of the streetlights, they paused to catch their breath. "We need to get back to the office and secure this information," Alex said, adrenaline coursing through his veins. "If we can confirm the shipment and its purpose, we might finally have the evidence we need to take Kline down."

Sarah nodded, her expression serious. "Let's get to work. We can't let this opportunity slip away."

As they drove back to the office, the weight of the informant's revelation settled over them like a shroud. They were stepping into dangerous territory, but with each piece of evidence they uncovered, the possibility of exposing The Benefactor grew closer. In the world they were navigating, danger lurked at every corner, but so did the truth—a truth that might change everything.

Back in the office, Alex and Sarah pored over the informant's information, cross-referencing it with their existing data. They worked tirelessly, fueled by coffee and the desire for justice. Every hour that ticked by felt like a countdown, intensifying their urgency.

As dawn broke, painting the sky with hues of pink and gold, they finally pieced together a clearer picture. The shipment was set to arrive at a secluded dock, a location that Kline used for illicit dealings. With this knowledge, they could orchestrate a sting operation, but they had to act swiftly and strategically.

"Let's get a team together and move," Alex said, determination etched on his face. "This could be our chance to finally unravel the web of deceit that surrounds Kline and The Benefactor."

As they prepared to face whatever lay ahead, Alex couldn't shake the feeling that they were on the precipice of something monumental. The first clue had set them on a path fraught with peril, but it also ignited a fire within him—a desire to seek the truth, no matter the cost. The game was afoot, and he was ready to play.

5. Old Friends, New Enemies

The rain poured down, a steady rhythm that matched the tumult in Andrew's mind as he stood outside the coffee shop. The familiar scent of roasted beans wafted through the air, drawing him back to a time when life was simpler, when the biggest threat was midterms and late-night study sessions. But that was before the past caught up with him, before he'd lost his way amid the tangled web of crime and corruption that now enveloped the city.

He pushed the door open, and the warm air enveloped him, a stark contrast to the cold drizzle outside. Inside, the shop bustled with life—students huddled over laptops, couples engaged in quiet conversation, and baristas chatting amiably as they crafted frothy lattes. Yet Andrew felt like a ghost, haunting the space that had once felt like home. His eyes searched for a face he hadn't seen in years.

"Andrew!" A voice broke through his reverie. It was Claire, his college roommate, her face lighting up with surprise. She rushed over, her hair a cascade of curls that bounced with every step. "What are you doing here?"

"Just needed a break from work," he replied, forcing a smile. They embraced, the warmth of their friendship momentarily dispelling the weight of his troubles.

"Let's grab a table." They settled into a corner booth, the ambient noise creating a bubble around them. As they caught up on each other's lives, Andrew felt a flicker of normalcy. But the conversation inevitably drifted toward the darker currents that had begun to taint their lives.

"Have you heard about the recent unrest?" Claire asked, her expression turning serious. "It's getting worse. People are scared."

Andrew nodded, his mind racing. The city had become a battleground, where rival factions vied for power and territory, and the violence spilled into the streets. What had started as whispers of corruption had escalated into a full-blown crisis, one that threatened to unravel everything he held dear.

"I'm working on a case that might shed light on it," he admitted, his voice low. "It involves some pretty high-level players. People I thought I could trust."

"Who?" Claire's eyes widened, a mix of concern and curiosity. Andrew hesitated, weighing the consequences of revealing too much. But the walls felt like they were closing in, and he needed to share the burden.

"It's connected to the mayor's office and some shady deals. I'm not sure how deep it goes, but there are names I recognize—friends from college who've turned into... well, something else entirely."

Claire leaned closer, her voice a whisper. "You're not talking about Ryan, are you? He was always ambitious, but..."

"Yeah, Ryan," Andrew said, his voice strained. "He's in the thick of it. I never thought he'd cross that line. It's like I don't even know him anymore."

The conversation turned heavy, filled with unease. Andrew could feel the tension building, the realization that old friendships could morph into new enmities. Ryan had once been a brother in arms, a partner in crime-solving during their college years, but now he was entangled in a world of greed and betrayal.

As they spoke, Andrew felt a pang of nostalgia. Their college years had been filled with idealism, a belief that they could change the world. But now, that innocence felt like a distant memory. The very friends who had once stood by him were now potential adversaries, each chasing their own dreams, even if those dreams were built on the suffering of others.

After their coffee cooled, Claire took a deep breath, her brow furrowed with worry. "You have to be careful, Andrew. If Ryan is involved, it could get dangerous. People like him don't just walk away from this kind of life."

"I know," he replied, his voice heavy with realization. "I'm trying to gather evidence, but every lead seems to lead me deeper into the chaos. It's like stepping into a pit of vipers."

"Do you think he knows you're investigating?" she asked, her gaze steady.

"Maybe. I can't shake the feeling that I'm being watched. It's as if the shadows are closing in, and every move I make echoes through the darkness."

Claire reached across the table, her hand resting on his. "Promise me you'll be careful. You can't trust anyone in this game. Not even the people you thought you knew."

"Yeah," Andrew murmured, the weight of her words settling heavily on his shoulders. "I'll be cautious."

As they parted ways, Andrew stepped back into the rain, feeling the droplets mingle with the uncertainty swirling in his mind. The city felt different now—more menacing, with every corner hiding potential threats. He couldn't shake the feeling that old friends were becoming new enemies, and that trust was a luxury he could no longer afford.

Days turned into weeks, and the investigation intensified. Andrew spent late nights poring over documents, tracking financial transactions, and piecing together the puzzle of deceit that seemed to stretch infinitely. He delved deeper into the underbelly of the city, uncovering layers of corruption that threatened to consume everything.

But as he dug, he also felt the noose tightening. Whispers reached his ears about a new player in town, someone who was pulling strings from the shadows. It became clear that the stakes were higher than he had anticipated. The people he once called friends were now entrenched in a world where loyalty was a liability, and betrayal was the currency.

During a particularly tense meeting, Andrew confronted Ryan. They met in a dimly lit bar, the air thick with tension and unspoken words. Andrew studied Ryan's face, searching for remnants of the friend he once knew. "What happened to you, man? This isn't who you are."

Ryan smirked, but it didn't reach his eyes. "You don't understand, Andrew. This is survival. You either play the game or get left behind."

"But at what cost?" Andrew challenged, his voice rising. "You're destroying lives for money. How can you justify that?"

Ryan leaned back, crossing his arms. "You think you're any different? You're just as deep in this as I am. You're investigating me, risking everything. Don't act like you're the moral high ground."

The words cut deep, and Andrew felt the truth in them. He was navigating treacherous waters, torn between seeking justice and confronting the harsh reality of the world they lived in. As he stared into Ryan's cold gaze, he realized that the bonds of friendship had frayed, replaced by an abyss of distrust.

That night, Andrew returned home, haunted by the encounter. The shadows felt more oppressive, and he couldn't shake the feeling of impending doom. He realized that the line between friend and foe was blurring, and every decision he made could lead him further down a path of no return.

Days passed, each bringing new challenges and revelations. Andrew found himself entangled in a web of deceit, where every connection led to more questions than answers. The city was alive with rumors, and the atmosphere crackled with tension. He began to receive cryptic messages—warnings to back off, to let go of the investigation.

But surrender wasn't in his nature. He pushed forward, determined to expose the truth, no matter the cost. Yet, with every step, the shadows grew longer, the enemies more defined. Andrew was not just battling corruption; he was facing the very people he had once called friends.

In a chilling twist of fate, he discovered that Ryan wasn't the only one involved. Claire had her own ties to the underground world, and the realization hit him like a punch to the gut. The very people he relied on had become entwined in the chaos, blurring the lines of loyalty and morality.

In a desperate attempt to confront her, Andrew found himself standing outside her apartment, grappling with the betrayal that cut deeper than any knife. The rain began to fall again, mirroring the turmoil within him as he prepared for a confrontation that could change everything.

Inside, the air felt thick with tension as he faced Claire. "Why didn't you tell me?" he demanded, the hurt evident in his voice.

"I didn't want to drag you into this," she replied, her voice barely above a whisper. "I thought I could handle it. I thought it was just a job."

"A job that involves dangerous people!" he retorted, feeling the weight of betrayal settle heavily in the room.

"I didn't think it would get this far, Andrew. I was trying to protect you," she admitted, tears glistening in her eyes.

"Protect me? Or protect yourself?" he shot back, unable to hide his anger. "You've been living a lie, and now I'm in the middle of it."

As the argument escalated, Andrew realized that every relationship he had once cherished was now steeped in uncertainty. The old friends he had once relied on were morphing into new enemies, and the city he loved was spiraling into chaos.

The confrontation left him shaken, and he stepped out into the rain once more, feeling the cold droplets wash over him. He was now adrift in a sea of betrayal, unsure of whom to trust. The friendships that had once anchored him were slipping away, replaced by shadows that whispered of danger at every turn.

In the days that followed, Andrew continued to gather evidence, but the looming specter of mistrust overshadowed every move he made. Each encounter felt like a dance on a razor's edge, where one misstep could lead to disaster. He found himself questioning the motives of everyone around him, haunted by the realization that even the people closest to him were not what they seemed.

As the investigation progressed, Andrew learned of a meeting—a gathering of the key players in the city's corruption. It was an opportunity

to uncover the truth, to expose the connections that ran deep through the veins of power. But it also meant stepping into the lion's den, where loyalty was a distant memory, and danger lurked behind every corner.

He arrived at the venue, a nondescript warehouse on the outskirts of town, shrouded in darkness and secrecy. The air was thick with tension as he entered, his heart pounding in his chest. He had come too far to turn back now.

Inside, he moved through the shadows, keenly aware of the stakes. Each face he recognized felt like a knife twisting in his gut—friends turned adversaries, allies turned foes. He was no longer the idealistic young man who believed in justice; he was a player in a high-stakes game where betrayal was inevitable.

As the meeting commenced, Andrew watched from the shadows, piecing together the connections and alliances that formed a treacherous web of deceit. The air crackled with tension as the power players discussed their plans, their ambitions laid bare. The very fabric of the city's future hung in the balance, and Andrew was determined to expose their corruption.

But as the night wore on, the danger became palpable. He felt eyes watching him, a sense of foreboding creeping over him. The shadows that had once felt like familiar territory now felt suffocating, and he knew he had to act before it was too late.

In a desperate bid for the truth, Andrew made his move. He stepped into the light, confronting the group with the evidence he had gathered. The gasps that followed were drowned out by the pounding of his heart, the realization that he had crossed a line from which there was no return.

"Enough!" he shouted, his voice echoing in the cavernous space. "You think you can run this city with your lies and corruption? I'm here to expose you."

The room erupted in chaos, voices rising in anger and disbelief. Friends turned enemies, allies turned traitors—Andrew was now in the center of a storm that threatened to consume him. He had opened Pandora's box, and there was no going back.

In the chaos that ensued, Andrew realized the true cost of betrayal. The friendships he had once cherished were now shattered, replaced by a landscape of animosity and distrust. As he fought to maintain his ground, he couldn't help but reflect on the choices that had brought him to this moment.

In the end, the storm passed, but the scars remained. The city would never be the same, and neither would he. Old friends had become new enemies, and in the ruthless world of ambition and greed, trust had become a fleeting illusion.

As Andrew walked away from the wreckage of that night, he knew that he would have to forge a new path, one where the shadows no longer held sway over his life. The fight for justice was far from over, but he was no longer the naïve idealist he had once been. The game had changed, and he was ready to confront the darkness head-on.

6. Crossing Paths

In the dim light of the bar, the air was thick with the smell of stale beer and the low hum of murmured conversations. Detective Alex Carter leaned against the counter, his gaze scanning the room for familiar faces. It was a haven for those who wanted to hide from the world, a place where secrets were shared like currency. Tonight, he was on the hunt—not for a criminal, but for answers that had eluded him for far too long.

The case had spiraled into a labyrinth of lies, each turn leading to another dead end. He was investigating the disappearance of several key witnesses in a high-profile money-laundering case, and the deeper he dug, the more he realized he was stepping into a world where power and greed overshadowed the truth. As he took a sip of his whiskey, his phone buzzed. A text from his partner, Sarah, flashed on the screen: "Meet me at the usual spot. I've got something."

Alex pushed himself off the bar and made his way to the back booth, a shadowy corner that offered both privacy and danger. Sarah was already there, her expression serious, a stark contrast to her usual lighthearted demeanor. He slid into the seat opposite her, instinctively lowering his voice.

"What did you find?" he asked, his heart racing at the thought of new information.

"They're onto us, Alex," she replied, her eyes darting around the room as if expecting someone to eavesdrop. "I've been following the money trail, and it leads to a shell corporation linked to the Westbrooks."

The name sent a chill down his spine. The Westbrooks were a powerful family known for their extensive connections in the city—business, politics, and even the underworld. They had a reputation for being untouchable, and anyone who dared to challenge them often found themselves in dire straits.

"Are you sure?" he pressed, feeling the weight of the implications.

Sarah nodded, her brow furrowed. "I've traced several transactions, all leading back to them. But it gets messier. There's someone else involved—someone high up in the police department."

"Corruption within our ranks?" Alex's voice was barely a whisper, the reality hitting him hard. If true, it meant that every step they took could be monitored, their investigation compromised.

"Yeah. I don't know who, but I'm working on it. We need to tread carefully. I suggest we keep this between us for now."

Just then, a figure entered the bar, drawing Alex's attention. It was a man in a dark coat, his face obscured by the shadows. He scanned the room with an intensity that made Alex's instincts flare. There was something off about him. The way he moved, the way he observed—it screamed danger.

"Sarah, stay close," he whispered, his eyes fixed on the newcomer.

The man approached the bar, his posture relaxed, but Alex could sense the tension radiating from him. He ordered a drink, but the moment he turned to face the crowd, Alex felt an unsettling familiarity. It was as if he had crossed paths with this man before, though he couldn't place where.

"Who is that?" Sarah asked, her voice barely audible over the din.

"Not sure. But I have a feeling he knows something," Alex replied, watching intently. The man's gaze flickered around the room, landing briefly on their booth before shifting away. A moment later, he pulled out his phone and began typing furiously.

"Let's get out of here," Alex said, urgency creeping into his voice. "I don't like this."

They stood up to leave, but before they could make their way to the exit, the man suddenly turned and approached them, a confident smirk on his face. Alex felt a rush of adrenaline as he braced himself for confrontation.

"Detective Carter, isn't it?" the man said, his tone casual but laced with a hint of mockery. "I've heard quite a bit about you."

"Who are you?" Alex asked, trying to maintain an air of authority despite the unease tightening his chest.

"Let's just say I'm someone who knows a thing or two about your current investigation. And I think we can help each other."

Alex glanced at Sarah, who looked equally wary. "Help us? Why would you want to do that?"

The man leaned in closer, lowering his voice. "Because the Westbrooks are not the only players in this game. You're in over your head, and I can provide you with the information you need to take them down. But you need to trust me."

"Trust is earned, not given," Alex retorted, narrowing his eyes. He was not about to let this stranger manipulate him.

"Fair enough. But time is running out. If you don't act soon, there will be nothing left to save. Meet me at the old warehouse by the docks tomorrow night. If you're smart, you'll come alone." With that, the man turned and walked away, leaving a trail of questions in his wake.

"What the hell just happened?" Sarah said, her voice a mixture of disbelief and concern.

"I don't know, but I have a bad feeling about this," Alex admitted, rubbing the back of his neck. "We can't ignore this lead. If he's telling the truth, we might finally get the break we need."

"But meeting him alone? That's risky," Sarah cautioned. "What if it's a trap?"

"Every step we take is a risk, Sarah. We can't afford to back down now."

As they left the bar, Alex felt the weight of their situation pressing down on him. The shadows seemed to stretch longer, the air heavier with the scent of danger. He knew he was walking a fine line between uncovering the truth and being consumed by it.

The next day, Alex prepared himself for the meeting. The warehouse loomed in the distance, its once-bustling exterior now a shell of its former self. As he approached, every instinct screamed at him to turn back, but he pushed through the trepidation. He had to see this through.

Inside, the air was cold and damp, and the sound of dripping water echoed in the emptiness. Alex stepped cautiously, every creak of the floorboards amplifying his anxiety. He found a corner where shadows gathered, waiting for the man from the bar.

Minutes passed like hours, and just when he began to doubt his decision, the man emerged from the darkness.

"Glad you came," he said, his expression unreadable. "I was starting to think you were too smart for your own good."

"I'm here," Alex said tersely. "Let's get to the point."

The man smiled, but there was no warmth in it. "The Westbrooks are planning something big—something that could tip the balance of power in this city. You need to stop them before it's too late."

"What do you know?" Alex pressed, his heart racing.

"I have documents, names, and locations. But first, I need to know that you're willing to do what it takes to bring them down. It won't be easy, and it will get messy. Are you prepared for that?"

Alex hesitated, considering the implications. If he said yes, he was crossing a line that could shatter everything he believed in. But the weight of the corruption he had already witnessed pushed him forward. "Yes," he finally said. "I want to end this."

"Then we'll need to move fast. There's no time to waste."

As they began to discuss the details, Alex felt a spark of determination igniting within him. He was stepping into a world of shadows, but this time, he would not be the one lost in the dark.

The paths he had crossed were leading him toward a reckoning—a chance to unveil the chaos that had taken root in the heart of the city. He would bring the truth to light, even if it meant facing the darkest corners of his own soul.

Chapter 2: The Underbelly of the City

1. Hidden in Plain Sight

In the heart of the bustling city, where shadows danced between towering skyscrapers, life went on with a deceptive normalcy. Streets thrummed with the rhythm of commuters and the buzz of countless conversations, each person engrossed in their own narrative. Yet, beneath this veneer of everyday life, something sinister lurked, hidden in plain sight, waiting for the right moment to strike.

For Michael, the young prosecutor tasked with uncovering the city's criminal underbelly, this façade was all too familiar. He had grown accustomed to the duality of existence—the public smiles and private despair. The streets held secrets, whispered only to those who dared to listen. With a determined stride, he navigated the throngs of people, his mind racing with the implications of his latest case.

Weeks earlier, a shocking incident had rocked the city. A prominent business mogul was found dead in his luxurious penthouse, the apparent victim of a heart attack. Yet, the circumstances surrounding his demise were shrouded in mystery. An anonymous tip had led Michael to believe there was more to the story—something deeper than a simple medical mishap. He had spent sleepless nights piecing together the fragmented clues, and now, he felt the weight of impending revelations bearing down on him.

As he arrived at his office, the scent of freshly brewed coffee mingled with the stale air of old files and documents. The walls were lined with portraits of former prosecutors, their stoic expressions almost daring him to step up to the challenge. Michael dropped his bag onto his desk and flicked on his computer, the screen illuminating his tired eyes. He began sifting through the information he had gathered, focusing on the business mogul's financial records. A pattern began to emerge—an intricate web of transactions that hinted at something more nefarious.

Hours passed in a blur of paperwork and intense focus. Michael's dedication was unwavering, his instincts sharpening with each passing minute. He discovered numerous offshore accounts, each one seemingly innocuous but leading to a trail of money that twisted like a serpent. As he delved deeper, he unearthed a series of shady deals and unreported payments that suggested a much darker side to the city's business elite. This was no mere accident; this was a conspiracy that extended beyond what he had initially imagined.

Determined to follow the thread, Michael arranged to meet with his informant, a former associate of the mogul who had recently come forward with shocking claims. They met in a dimly lit café, where the clinking of cups and the murmur of hushed conversations provided the perfect cover for their discussion. The informant, a gaunt man with haunted eyes, slid a folder across the table, his hands trembling.

"What you're looking for is in here," he whispered, glancing nervously around. "But you have to be careful. They're always watching."

Michael opened the folder, revealing a series of photographs and documents. As he perused the contents, a chilling realization washed over him. The images depicted clandestine meetings between the mogul and various shadowy figures, each one more menacing than the last. The documents detailed a network of influence that ran deep within the city's fabric, touching politicians, law enforcement, and even members of the judiciary.

The implications were staggering. Michael understood that he was standing on the precipice of something monumental. The longer he stared at the evidence, the more he felt the walls closing in around him. This wasn't just about uncovering the truth; it was about survival. The forces he was up against were powerful and ruthless, willing to do anything to protect their interests.

As he left the café, the weight of the folder felt heavier than ever. The bustling streets now seemed suffocating, each passerby a potential threat. Michael's instincts kicked in, urging him to stay vigilant. He began to notice the subtle signs of being followed—the unfamiliar car that seemed to circle the block, the figure lingering at the corner. It was a reminder that in this world of shadows, one could never be too careful.

Days turned into weeks, and Michael's investigation continued to spiral deeper into the heart of the city's corruption. He reached out to trusted colleagues, but found them hesitant, wary of the implications that came with diving too deep. Whispers of disloyalty and betrayal seeped through the ranks, and Michael began to realize that trust was a luxury he could no longer afford.

Determined to push forward, he sought out the one person he believed could offer him insights: a seasoned detective who had spent years navigating the city's criminal landscape. Their meeting took place in a forgotten part of town, a stark contrast to the glittering offices of the elite. The detective, a grizzled veteran with a no-nonsense demeanor, listened intently as Michael laid out the evidence he had collected.

"This city thrives on secrets," the detective said, his voice low and gravelly. "The truth is often obscured by layers of deceit. You need to peel those layers back, but be ready for what you find. Sometimes, it's better to leave things hidden."

Michael absorbed the warning, but his determination only grew stronger. He could feel the clock ticking, the pressure mounting with each passing day. The deeper he delved, the clearer it became that his life—and the lives of those he cared about—hung in the balance.

As he returned to his office, Michael felt a renewed sense of purpose. The evidence was there, waiting to be uncovered, and he was prepared to confront the darkness head-on. He meticulously organized the information, creating a comprehensive timeline of events that would lead him to the truth. Every detail mattered; every connection was a piece of the puzzle that could unlock the chaos surrounding him.

Then, one evening, as he pored over the files, a breakthrough arrived. A single name appeared repeatedly in the documents—a woman known only as "Veronica." She seemed to be the linchpin in the entire operation, a figure shrouded in mystery whose influence reached far and wide. Michael felt an urgency to find her, to uncover the role she played in the web of deceit.

With determination in his heart, he began his search for Veronica, knowing that in the world of shadows, she was the key to unraveling it all. Each lead brought him closer to her, and yet, he felt the walls of danger closing in. Every time he got close, it seemed as if the forces protecting her were always one step ahead.

As days turned into nights, the investigation began to consume him. The lines between work and personal life blurred, and Michael found himself withdrawing from friends and family. They noticed the change in him—the sleepless nights, the intense focus, the shadows under his eyes. But he pushed them away, convinced that he had to do this alone.

Finally, after weeks of relentless searching, Michael received an anonymous tip about Veronica's whereabouts. It was a risky move, but he felt the fire of determination igniting within him. He couldn't turn back now. The time had come to confront the elusive woman who had evaded him for so long.

He arrived at a nondescript building on the outskirts of the city, its exterior unassuming yet foreboding. Heart pounding, he pushed through the door and stepped into a dimly lit corridor. The air was thick with anticipation, and every step echoed in the silence.

As he reached the end of the corridor, he found himself face-to-face with a door marked only by a single, flickering light. Taking a deep breath, he knocked, his mind racing with questions.

What would he find on the other side? Would she be the key to unraveling the chaos, or would she plunge him deeper into the darkness?

The door creaked open, revealing a figure silhouetted against the light. Veronica stood there, an enigmatic smile playing on her lips. In that moment, Michael knew he was stepping into a world that could change everything—or cost him everything he held dear.

2. A Web of Lies

In the dim light of the underground café, the air was thick with smoke and whispers. It was here that secrets brewed alongside the bitter coffee, and truth was as elusive as the fleeting shadows on the walls. Jack Donovan, a seasoned prosecutor with a reputation for exposing corruption, leaned over his cup, eyeing the man across the table. Leo, an informant with ties to the criminal underworld, had always delivered valuable intel, but Jack sensed that tonight was different.

Leo shifted nervously, his eyes darting to the entrance. "You need to know what's coming, Jack. There's a network here that goes deeper than you think. They're not just running drugs or rackets—they're controlling everything."

Jack leaned in closer, intrigued yet cautious. "What do you mean by everything?"

"Their hands are in politics, finance, even the media. They weave a web of lies so intricate that it's nearly impossible to unravel," Leo replied, his voice barely above a whisper. "Every piece of information you think you know is manipulated to serve their agenda."

As Jack listened, he felt a knot tighten in his stomach. He had encountered deception before, but this sounded like a conspiracy that reached far beyond local crime. "So, who's at the center of this web?"

Leo hesitated, then took a deep breath. "I can't give you names, but I can tell you this: there's a woman. She's the mastermind behind it all. They call her 'The Architect.'"

The name struck a chord within Jack, echoing like a long-forgotten memory. He'd heard rumors of a shadowy figure who orchestrated chaos with a flick of her wrist, but he had always dismissed them as myth. Now, faced with Leo's intense gaze, he wondered if it was time to reevaluate everything he thought he knew.

As the conversation unfolded, Leo detailed the mechanics of the operation. It began with small lies—rumors planted in the media, disinformation spread through social networks. Gradually, these lies morphed into a vast tapestry of deception, obscuring the truth and manipulating public perception. Jack realized that the deeper he dug, the more he would have to confront the uncomfortable truth about the society he served.

"Why are you telling me this?" Jack asked, suspicion creeping into his tone.

Leo leaned back, his demeanor shifting from anxious to defiant. "Because you're the only one who can stop her. If you don't act, it'll be too late. They'll tighten their grip, and no one will be able to escape their reach."

Jack felt the weight of responsibility settle on his shoulders. The stakes were higher than ever, and he had a choice to make. He could walk away, pretend he hadn't heard anything, and continue his life in the shadows of ignorance. Or he could step into the light, armed with the knowledge that could either save or destroy him.

The decision crystallized in his mind. He couldn't ignore the call for justice. "What's the first step?" he asked, his voice steady.

Leo smiled faintly, a glimmer of hope flickering in his eyes. "We gather evidence. We build a case that exposes her web. But be careful—she has eyes everywhere. One misstep and we'll be the ones caught in her trap."

As the two men plotted their course, the café around them buzzed with the life of unsuspecting patrons, blissfully unaware of the chaos brewing beneath the surface. Jack's heart raced at the thought of what lay ahead. He had faced criminals, fought corrupt officials, but this was something entirely different. It was a battle of wits, a game where the rules were obscured, and every ally could potentially be a foe.

In the days that followed, Jack delved into the shadows of the city, piecing together fragments of information that Leo had shared. He scoured public records, contacted former associates, and followed the trails of financial transactions that led to dead ends. Each discovery seemed to confirm Leo's warnings—this was indeed a well-crafted web, spun with expertise and malice.

But as Jack continued his investigation, he found himself grappling with a haunting realization: the deeper he went, the more isolated he became. Colleagues who had once offered their support began to distance themselves, their eyes filled with suspicion. Rumors circulated, whispers of paranoia that suggested he had crossed a line no one dared to breach. Jack's instincts told him that the Architect's influence had seeped into every corner of the city, twisting loyalties and bending truths.

Days turned into weeks, and Jack's resolve was tested. Every time he thought he was close to a breakthrough, a new obstacle would appear, as if the universe conspired to protect the Architect's secrets. Yet, the more he struggled, the more determined he became. He knew that there was a truth waiting to be uncovered, and he was willing to risk everything to find it.

One late evening, as he pored over financial documents in his cramped office, Jack received an anonymous tip. A name—Nina Koroleva—floated to the surface, accompanied by a vague promise of connection to the web of lies. Intrigued, Jack set out to learn more about this mysterious figure.

What he discovered sent chills down his spine. Nina was a well-respected philanthropist, known for her charitable works and community involvement. Yet, behind the facade of kindness, Jack sensed something darker. Her foundation, it turned out, had deep ties to numerous corporations, many of which had been implicated in shady dealings. The more he learned, the more convinced he became that Nina was not just a player; she was a key player in the Architect's grand scheme.

Jack arranged to meet with an investigative journalist who had written extensively about Nina's activities. Over drinks at a quiet bar, they exchanged information, each piece fitting together like a puzzle. The journalist's insights unveiled a side of Nina that the public never saw—manipulation, intimidation, and a calculated approach to dismantling anyone who threatened her empire.

The conversation shifted when Jack mentioned Leo. The journalist's expression darkened. "Be careful with that one. Leo has a reputation for playing both sides. He's survived by navigating the murky waters of deceit, and he's not above using others for his gain."

Jack's heart raced. He had trusted Leo, but doubt crept in. Was he truly an ally, or just another pawn in the Architect's game? Determined to uncover the truth, he arranged a meeting with Leo, hoping to confront him about his past.

When they met in the same café where it all began, the atmosphere felt charged with tension. Jack's mind raced as he weighed his options. "You said you wanted to help me, but how can I trust you?" he asked, leaning across the table.

Leo's eyes narrowed. "You think I'm playing you? I've risked everything to come forward. The Architect will come for me next if I don't help you."

Jack hesitated. "But how do I know you're not working for her?"

Leo's expression softened, revealing a glimpse of vulnerability. "Because I want to see her downfall as much as you do. She's destroyed too many lives. You have to believe me."

In that moment, something shifted in Jack. He recognized the desperation in Leo's voice, the urgency of their shared mission. Perhaps trust would have to be a calculated risk, a necessary leap into the unknown.

As they resumed their planning, Jack couldn't shake the feeling that the walls were closing in. The web of lies was tightening around them, and every move they made drew them closer to the center of the storm. They discussed strategies, names, and potential allies, but Jack's mind remained clouded with doubt.

Days turned into sleepless nights, each filled with questions and revelations that left him both exhilarated and terrified. Jack felt the weight of responsibility pressing down on him. He wasn't just seeking justice; he was fighting against a formidable force that had orchestrated chaos for far too long.

As Jack continued to unravel the threads of deception, he felt a renewed sense of purpose. This wasn't just about exposing the Architect—it was about restoring faith in a system that seemed irreparably broken. With each piece of evidence he gathered, he saw a flicker of hope: the possibility of a future free from the clutches of those who wielded power through lies.

But as he delved deeper, he knew he was playing a dangerous game. The Architect was watching, and every move he made could bring him closer to either victory or destruction. As he stood on the precipice of revelation, he understood that the web of lies was not just a threat; it was a challenge—one that would define his legacy as a prosecutor and a defender of truth.

In the end, Jack knew that the path ahead would not be easy. But armed with the knowledge he had gathered, he felt ready to confront the darkness that lurked just beyond the shadows, determined to expose the web of lies that had ensnared so many. As he prepared for the battles to come, he reminded himself that truth, no matter how buried, always has a way of rising to the surface. And with it, he would stand firm against the chaos that sought to consume everything he believed in.

3. Meeting the Informant

The air was thick with tension as Prosecutor Alex Reed stepped into the dimly lit café on the outskirts of the city. It was the kind of place that wore its secrets like a well-tailored suit, with its walls echoing whispered conversations and its corners shadowed by the weight of untold stories. Today, it would serve as the stage for a meeting that could alter the course of his investigation.

He scanned the room, searching for the informant who had promised crucial information about the intricate web of corruption and crime that had ensnared the city. A familiar figure caught his eye—a man in his late forties, wearing a weathered leather jacket and a cap pulled low over his brow. Mike "The Weasel" Thompson had a reputation that preceded him. A small-time hustler turned whistleblower, he had danced along the edges of the law for years, accumulating a wealth of knowledge about the city's underbelly.

As Alex approached, he noticed the way Mike's eyes darted around the room, alert to every movement, every change in the atmosphere. It was a behavior borne of survival, a reminder that in their line of work, paranoia was often the best form of self-defense.

"Mike," Alex greeted, taking a seat across from him. "Thanks for meeting me."

"Cut the pleasantries, Reed. You know I don't do this for fun," Mike replied, his voice a gravelly whisper. He leaned closer, as if the very walls had ears. "I've got information, but it doesn't come cheap."

Alex studied him, weighing the risks of what he was about to engage in. "I know the score. Just tell me what you've got."

Mike hesitated, glancing over his shoulder before speaking. "You're digging into something much deeper than you realize. There's a reason the higher-ups want this investigation buried. You're not just up against street thugs; you're tangling with people who have power—real power."

The mention of power sent a shiver down Alex's spine. It wasn't news to him that the crime families operating in the shadows of the city had their fingers in more than just illicit activities; they had ties to influential politicians and business leaders, creating a fortress of corruption that was nearly impossible to penetrate.

"Who are we talking about?" Alex pressed, his tone firm yet cautious.

"The Eastside Syndicate," Mike replied, his eyes narrowing. "They've got a new player in town—a woman named Elena Vasilev. She's been pulling strings behind the scenes, orchestrating moves that could destabilize everything you've worked for."

Alex felt a tightening in his chest at the name. He had heard whispers of Elena Vasilev, a shadowy figure whose reputation for ruthlessness was almost mythological. Some said she had ties to international crime networks, while others claimed she was a mastermind in her own right. Whoever she was, she was a force to be reckoned with.

"What's her game?" Alex asked, leaning forward.

"She's been funneling money through legitimate businesses, disguising the operations as front companies," Mike explained, his voice lowering to a conspiratorial tone. "But there's something bigger at play. She's got connections that reach far beyond the Eastside. If you're not careful, you'll find yourself caught in a crossfire you can't escape."

The implications of Mike's words hung heavy in the air. Alex knew that if he wanted to dismantle the Syndicate's operations, he needed more than just information; he needed a strategy that could outmaneuver the formidable forces he was up against.

"Do you have evidence?" he asked, urgency creeping into his voice.

Mike shifted uncomfortably. "I can get you something, but it'll take time. I need to be sure I'm not stepping on anyone's toes."

"Time isn't a luxury I have," Alex replied, frustration seeping through. "Every moment we waste gives them an opportunity to tighten their grip. You have to understand what's at stake here."

Mike leaned back, crossing his arms defensively. "You think I don't know what's at stake? I'm risking my neck by talking to you. But I'm not some charity case, Reed. I need protection. If they catch wind of this, I'm a dead man."

Alex weighed his options, realizing that the line between right and wrong had blurred significantly. "I can arrange for protection, but you need to be straight with me. No more games."

Mike nodded slowly, the tension in his posture easing slightly. "Fine. But you'll owe me. I want guarantees—money, resources, whatever it takes to keep me safe."

"Deal," Alex replied, extending his hand. "But you have to deliver the information quickly. We're running out of time."

As they shook hands, Alex felt a mixture of hope and apprehension. The conversation had opened a door to a world he had only glimpsed from a distance, and yet he couldn't shake the feeling that with each step deeper into the shadows, he risked losing himself to the chaos that loomed ahead.

After they parted ways, Alex walked out into the street, the city lights flickering like stars against the backdrop of an impending storm. He had a lead, but with it came a weight of uncertainty. What had begun as a straightforward investigation was spiraling into a labyrinth of danger and intrigue.

His mind raced as he headed back to his office. Elena Vasilev would not be an easy opponent, and he had no illusions about the price of failure. The stakes had never been higher, and he needed to prepare himself for the challenges that lay ahead.

As the night enveloped the city, Alex understood that the shadows were closing in. He had made a pact with the informant, but every promise came with a price, and the cost of this particular alliance could prove catastrophic. It was a game of chess, and he was determined to be several moves ahead.

With renewed resolve, he sat at his desk and began mapping out his next steps. He needed to connect the dots between the Syndicate's operations and the powerful figures in the city who had turned a blind eye. The path to justice would be fraught with danger, but he was ready to face whatever came next.

4. Secrets of the Street

In the dimly lit alleyways of the city, secrets festered like the dampness that clung to the bricks. The streets were alive with whispers, an unspoken language understood by those who roamed them. For the uninitiated, the city was merely a collection of buildings and roads; for others, it was a labyrinth of hidden truths, where every corner held the promise of revelation—or danger.

Alex had learned early on that information was the currency of survival. As a prosecutor, he walked a fine line between the law and the murky world of the underbelly. Tonight, he felt the weight of that dual existence more than ever. A heavy fog rolled in, cloaking the streetlights in a ghostly glow, making the city feel both familiar and alien. He was on his way to meet an informant who had promised to unveil a thread in a complex web of corruption.

The meeting point was a small diner tucked away from the main roads. It had a reputation for greasy fries and strong coffee, but what really drew Alex was the clientele—the kind of people who had seen too much and said too little. As he pushed open the door, the bell chimed, a jarring note in the soft murmur of conversations. He scanned the room, searching for a familiar face.

In a booth at the back, shrouded in shadows, sat Marissa, a former street hustler turned informant. Her sharp green eyes flicked up to meet his, a mix of curiosity and caution evident in her expression. He slid into the seat opposite her, the vinyl sticky against his skin.

"You're late," she said, her tone laced with irritation.

"Traffic," he replied, knowing full well it was a weak excuse. The truth was, he had hesitated, wrestling with the implications of their meeting. Marissa had a way of digging up dirt that could either help or bury him.

She leaned closer, lowering her voice. "I have something you need to hear, but it's not going to come cheap."

Alex sighed, bracing himself for the cost of her information. "Just tell me what you know."

Marissa smirked, enjoying the moment. "You know the Reyes family? The ones with the big shipping company?"

He nodded, the name striking a chord. The Reyes family was notorious—its tentacles spread through various sectors, their influence felt in boardrooms and back alleys alike.

"They're laundering money," she continued, her voice barely above a whisper. "I've seen the books. They're moving millions through shell companies and fake charities."

Alex leaned in, his interest piqued. "Do you have proof?"

"Proof? That's tricky. But I can get you names—contacts who can confirm what I'm saying."

His instincts kicked in. If what she was saying was true, it could lead to a major breakthrough in his investigation. But trusting Marissa was a gamble. "What's the catch?"

She hesitated, her eyes narrowing. "I want immunity for my sister. She's mixed up in this, and if they find out I talked to you, she'll be in deep trouble."

Alex considered her request. The stakes were high, but the potential reward was worth the risk. "Fine. If you give me the names, I'll see what I can do."

Marissa nodded, satisfaction flickering across her face. "Alright. But I need you to understand—this isn't just some petty crime. This is big, and there are people who won't like it when they find out someone is talking."

A chill ran down Alex's spine. He knew the price of digging too deep. The streets were ruthless, and the people who lived by their codes were even more so. "Tell me what you have," he urged.

For the next hour, Marissa unraveled a narrative that intertwined greed, deception, and desperation. She spoke of secret meetings, coded messages, and vast sums of money that slipped through the cracks of legality like water through a sieve. Each name she dropped felt like a dagger, piercing the facade of respectability that the Reyes family had carefully constructed.

As she spoke, Alex's mind raced. The implications of her information could shatter the surface of calm that enveloped the city's elite. But it also meant he would have to tread carefully; one misstep could cost him everything.

When they finished, he leaned back, the weight of the revelation pressing down on him. "I need to follow up on this."

Marissa waved a hand dismissively. "Just remember, you're not the only one hunting for answers. There are eyes everywhere."

As he left the diner, the air felt different, charged with a sense of impending chaos. The streets held their breath, and Alex couldn't shake the feeling that the secrets lurking in the shadows were about to emerge into the light. The web of lies was tightening, and he was now at the center of it.

That night, as he returned home, he replayed Marissa's words in his mind. The city felt like a character in its own right, alive with stories waiting to be told. But beneath its vibrant surface lay a darkness that could swallow him whole. He needed to be careful, not just for himself but for those he loved.

Days turned into nights, and as he delved deeper into the Reyes family's operations, the stakes grew higher. Each discovery opened new avenues of inquiry, but also brought fresh threats. His phone buzzed with messages from unknown numbers, cryptic warnings that made his skin crawl.

The streets he once navigated with confidence became a minefield of danger. The secrets of the street had a way of revealing themselves, but they also had a way of ensnaring those who sought them. Alex had to keep moving, piecing together the puzzle while avoiding the traps set by those who thrived in the shadows.

The hunt was on, and the streets would not give up their secrets easily. Each turn brought new risks, and he had to decide how far he was willing to go for the truth. In a world where loyalty was as fragile as glass, trusting the wrong person could lead to devastating consequences.

As the fog rolled in again one evening, Alex found himself at a crossroads. The secrets of the street were no longer just whispers; they were a call to action. With every piece of information he uncovered, he was drawing closer to the heart of the chaos. And while he was determined to seek justice, he knew that justice often came with a heavy price.

5. The Price of Silence

In the dimly lit backroom of a dilapidated bar, a heavy silence lingered, punctuated only by the occasional clink of glasses and hushed whispers. The air was thick with the scent of stale smoke and desperation. Here, in the underbelly of the city, secrets had a price, and tonight, that price was steep.

Lucas Harrington leaned back in his chair, a weary expression etched on his face. He had spent years as a prosecutor, dedicated to unearthing the truth and serving justice. Yet, as he stared into the depths of his whiskey, he couldn't shake the feeling that the very system he believed in was as corrupt as the criminals he pursued. It was a bitter realization, one that gnawed at him relentlessly.

He remembered the case that had brought him here—a prominent business tycoon found dead in his penthouse, surrounded by a sea of unanswered questions. The police had deemed it a suicide, but Lucas had his doubts. The whispers he heard suggested something much darker. It was a tale woven with deception, a plot that reached into the highest echelons of power.

As he contemplated the evidence, a figure slipped into the booth across from him. It was Eva, a former informant with connections to the criminal underworld. Her reputation for gathering intel was unmatched, but she was equally known for her willingness to disappear when things got too hot. Lucas could sense her unease the moment she sat down.

"Lucas," she said, her voice barely above a whisper, "you need to stop digging. Some things are better left buried."

He studied her, noting the tremor in her hands and the shadows under her eyes. "You know I can't do that. If there's something wrong, I have to bring it to light."

"Bringing it to light can get you killed," she replied, glancing over her shoulder as if expecting someone to appear from the shadows.

"You're playing a dangerous game, and the stakes are higher than you realize."

"Tell me what you know," he insisted, his voice firm. "I can't act on assumptions. If there's evidence of foul play, I need it."

Eva hesitated, her gaze drifting towards the door. "There's a price for silence, Lucas. The higher you climb, the more they'll want to keep you quiet."

"Who's they?" he pressed, sensing her reluctance. "What's really going on?"

She leaned in closer, her voice low and urgent. "There's a network of powerful people who will do anything to protect their interests. If you keep pushing, you won't just be risking your career—you'll be risking your life."

Lucas felt a chill run down his spine. He had seen too many good men and women lose their way in pursuit of the truth, their dreams shattered by the very system they sought to protect. "I'm not afraid of them," he declared, though the conviction in his voice wavered.

"Maybe you should be," she said, her eyes locking onto his with an intensity that made him uneasy. "You're not just a prosecutor anymore; you're a threat. They'll silence you before you can expose what they've done."

As the weight of her words sank in, Lucas realized the enormity of the situation. The price of silence was not just a figure on a balance sheet; it was the lives of those who dared to speak out, the dreams of those who sought justice, and the very fabric of a society that claimed to uphold the rule of law.

He thought of the dead tycoon, of the secrets he had taken with him to the grave. There were whispers of illicit deals and hidden agendas, a maze of corruption that twisted through the heart of the city. The more he uncovered, the more he understood that the truth was not just elusive; it was dangerous.

"Have you seen anything? Heard anything?" he asked, desperation creeping into his tone.

She shook her head. "All I know is that people are disappearing. Those who get too close to the truth... they just vanish. It's as if they never existed."

Lucas felt a surge of determination. "I can't walk away. Not now. If I don't stand up to them, who will?"

"Then you better be prepared," Eva warned, her expression grave. "They won't just come after you. They'll come after everyone you care about. Your friends, your family—no one is safe."

The weight of her words settled heavily on his shoulders. He had always known that pursuing justice came with risks, but he had never anticipated the depths of betrayal that lurked beneath the surface. The more he fought for the truth, the more he realized that the system was rigged against him.

As the night wore on, Lucas felt the walls closing in. He needed to find a way to navigate the treacherous waters ahead, but the question loomed large: at what cost?

He finished his drink and pushed the glass aside, determination coursing through him. "I need to go. I have to follow the leads. I can't let fear dictate my actions."

Eva's eyes widened in alarm. "You're making a mistake, Lucas. Please, think about what you're doing."

"Silence is not an option," he replied, his voice steady. "If I don't fight for justice, who will?"

With that, he left the bar, stepping into the chilly night air, the weight of his decision settling heavily upon him. He was acutely aware that the road ahead would be fraught with danger, but he refused to let fear hold him back.

As he walked through the dimly lit streets, Lucas couldn't shake the feeling that he was being watched. The shadows seemed to stretch and flicker around him, whispering secrets he wasn't yet ready to uncover. He had crossed a line, and there was no turning back.

The price of silence was steep, but he would pay it if it meant exposing the truth. He had to believe that justice would prevail, even in a world where shadows loomed large and danger was a constant companion. The battle for truth had begun, and he was determined to see it through, no matter the cost.

6. Uncovering Connections

The dim light of the office cast long shadows as the young prosecutor leaned over the cluttered desk, papers strewn about like fallen leaves. Each document told a fragment of a story, but piecing them together felt like trying to assemble a jigsaw puzzle in the dark. The hum of the city outside faded into the background, replaced by the quickening pulse of his thoughts. He felt it in his bones—something larger was at play.

A recent tip from an informant had led him here, to the heart of the matter. It wasn't just about the money laundering or the murders linked to the syndicate; it was the network that connected them all, a web woven with the finest threads of deceit. He had glimpsed the edges of this network, but it was time to dive deeper.

As he rifled through the files, one name kept resurfacing: Elena Veranova. A woman shrouded in mystery, she seemed to move through the shadows, leaving behind only whispers and rumors. The connections were elusive, yet unmistakable. Elena was not just a player in this game; she was at its center. He had to learn more.

His fingers grazed a photograph of her, taken at a gala last year. She looked poised and confident, surrounded by politicians and business magnates. Her smile was captivating, yet there was something in her eyes—an unsettling glint that suggested she was more than she appeared. He remembered the conversations he had overheard in hushed tones about her influence, how she had ties to powerful individuals who would go to great lengths to protect their secrets.

Hours slipped away as he meticulously traced the paths connecting Elena to various players in the city. There were the usual suspects: high-ranking officials whose palms were greased with dirty money, and local crime lords whose ambitions were matched only by their ruthlessness. But there were also more surprising connections—philanthropists with pristine public images and CEOs of major corporations, all linked to her in one way or another. Each name was a clue, a piece of the puzzle that hinted at a larger conspiracy.

Suddenly, a knock on the door pulled him from his thoughts. It was his assistant, Jake, a keen observer with a knack for digging up information. "I found something," he said, excitement bubbling in his voice. He handed over a folder, and the prosecutor quickly scanned the contents. Inside was a report detailing a series of anonymous donations to political campaigns, all traced back to shell companies. The common thread? They all led to Elena.

"This can't be a coincidence," the prosecutor murmured, his mind racing. "If she's financing these campaigns, she's positioning herself in a way that gives her influence over policy decisions. This could explain the lack of action against the syndicate."

Jake nodded, eyes wide. "And if she's pulling the strings, we need to figure out how deep this goes."

The two men spent the next few days unraveling the connections, gathering evidence piece by piece. Late nights were fueled by takeout and strong coffee as they connected dots that revealed a sprawling network of corruption. Every lead seemed to uncover another layer, each more troubling than the last. It was a game of chess, and Elena was always several moves ahead.

As the investigation progressed, the prosecutor found himself drawn into Elena's world. He attended social events under the guise of a concerned citizen, observing her interactions and collecting intelligence. She was charming, with an easy laugh that disarmed those around her. But there was a predatory glint in her eye whenever she spoke to powerful men, as if she were assessing them, deciding who would be useful to her plans.

One evening, at an extravagant gala, he watched her from a distance. She was captivating, surrounded by admirers, her laughter ringing like a siren's call. Yet, he couldn't shake the feeling of danger that hung in the air. As the evening wore on, he approached her, pretending to be drawn into her orbit. Their conversation flowed easily, but he remained cautious, aware that every word could be a double-edged sword.

"You have an impressive network," he remarked, attempting to gauge her reaction. "It must be quite advantageous for your ventures."

Elena's smile widened, but it didn't reach her eyes. "Connections are everything in this world. One must know how to navigate the waters." Her words were smooth, but there was a steely undertone that hinted at her true nature.

As the night drew to a close, he found himself both intrigued and wary. She was dangerous, a master manipulator, and he was playing a game he could not afford to lose. The connections he uncovered were leading him down a path fraught with peril, but he was determined to expose the truth, no matter the cost.

Back at the office, the prosecutor and Jake reviewed their findings. They had enough evidence to implicate several key figures in the scheme, but the question remained—could they get to Elena? She was the linchpin, and without her, the entire operation might collapse. Yet, getting close to her would require a careful strategy. They needed to outsmart her, to anticipate her moves.

Days turned into weeks as they continued to build their case, each discovery more shocking than the last. The web of connections was far more intricate than they had initially imagined, and every time they thought they had cornered Elena, she slipped away like smoke. The prosecutor began to wonder if he would ever truly grasp the extent of her influence.

Just when they thought they had made progress, a new player entered the game—an anonymous tipster who claimed to have information about Elena's dealings. The prosecutor was both excited and cautious. This could be the breakthrough they needed, but it also felt like a trap. They arranged to meet in a secluded location, nerves tingling with anticipation.

As the meeting approached, he couldn't shake the feeling that someone was watching him. He felt it in the air, a weight of suspicion that pressed against his chest. Elena's reach seemed to extend into every corner, and he had to tread carefully. The night was dark, the streets eerily quiet as he made his way to the meeting spot. Shadows danced under the flickering streetlights, making him acutely aware of the dangers that lurked in the unknown.

When he arrived, the informant was already waiting. The figure emerged from the darkness, a hooded silhouette that concealed their identity. "You're looking for Elena," the voice rasped, a mix of fear and urgency. "But she's not what she seems. She's connected to something much bigger."

The prosecutor's heart raced as he listened intently. "What do you know?"

"She has ties to a global network, one that stretches beyond borders. They're involved in trafficking, money laundering, and much more. If you dig too deep, you won't just be facing her; you'll be facing a whole system designed to protect her."

The weight of the informant's words settled heavily in his gut. The connections were not just local; they were global, intricately woven into the fabric of power itself. As the informant divulged more details, the prosecutor's mind raced with the implications. This was no longer just about corruption in the city; it was about an entire criminal enterprise that spanned continents.

With this new information, the stakes had never been higher. Elena was not just a woman of influence; she was the epicenter of a chaotic storm that threatened to engulf everything in its path. The prosecutor realized that uncovering her connections would require not only skill but also bravery, as the truth he sought could lead him into the very heart of darkness.

As he left the meeting, the adrenaline coursed through him. He had a newfound determination to bring the web of corruption to light. But he also knew he had to be careful; one misstep could spell disaster. The connections he was uncovering were fraught with danger, and the closer he got to Elena, the more perilous his journey would become.

Days turned into sleepless nights as the investigation deepened. The prosecutor and Jake worked tirelessly, following leads, interviewing sources, and piecing together the connections that defined the syndicate. Each discovery fueled their resolve, but it also made them acutely aware of the risks they faced.

Then, one fateful night, as the prosecutor returned home, he noticed a car following him. Heart pounding, he took a detour, weaving through alleys and side streets, trying to shake off the tail. He could feel the weight of unseen eyes, a constant reminder that he was not alone in this battle.

Just as he thought he had lost them, he turned a corner and found himself face-to-face with an ominous figure blocking his path. It was a warning—a clear signal that he was getting too close. The connections he had begun to uncover were not just links in a chain; they were tendrils of a monstrous entity determined to protect its secrets.

Yet, fear only fueled his determination. With each connection unveiled, the prosecutor knew he was not just fighting for justice; he was battling against a system that thrived on chaos. He would not be intimidated. The truth would be revealed, and he would expose Elena and her sinister network, no matter the cost.

Chapter 3: A Dangerous Alliance

1. Trusting the Untrustworthy

In the dimly lit café nestled in a forgotten corner of the city, the air was thick with tension. Prosecutor Alex Carter sat across from a figure cloaked in shadows, a man whose reputation teetered between infamy and indispensability. This was Anton, an informant known for his slippery allegiances and murky past. Alex's heart raced; he had always been wary of Anton, but desperation pushed him to this meeting. With the city spiraling into chaos and corruption seeping into every crevice, he had little choice but to embrace the untrustworthy.

Anton sipped his espresso, his eyes darting around as if expecting an army of enforcers to burst through the door at any moment. "You want to know about the hand that pulls the strings? I can help, but my information doesn't come cheap," he said, his voice a low rumble. Alex clenched his jaw, a mixture of frustration and intrigue churning within him. Trusting Anton felt like walking a tightrope over a bottomless pit; one misstep could cost him everything.

"Just tell me what you know," Alex replied, forcing calm into his voice. The stakes were too high for games. "I don't have time for your theatrics." Anton leaned in, a sly smile creeping onto his face. "You think you're the only one chasing the truth? Everyone's got a price, Alex. Even you."

As the conversation unfolded, Alex's mind raced with questions. Who could he really trust? He had spent years building a reputation for integrity, but the world he navigated was riddled with deception. Corruption twisted the very fabric of justice, and he found himself ensnared in a web where allies were often enemies in disguise. The lines between right and wrong blurred as he delved deeper into the heart of the chaos.

Anton revealed a network of underground transactions, money laundering, and power plays that reached far beyond what Alex had anticipated. Each name Anton dropped felt like a dagger, exposing the raw nerve of the city's criminal underbelly. Yet, with each revelation, Alex's apprehension grew. What if Anton was leading him into a trap? The informant thrived in a world where loyalty was an illusion, and betrayal was currency.

"I can get you in touch with the big players," Anton offered, his voice dripping with false sincerity. "But you need to understand—trust no one. They'll eat you alive if they catch a whiff of your intentions." Alex studied Anton, wondering if this was yet another mind game. The man thrived on manipulation, and every word dripped with a duality that left Alex feeling exposed.

Days turned into a blur of late nights and whispered meetings as Alex sought to verify Anton's claims. He connected the dots between the names Anton had provided, uncovering a trail of deception that wound its way through the city's elite. The deeper he went, the more he understood the cost of seeking the truth. Each revelation came with its own set of dangers, and the shadows lengthened around him.

Meanwhile, his personal life began to crumble. Late nights and endless investigations took a toll on his relationships. Friends turned into strangers, and trust—once a cornerstone of his existence—became a fragile memory. Each time he returned home, the silence echoed louder, reminding him of the isolation that came with pursuing justice in a world soaked in greed and corruption.

Then came the moment of reckoning. A tip-off led Alex to a clandestine meeting in an abandoned warehouse on the outskirts of the city. Armed with nothing but his wits and a burning desire for truth, he approached the location. Shadows danced across the walls, and the air hummed with an electric tension. The stakes had never been higher.

Inside, he discovered a gathering of powerful figures discussing plans that would shake the very foundation of the city. As he stealthily listened, he realized Anton's web of lies was even more intricate than he had imagined. They spoke of control, influence, and the ways they planned to maintain their grip on power. It was a chilling reminder of the treacherous game he had willingly entered.

Just as he was about to retreat, a sudden noise made his heart race. A gunshot rang out, followed by chaos. Alex ducked behind a crate, adrenaline coursing through his veins. The untrustworthy players he had sought to expose were now entangled in their own web of violence. Trust had always been a gamble, and in this moment, he was witnessing the deadly stakes firsthand.

He had to escape. The urgency to get the information he'd gathered to the authorities ignited a primal instinct within him. In the heat of the moment, he dashed toward the exit, the cacophony of shouting and gunfire echoing in his ears. Just as he reached the door, a figure emerged from the shadows—a familiar silhouette that sent a chill down his spine.

Anton stood there, a smirk plastered across his face. "Did you really think you could play this game without me?" he taunted, his eyes gleaming with a mixture of menace and amusement. In that instant, Alex felt the full weight of betrayal crushing down on him. Trusting the untrustworthy had led him here, into the maw of danger with no clear path to safety.

In a moment of desperation, Alex realized he had only one option left: to confront Anton and turn the tables. "You think you control this, Anton? You're just another pawn in a game far bigger than you understand," he shot back, his voice steady despite the chaos surrounding them. It was a gamble, but if he wanted to survive, he needed to seize the upper hand.

With a calculated move, Alex feigned a distraction, using the noise to his advantage. As Anton turned to gauge the situation, Alex lunged, wrestling for control of the gun that Anton had drawn. A struggle ensued, and with every ounce of strength, Alex pushed back, fueled by the need to reclaim his narrative.

In that tense moment, clarity washed over him. Trust was a fragile illusion, and those who wielded it as a weapon would ultimately be their own undoing. The fight for survival wasn't just against the chaos of the world around him, but also against the insidiousness of betrayal within.

As the dust settled, Alex found himself standing over Anton, the weapon clutched tightly in his hands. "You played your game, but it's over now," he declared, a newfound resolve igniting within him. Trusting the untrustworthy had taught him a valuable lesson: the path to justice was riddled with shadows, but he would emerge stronger, ready to face the darkness that lay ahead.

And so, as he walked away from that warehouse, the echoes of betrayal still reverberating in his mind, Alex Carter understood that in a world where trust was a dangerous game, it was his own convictions that would guide him toward the light. The battle was far from over, but now he was armed not just with information, but with a fierce determination to dismantle the chaos that threatened to consume everything he held dear.

2. The Agent's Proposal

As the sun dipped below the horizon, casting long shadows across the city, Daniel stood in front of the sprawling glass skyscraper that housed the offices of the city's most powerful law firm. The lights flickered on one by one, illuminating the rows of desks inside, where attorneys poured over documents that held the secrets of the powerful and the corrupt. Daniel's mind raced as he recalled the message he had received that morning—a meeting request from a man named Victor Kane, a figure shrouded in mystery and rumored to be connected to both the criminal underworld and the highest echelons of power.

Victor was a former intelligence officer, now a private consultant known for his ability to navigate the murky waters of corruption and deceit. Rumors floated around about his involvement in cases that never saw the light of day—cases where the law was more of a suggestion than a rule. Daniel had heard whispers of Victor's expertise, but also of the danger that came with crossing paths with him.

The meeting was set for the rooftop bar, a trendy location that offered breathtaking views of the city. Daniel stepped inside, the warmth and the soft hum of conversation enveloping him like a familiar cloak. He spotted Victor immediately—a tall man with a chiseled jaw, dressed in a tailored suit that seemed to blend into the ambiance of wealth and power surrounding him.

"Daniel, I presume," Victor said, his voice smooth like aged whiskey. He gestured for Daniel to take a seat, his eyes assessing him with an intensity that made Daniel uncomfortable.

"Thank you for meeting with me," Daniel replied, trying to maintain his composure. "I wasn't sure if you'd want to discuss this in public."

Victor leaned back, his expression inscrutable. "In this city, everything is public. Trust is a currency, and I prefer to keep my dealings as transparent as possible—at least until the stakes rise."

Daniel swallowed hard. The stakes were already high, and he knew that. His recent investigation into a money laundering operation had revealed connections that reached far beyond his initial expectations, drawing him closer to a network of corruption that entangled politicians, businessmen, and, possibly, the mafia.

"I've stumbled onto something," Daniel said cautiously, choosing his words with care. "There's a flow of money that doesn't make sense. It leads back to certain politicians and firms. I believe they're using shell companies to mask their dealings."

Victor's gaze sharpened, his interest piqued. "And you want to take them down?"

"Of course," Daniel said, feeling the weight of his mission pressing down on him. "But I can't do it alone. I need information, resources... connections."

Victor nodded slowly, a slight smile playing on his lips. "That's where I come in. I have access to networks you wouldn't even know to look for. But my help comes at a price."

"What kind of price?" Daniel asked, suddenly wary.

"Just a small favor in return," Victor replied, his tone casual but his eyes serious. "I need you to gather information on someone for me—someone who has their hands in far too many pies. If you can do that, I'll provide you with everything you need to dismantle this operation."

Daniel felt a knot form in his stomach. He was already walking a fine line, and now Victor wanted him to step deeper into the shadows. "Who are we talking about?"

"Let's just say, they're connected to some very dangerous people," Victor said, his voice dropping to a whisper. "But they also have something I need. You'll be doing both of us a favor."

"What if I refuse?" Daniel asked, trying to gauge the risk involved.

Victor chuckled softly. "Then you'll have to navigate this web of deceit on your own. I'm sure you're resourceful, but these are not your ordinary players. They're ruthless. Trust me when I say you'd be safer with me in your corner."

As the city twinkled beneath them, Daniel weighed his options. He could walk away, but he also knew he was already in too deep. The threads he had begun to unravel were pulling him into a world of chaos, one that he couldn't escape unscathed.

"What's the catch?" Daniel finally asked, feeling the air between them thicken with tension.

Victor leaned forward, his voice dropping to a conspiratorial tone. "The catch is that once you step onto this path, there's no turning back. You'll have to make sacrifices—potentially lose people you care about. But if you want to achieve justice in this city, you'll need to embrace the chaos. It's the only way to cut through the lies."

Daniel's heart raced as he considered the implications of Victor's words. He thought of the lives that hung in the balance, of the victims of the corruption he had seen firsthand. Could he really turn down an opportunity to make a difference, even if it meant risking everything he held dear?

"Fine," Daniel said finally, his resolve hardening. "I'll do it. But I need guarantees that I won't end up as collateral damage."

Victor smiled, a glimmer of approval in his eyes. "Smart man. We'll draw up an agreement. And remember, Daniel—when you play with fire, you should expect to get burned. But I promise you, the heat can also forge something stronger."

As they shook hands, Daniel felt a mixture of anticipation and dread. He was stepping into a world where trust was a commodity and betrayal lurked around every corner. But for the sake of justice, he was willing to embrace the chaos that lay ahead.

The meeting ended, but Daniel knew this was just the beginning. He had crossed a threshold into a realm where every decision would be a dance with danger, and every ally could be a potential enemy. The city glimmered below, but all he could see was the darkness creeping in at the edges, whispering promises of power and peril.

With his heart racing, he walked out of the bar, the weight of Victor's proposal pressing heavily on his shoulders. He had made his choice, and now he would have to navigate the treacherous waters of intrigue, deceit, and violence that lay ahead. Each step forward felt like a step deeper into the abyss, but the hope of bringing light into the darkness urged him onward.

3. A Game of Cat and Mouse

The city at night was a different beast—one cloaked in shadows, where the line between predator and prey blurred. Streetlights flickered, casting brief halos of light that were quickly swallowed by the inky darkness. Each footstep echoed, a reminder that in this part of town, everyone was being watched. Somewhere out there, someone was pulling the strings, orchestrating the chaos like a silent conductor. And for Thomas Calloway, the young prosecutor caught in the middle of it all, it felt like the walls were closing in.

He had known when he took the case that it would be dangerous. The trail of corruption, blood money, and secrets hidden behind locked doors stretched farther than he had initially imagined. What he hadn't anticipated was the personal nature of the hunt. It had started with a few threats, the usual warnings from the shadows to back off, leave the investigation alone. But then things took a darker turn. A break-in at his apartment, a car following him too closely at night, the unmistakable sensation that he was always being watched. It wasn't paranoia if it was true.

The game had begun in earnest, and the rules were simple: trust no one.

Calloway knew that the woman at the center of it all, the enigmatic figure who had eluded law enforcement for years, was more than just a criminal mastermind. She was a ghost, her name whispered but never spoken aloud, her face unseen. Her fingerprints were on everything—the laundering of billions, the destruction of lives, the manipulation of power on a global scale—but no one had ever come close to catching her. She played the game with an elegance that few could match, always staying one step ahead, leaving her pursuers chasing phantoms.

But Calloway wasn't just any pursuer.

He had spent months meticulously piecing together a trail that led to her door—or at least, he thought he had. Every lead had seemed like a breakthrough until it evaporated into nothing, leaving him with more questions than answers. It was as if she knew his every move before he made it. Frustration gnawed at him. This wasn't just about the case anymore; it was about proving that he could outsmart her, that he could finally be the one to bring her down. She was the cat, and he was determined not to be the mouse.

But with each step forward, the game became more dangerous. His sources began disappearing—people who had been willing to talk suddenly turned silent, terrified of what might happen if they were caught cooperating. And when one of them turned up dead, Calloway knew the stakes had escalated.

He sat in his dimly lit office, surrounded by case files, his mind racing through the possibilities. Every piece of evidence was laid out in front of him like a twisted puzzle, but the pieces refused to fit together. He reached for his phone, dialing the one person he thought he could trust: Sarah Jacobs, an old friend and fellow prosecutor who had been by his side since law school. She had a way of cutting through the noise, seeing things he might have missed.

"Thomas," her voice crackled through the line, "you sound like hell."

"I feel worse," he replied, rubbing his temples. "I'm starting to wonder if this whole thing is a wild goose chase. Every lead I follow just ends in smoke."

"She's toying with you," Sarah said, her voice steady. "She knows you're close, and she's trying to shake you off. This is her game."

"But how do you catch someone who's always a step ahead?" Calloway asked, the frustration bleeding through in his tone.

"You don't play by their rules," she answered simply. "You make your own."

Her words lingered in the air as he hung up. It was the truth he didn't want to admit—he had been playing right into her hands, chasing after the breadcrumbs she had left behind. If he wanted to catch her, he needed to change the game entirely.

The next few days were a blur of frantic activity. Calloway worked tirelessly, combing through every file, re-interviewing every source, looking for the one thing he had missed. His gut told him that there was a pattern somewhere, a thread that connected everything, but it was so deeply buried beneath layers of misdirection and deception that finding it felt impossible.

And then, late one night, as he pored over yet another batch of documents, he saw it—a name, buried in the fine print of a financial transaction. It was a name he hadn't seen in years, one he thought he had forgotten. It was the name of someone he had once known, someone he had trusted.

The revelation hit him like a freight train. All this time, she hadn't just been toying with him; she had been using him. The people he had reached out to, the leads he had followed—they hadn't been dead ends. They had been carefully constructed traps, designed to lead him exactly where she wanted him to go. And now he was staring at the name of the person who had been pulling the strings all along.

A surge of anger flooded through him. He had been played, and the realization was both humiliating and infuriating. But now, at least, he knew who he was really after. The question was, what was he going to do about it?

He couldn't go to his superiors. If this person was involved, there was no telling how far the corruption had spread. Calloway was on his own, and if he made one wrong move, it could cost him everything.

For the next week, he moved carefully, keeping a low profile, avoiding his usual haunts. He didn't trust anyone—not his colleagues, not his friends. He even stopped calling Sarah, afraid that somehow the information might be intercepted. The game was no longer just about outsmarting the woman in the shadows; it was about surviving long enough to bring her down.

Every night, he checked his surroundings before leaving the office, taking different routes home, never using the same routine twice. Paranoia had become his constant companion, but it was the only way to stay ahead. He knew they were watching, waiting for him to slip up.

And then, just as he felt the pressure becoming unbearable, he received a message. It was delivered in the most mundane way possible—a simple envelope slipped under his door, no return address, no markings. Inside was a single piece of paper with a date and a location.

Calloway knew what it meant. She was inviting him to the final act.

The night was cold as he made his way to the abandoned warehouse on the edge of the city. The air was thick with tension, every step echoing in the emptiness around him. He wasn't sure what he would find, but he knew that this was it—this was where the game would end.

Inside, the warehouse was dimly lit, the flickering light casting long shadows across the floor. And there, standing in the center of the room, was the woman he had been chasing for months. She was as enigmatic as ever, her face obscured by a hood, her posture relaxed, as if she had been expecting him all along.

"Thomas," she said, her voice soft but commanding. "You've come a long way."

"Cut the games," he replied, stepping closer. "It's over."

She laughed, a low, melodic sound that sent a chill down his spine. "Oh, it's far from over. You've only just begun to understand."

Before he could react, the lights went out, plunging the room into darkness. And in that moment, Calloway realized the truth—he was still the mouse, and the game was far from finished.

4. The Risks of Collaboration

The weight of the decision pressed on his shoulders like an iron shackle. Prosecutor Daniel Reed had never thought he would be in this position—teetering on the edge of a dangerous collaboration that could either bring the entire operation to its knees or bury him in the underworld he had sworn to dismantle. The air in the room felt thick with unspoken tension, every breath measured, every glance scrutinizing. He was no stranger to risky partnerships, but this was different. The stakes were higher, the players more cunning, and the consequences far more dangerous.

The meeting had been set in an inconspicuous bar at the edge of the city, a place where anonymity was guaranteed by the very nature of its clientele. Faded lights flickered overhead, casting an eerie glow on the cracked leather seats. In the corner sat a figure he had only ever seen in whispers and confidential files—Lucien Kovac, a man whose influence stretched far beyond the criminal world, a man who controlled the unseen currents of chaos.

Kovac's presence in the bar was a calculated risk in itself. He never showed his face unless he believed he was holding all the cards. Daniel's nerves, normally steeled against intimidation, quivered as Kovac raised his eyes, cold and sharp, and fixed them on him.

"You're not a fool, Reed," Kovac began, his voice smooth like silk, but underneath there was a hardness that promised ruthlessness. "So let's skip the pleasantries. You need me. I can offer you a way in, deeper than you've ever gone before. But I won't pretend this comes without strings."

Daniel shifted in his seat, keeping his expression unreadable. His mind raced, weighing every possible outcome. Kovac was known for his ability to turn alliances into traps. The prosecutor had seen it before—those who aligned themselves with Kovac found themselves entangled in webs they couldn't escape. But this time, it felt like he had no choice. The network he was trying to take down was bigger than any operation he'd encountered. Without Kovac's connections, the investigation would be dead in the water.

"You think I trust you?" Daniel asked, his voice steady despite the churn of anxiety within him. "Your reputation isn't exactly built on keeping your word."

Kovac smirked, leaning forward, his elbows resting on the table between them. "Trust? No, trust is for the weak. I expect you to be smart enough not to trust me. But what I offer is power—information that can tear down the empire you've been chasing for years. You want to stop the chaos? This is the only way."

The words hung between them, each one a carefully crafted hook. Kovac was a master at this game, a predator circling his prey, offering just enough to lure them in, but never enough to keep them safe. Daniel's pulse quickened as he considered the implications. To work with Kovac would mean compromising everything he stood for as a prosecutor. Yet, to walk away now would mean letting the criminals slip further into the shadows, their hands still dripping with blood.

"I need to know what you're after, Kovac," Daniel said, keeping his tone level, though the intensity of the moment gripped him tightly. "Why help me? What's in this for you?"

The smirk remained on Kovac's face, a glint of amusement flashing in his dark eyes. "You think I'm doing this out of the goodness of my heart? Please. Let's not insult each other's intelligence. What I want is survival. The empire you're targeting... they've overstepped. Even the most powerful need to remember there's always someone stronger. Someone smarter. I help you take them down, and in return, I get to keep playing the game. Without interference."

It was a precarious balance. Kovac, for all his crimes, understood the necessity of maintaining a certain order in the underworld. He thrived in chaos but knew better than to let it spiral beyond control. Daniel's mind raced through the possibilities. With Kovac's help, they could penetrate the deepest layers of the criminal organization, exposing the financial pipelines that fueled corruption at the highest levels. But what would be the cost? What compromises would he have to make?

"I can't promise you immunity," Daniel said carefully. "If I take this deal, we play by my rules. You cross a line, and I'll take you down with the rest of them."

Kovac chuckled, shaking his head. "Your rules, Reed? You and I both know that once you start down this path, the lines blur. Your precious rules will be tested. But let's not pretend you have much of a choice here. Without me, you're stumbling in the dark. With me, you might just find the light at the end of the tunnel."

The truth of Kovac's words stung. Daniel knew he was right. He had already been chasing ghosts for months, with no solid leads and every step forward met by an impenetrable wall. The criminal network was vast, their power rooted in secrecy and the complicity of those in high places. Kovac's offer was his only shot at breaking through.

"Fine," Daniel said, the weight of his decision pressing down on him like a vice. "But we do this my way."

Kovac's smile widened, but there was no warmth in it. "Of course, prosecutor. Your way."

They sealed the deal with a curt nod, but Daniel couldn't shake the unease that settled deep in his gut. The risks of collaboration were real, and he knew that once he entered into this partnership, there was no turning back. Kovac would be watching, waiting for any moment of weakness, ready to twist the situation to his advantage.

In the weeks that followed, Daniel found himself caught in a whirlwind of activity. With Kovac's guidance, they began dismantling the financial networks that propped up the criminal empire. Offshore accounts, shell companies, illicit trade routes—it all started to unravel, each thread pulled with precision and care. But with every victory came a sense of growing dread. The deeper they went, the more dangerous the players became.

Kovac's influence was everywhere. He seemed to know things before they happened, predicting the movements of their enemies with uncanny accuracy. Daniel couldn't help but wonder how much of this Kovac had orchestrated himself. The prosecutor had expected manipulation, but the extent of Kovac's reach was staggering.

Late one night, as Daniel reviewed the latest intelligence reports, his phone buzzed on the desk. It was an encrypted message from Kovac.

"They know. Be ready."

His heart sank. The criminal organization had caught wind of their moves. The game had just escalated, and now, the hunters were becoming the hunted.

The following day, the first blow came in the form of a car bomb—targeted at one of Daniel's key informants. The man had been instrumental in tracing the money trails, and now he was gone, reduced to nothing more than ash and debris. The message was clear: back off, or face the consequences.

Daniel stared at the scene of destruction, his jaw clenched in anger. This was the cost of collaborating with Kovac—the line between justice and corruption was becoming more difficult to discern. And yet, he had no choice but to push forward. The only way to survive this storm was to see it through to the end.

As the tension mounted, Daniel realized that the real battle wasn't just against the criminal organization—it was against the pull of the darkness that came with working alongside Kovac. Every step forward, every victory, came with a cost. And as the bodies began to pile up, Daniel couldn't shake the feeling that he was losing a piece of himself with each decision he made.

Kovac, for his part, seemed unbothered by the chaos around them. He thrived in it, navigating the destruction with the same cold calculation that had made him a legend in the underworld. But Daniel knew that their partnership was fragile, and that the moment Kovac saw an opportunity to turn on him, he would take it.

The final test came when they cornered the last of the key figures in the criminal organization. It had been a long and bloody road to get there, but now, victory was within reach. All they had to do was take down the man who had orchestrated the entire operation.

5. Following the Trail

The trail was faint, barely discernible in the chaos of city life. But it was there, waiting to be followed, if only someone had the patience and the eye to see it. For Daniel Mercer, a prosecutor with a reputation for persistence, it was more than just a lead—it was a lifeline. Every case he had taken on felt like a challenge, but this one was different. The stakes were higher, the players more dangerous, and the consequences of failure—unthinkable.

He had been tracking the movements of one of the most elusive crime syndicates in the world, a group so well-organized that even their failures seemed intentional. Every dead end, every false lead—it all seemed orchestrated, as if they were always one step ahead. Yet something had changed. He could feel it. For the first time in months, Mercer believed he was the one holding the advantage, however slim. But there was a fine line between confidence and hubris, and he knew the line was razor-thin.

Mercer's first break had come from an unlikely source. A low-level money launderer, someone barely known outside the underbelly of the city, had slipped. It wasn't much, just a casual name drop during a surveillance operation, but it was enough. "Lydia," he had muttered, barely aware of his own words. That single name had set Mercer on a path that had led him here, standing outside a small, nondescript bar on the outskirts of the city.

The bar was one of those places that seemed to thrive on being forgotten. The kind of establishment where the lights were dim, the conversations hushed, and nobody asked questions. It was the perfect hiding place for someone who didn't want to be found. And yet, Mercer was here, certain that Lydia, whoever she was, had left traces of her presence.

He stepped inside, the stale smell of alcohol and cigarette smoke immediately assaulting his senses. The patrons barely glanced in his direction, a testament to the bar's regular clientele. Mercer approached the counter, his eyes scanning the room, noting the exits, the faces, the potential threats. It was second nature by now.

"What can I get you?" The bartender's voice was gruff, his tone indifferent. He looked like he'd seen his fair share of trouble but had learned not to get involved.

Mercer ordered a drink, not because he wanted one, but because it was the expected thing to do. He needed time to observe, to listen. He had learned over the years that people revealed far more in their silences than they did in their words. And sure enough, after a few minutes, he noticed the first crack. A man sitting at a table in the corner, his posture tense, his eyes flicking nervously toward the door every few seconds. He was waiting for something—or someone.

Mercer sipped his drink, pretending not to notice, but his attention was fully on the man. He had the look of someone who didn't belong here, not really. His clothes were too clean, his demeanor too skittish. He was hiding something, and Mercer had a good idea what it was.

The minutes ticked by, and Mercer felt the tension in the air grow thicker. Something was about to happen, and he needed to be ready. He shifted in his seat, casually adjusting his jacket to ensure his badge and gun were within easy reach. Just as he did, the door creaked open, and a woman walked in.

Mercer knew immediately that this was Lydia. There was something about her that commanded attention, even in a place like this. She was tall, with sharp features and an air of confidence that bordered on arrogance. Her eyes, cold and calculating, swept the room before settling on the man in the corner. She moved toward him with purpose, her steps deliberate, like a predator stalking its prey.

The man stood as she approached, his nervous energy almost palpable. They exchanged a few quiet words, and then, without warning, she slapped him across the face, hard enough to draw the attention of everyone in the bar. The man winced but didn't retaliate. He merely stood there, frozen, as Lydia leaned in and whispered something in his ear. Whatever she said, it worked. The man nodded furiously, his entire demeanor shifting from defiance to submission in a matter of seconds.

Mercer didn't need to hear the words to know what had just happened. Lydia had just asserted her dominance, and the man was now firmly under her control. He watched as she turned and left the bar, not sparing a glance at anyone else. The man, visibly shaken, downed his drink in one gulp before hurriedly following her out.

Mercer waited a moment before slipping out after them. He kept his distance, careful not to draw attention, but close enough to maintain visual contact. The streets outside were dark and quiet, with only the occasional car passing by. Lydia and the man walked quickly, their footsteps echoing against the pavement. They turned a corner, disappearing into an alleyway, and Mercer quickened his pace, his hand instinctively resting on his gun.

As he rounded the corner, he saw them standing near the back of a building, engaged in what appeared to be a heated conversation. Mercer crouched behind a dumpster, straining to hear their words.

"You said you'd handle it," Lydia's voice was sharp, laced with anger. "You promised me there wouldn't be any problems."

The man mumbled something in response, but his words were too soft for Mercer to catch.

"I don't care about your excuses," Lydia snapped. "You're going to fix this, or I'll make sure you regret ever getting involved."

There was a long pause, and then the man nodded, defeated. Lydia, satisfied, turned and walked away, leaving the man standing there, looking like he'd just been given a death sentence.

Mercer stayed hidden, waiting until Lydia was out of sight before emerging from his hiding spot. The man was still standing there, his shoulders slumped, lost in thought. Mercer approached him quietly, his badge already in hand.

"Don't move," Mercer said, his voice firm but calm.

The man spun around, his eyes wide with fear. "I didn't do anything," he stammered, raising his hands in surrender.

"I'm not here to arrest you," Mercer replied, though he wasn't entirely sure that was true. "I just want to talk."

The man hesitated, glancing nervously down the alleyway as if expecting Lydia to reappear at any moment. "I can't," he muttered. "She'll kill me if she finds out."

"She'll kill you anyway," Mercer said bluntly. "But if you help me, I can protect you."

For a moment, the man looked as though he might bolt, but then his shoulders sagged in resignation. "You don't know what you're getting into," he said quietly. "This isn't just some gang. They control everything—money, people, even the law. If you go after them, they'll destroy you."

Mercer stepped closer, his gaze unwavering. "Let me worry about that. Just tell me what you know."

The man took a deep breath, his eyes darting nervously around the alley as if the walls themselves were watching him. "There's a shipment coming in," he said finally. "Tomorrow night. It's big—guns, drugs, money, you name it. Lydia's the one handling it, but she's not the one in charge. There's someone else... someone higher up. I've never met him, but they call him 'The Hand.'"

Mercer's mind raced. He had heard whispers of this elusive figure before, a shadowy leader pulling the strings from behind the scenes. But until now, he had no proof that The Hand even existed.

"Where's the shipment coming in?" Mercer asked, his voice tense with urgency.

The man hesitated, glancing around once more before answering. "Pier 17, down by the docks. Midnight."

Mercer nodded, slipping his badge back into his pocket. "You're coming with me," he said. "You're safer in custody than out here."

The man didn't argue. He simply followed Mercer out of the alley, his fate now tied to the prosecutor's. Mercer could feel the weight of the decision he had just made pressing down on him. He was following the trail, but where it would lead—he wasn't sure. One thing was certain, though. The deeper he went, the more dangerous the game became. And he was running out of time.

6. A Deadly Encounter

The night was unnaturally quiet, as if the city itself had paused to hold its breath. The narrow alleyways of the old district, usually humming with the soft murmur of distant conversations and the occasional clatter of footsteps, were now cloaked in an eerie silence. Even the wind, which typically howled through the cracks between the dilapidated buildings, was still.

Tomás Herrera moved through the darkness, his footsteps muffled by the thick fog that had rolled in from the bay. His heart pounded in his chest, each beat a reminder of the danger that surrounded him. He had been here countless times before, navigating the underworld of crime and deceit, but tonight was different. Tonight, the air felt heavier, and his instincts screamed at him to turn back, to walk away from the inevitable.

But there was no turning back now.

He could feel the cold steel of the revolver tucked into the waistband of his jeans, a weight that had become almost familiar to him over the years. It was both a comfort and a curse, a reminder of the line he had crossed long ago when the law had stopped being enough to protect the innocent. He had made peace with it—or at least, that's what he told himself in the sleepless hours before dawn. Now, as he approached the shadowed figure at the end of the alley, Tomás wondered if tonight would be the night he finally paid the price for all the deals, all the betrayals.

The figure leaned casually against a lamppost, the faint orange glow of a cigarette flickering in the darkness. He was tall, with broad shoulders and a face shrouded in the shadows of a low-brimmed hat. Despite the relaxed posture, Tomás could feel the tension radiating from the man, like a coiled snake waiting to strike. The smell of cheap tobacco mixed with the dampness in the air, creating a nauseating cocktail that turned Tomás's stomach.

He stopped a few feet away, close enough to see the man's cold, calculating eyes, but far enough to draw his gun if necessary. The man exhaled a long stream of smoke, the cloud swirling and then disappearing into the fog.

"You came alone," the man said, his voice low and rough, like gravel scraping across metal.

Tomás nodded, his eyes never leaving the man's hand, which rested a little too comfortably inside the pocket of his coat. "Just like you asked."

A slow smile spread across the man's face, but it never reached his eyes. "I was expecting your boss to send someone more... intimidating. Guess I overestimated him."

"Guess so," Tomás replied coolly. His hand hovered near the waistband of his jeans, fingers twitching with the familiar urge to reach for his gun. But he knew better. Pulling a weapon too soon could turn a tense conversation into a bloodbath. Timing was everything.

The man chuckled, a deep, guttural sound that sent a chill down Tomás's spine. "You've got guts, kid. I'll give you that. But guts won't save you out here."

Tomás swallowed hard, keeping his voice steady. "I'm not looking for trouble. I'm just here to deliver a message."

"Message?" The man took a step closer, his boots crunching on the gravel beneath his feet. "You don't think I already know what your boss wants? He's been poking his nose into places it doesn't belong. Places he doesn't understand. This isn't some game, Herrera."

Tomás's jaw tightened. "Then maybe you should tell him that yourself."

The man's smile vanished, replaced by a hard, dangerous look. He pulled his hand from his pocket, revealing a gleaming switchblade. "Maybe I will. After I carve it into your skin."

Before Tomás could react, the man lunged at him, the blade flashing in the dim light. Instinct took over, and in one fluid motion, Tomás yanked the revolver from his waistband and fired. The crack of the gunshot echoed through the alley, louder than he expected, shattering the silence.

The man stumbled, a look of shock crossing his face as he clutched his side. Blood seeped between his fingers, staining the dark fabric of his coat. He took a step back, then another, before collapsing against the wall.

Tomás stood frozen, his breath coming in short, ragged bursts. The gun still trembled in his hand, smoke curling from the barrel. He had fired before—plenty of times, in fact—but this was different. This wasn't a nameless thug or a distant target. This was personal.

The man groaned, his voice weak and strained. "You... you're making a big mistake, kid. You have no idea... what you've done."

Tomás lowered the gun slightly, his mind racing. He could feel the adrenaline surging through his veins, the fight-or-flight response overwhelming his senses. But the man's words cut through the fog in his mind, and for a brief moment, doubt flickered in his chest.

"What do you mean?" Tomás demanded, his voice harsher than he intended.

The man coughed, blood splattering his lips. "You think... you think your boss is the only one pulling strings? There's a bigger game here... and you just became a pawn."

Tomás frowned, stepping closer despite the warning bells ringing in his head. "Who are you working for?"

The man's eyes flickered with something—fear, maybe, or regret. "Doesn't matter now. You're already in too deep. We all are."

And with that, the man's head lolled to the side, his body going limp as the last breath escaped his lungs. The alley fell silent once more, save for the distant hum of traffic and the faint rustle of the fog.

Tomás stared at the lifeless body in front of him, a cold sweat breaking out on his forehead. He had gotten what he came for—a message, albeit a cryptic one—but it left him with more questions than answers. Who was pulling the strings? And what had he just stepped into?

Holstering his gun, Tomás turned and disappeared into the fog, his mind racing with the possibilities. The deadly encounter had been just the beginning. The deeper he dug, the more dangerous it became—and now, there was no way out.

Hours later, Tomás found himself at a run-down bar on the outskirts of the city, nursing a whiskey that burned as it went down. The bar was mostly empty, save for a few regulars slumped over their drinks, lost in their own troubles. It was the kind of place where questions weren't asked, where people came to forget, not to be remembered.

He ran a hand through his hair, the weight of what had just happened still settling on his shoulders. The man's dying words echoed in his mind, a cryptic riddle that gnawed at him. There was more to this—much more—and now he was right in the middle of it. But that was the problem with this world. Once you stepped in, it was almost impossible to step out.

As the bartender slid another drink his way, Tomás caught sight of a familiar face in the corner of the room. A woman, dressed in a sleek black coat, her hair pulled back in a tight bun. She was watching him, her eyes sharp and unreadable. He knew her, but from where?

She stood, crossing the room with the grace of a predator stalking its prey. As she approached, Tomás's hand instinctively moved to his side, brushing against the revolver hidden beneath his jacket. He didn't trust anyone anymore—especially not a stranger who seemed to know more than they should.

Without asking, she slid into the seat across from him, her lips curling into a sly smile. "Rough night?"

Tomás narrowed his eyes, his voice low. "Who the hell are you?"

She leaned forward, her eyes glinting in the dim light. "Someone who can help you. If you're willing to listen."

For a moment, Tomás considered walking away, leaving the woman to whatever game she was playing. But something in her gaze—something dangerous and alluring—kept him rooted to the spot.

"You've got two minutes," he said, his voice flat. "Make them count."

The woman's smile widened. "Oh, I will. But first, let's talk about what really happened tonight."

Tomás tensed. How did she know about the encounter in the alley? Was she part of the larger game the dying man had hinted at?

Chapter 4: The Dark Web

1. Digital Footprints

The digital world is like a vast, untamed wilderness. It stretches infinitely, filled with both hidden dangers and limitless possibilities, and at any given moment, thousands of people are leaving traces of their existence across this invisible landscape. Whether we realize it or not, every action we take online — a simple search, a quick message, a social media post — leaves behind a digital footprint, a trail that can be followed.

For most people, these footprints are harmless, innocuous. They browse online stores, chat with friends, watch the latest viral videos. But for others, these digital traces carry weight, leading directly to secrets best left buried. And for someone like Andrew Marcus, a prosecutor with a dogged determination to unearth those hidden truths, digital footprints were more than just data. They were breadcrumbs leading to the heart of something dark and dangerous.

Sitting at his desk, Andrew stared at his computer screen, the harsh glow reflecting off his glasses. Lines of code, email threads, and timestamps filled the display, each one a small piece of a much larger puzzle. He had been combing through this data for days, ever since the first whispers of a shadowy organization began to reach his ears. The media had started calling it "The Secret Hand," though its true nature remained elusive. What was known, however, was that billions of dollars were moving through invisible channels, fueling chaos in ways no one had ever anticipated.

Andrew leaned back, rubbing his temples as he tried to make sense of the fragmented clues before him. He had always believed that people couldn't hide forever. The digital age had made it nearly impossible to stay invisible, no matter how hard one tried. Somewhere, in the vast ocean of the internet, there would be a footprint, however small, that would lead him to the truth. All he had to do was find it.

It began innocently enough. A flagged transaction here, an encrypted email there. The deeper Andrew dug, the more he realized that this was no ordinary investigation. The web he had stumbled upon was vast, intricate, and meticulously crafted. Those behind it had gone to great lengths to ensure that they remained in the shadows, pulling strings without ever revealing themselves. But even the most careful criminals made mistakes. And Andrew was determined to find them.

The first significant break came when he stumbled across a series of seemingly unrelated emails. On the surface, they appeared to be nothing more than routine communication between business associates — short, impersonal, and filled with mundane details about meetings and contracts. But something about them felt off. Andrew had seen enough in his career to recognize when something wasn't right. The language was too formal, too measured. There was a sterility to the exchanges, a lack of personality that made the hair on the back of his neck stand on end.

He ran the emails through a decryption program, one that specialized in uncovering hidden metadata. At first, nothing jumped out, but after several hours of cross-referencing IP addresses and server locations, he hit upon something unusual. The emails, despite appearing to come from separate individuals across different countries, were all being routed through the same server — a nondescript data center located in a remote part of Eastern Europe.

Andrew's pulse quickened. This was the break he had been waiting for. With this information, he could start tracing the emails back to their original senders, peeling back the layers of anonymity that had so carefully been constructed. But the closer he got, the more dangerous things became.

He reached out to his tech expert, a former hacker named Lena, who had a reputation for being able to crack even the toughest digital barriers. They had worked together on several cases in the past, and though she operated in a moral gray zone, Andrew trusted her instincts. When he explained what he had found, she immediately began running her own diagnostics.

"This isn't just any encryption," Lena muttered, her fingers flying over the keyboard as she pulled up the email metadata on her own screen. "Whoever set this up knew what they were doing. It's designed to look like routine traffic, but it's layered. There's something buried underneath."

Andrew felt a surge of anticipation. "Can you crack it?"

Lena paused, her brow furrowing. "It's going to take time. And even then, there's no guarantee. But... if this is as big as you think it is, we're playing with fire. Whoever is behind this won't let us get too close without a fight."

He nodded, already prepared for the dangers ahead. This wasn't the first time he had gone up against powerful, dangerous people. But there was something different about this case. It wasn't just the money. It was the reach, the influence. These people weren't just criminals — they were something far worse. They were untouchable.

For the next several days, Andrew and Lena worked tirelessly, chasing down every lead, every tiny digital footprint that might point them in the right direction. Lena uncovered fragments of hidden code buried within the emails, encrypted messages that revealed meetings, wire transfers, and offshore accounts. It was a treasure trove of information, but it came with a price.

The deeper they dug, the more they realized that this wasn't just about money laundering or illegal deals. This was something far more insidious. The Secret Hand was funding uprisings, manipulating governments, and creating instability across the globe. And all of it was being done with near-perfect anonymity. Their digital footprints were faint, almost invisible, but they were there. And Andrew was getting closer to exposing them.

But just as they began to piece together the final clues, the unthinkable happened. One evening, as Andrew sat at his desk, his phone rang. It was Lena, her voice sharp with panic.

"We've been compromised."

His heart skipped a beat. "What do you mean?"

"They've been tracking us," she said, her voice shaking. "I don't know how, but they've known we were onto them for days. My system's been breached. Everything... everything I've been working on is gone."

Andrew's stomach dropped. He had known the risks, but he hadn't expected them to strike so quickly. "Are you safe?"

"For now," she replied, but he could hear the fear in her voice. "But Andrew, you need to back off. These people... they're not playing by any rules. If we keep pushing, they'll come for us."

Andrew clenched his fist, his mind racing. He couldn't back down now, not when they were so close. But Lena was right. They were up against something far more dangerous than they had anticipated. And the footprints they had been following? They were leading them straight into the lion's den.

For days after the breach, Andrew felt the weight of his choices pressing down on him. He knew that whoever was behind The Secret Hand had the resources to erase them without a second thought. But he couldn't walk away. Not now. He had spent too long chasing justice, uncovering truths that others wanted to keep hidden. This was no different.

Or was it?

The lines had begun to blur. Every move he made was being watched. Every step he took felt like it was being countered before he even knew he was making it. The digital footprints he had once relied on were now turning against him, as if the very trail he was following had been laid out for him to find — a trap, designed to lure him in deeper and deeper.

And yet, he couldn't stop. He was too far in.

2. A New Lead

The air in the dimly lit office felt thick with tension as prosecutor James Carter flipped through the stack of files spread across his desk. His eyes scanned over the countless reports, witness statements, and fragments of evidence that had been piling up for weeks. But today, something was different. A sense of anticipation simmered just beneath his skin, like an electric current buzzing through his veins. He had been chasing shadows for too long, hitting dead ends and running into walls. The elusive figures behind the city's most dangerous criminal network seemed to always stay one step ahead, slipping through his fingers no matter how close he came. Until now.

James leaned back in his chair, letting out a slow breath as his gaze settled on the new folder that had just landed on his desk that morning. It was thin—almost disappointingly so—but something about it felt promising. He didn't know why. Perhaps it was the cryptic note from his contact inside the police department, slipped under his office door in the dead of night: "You need to see this."

The folder was marked with a single word: "Confidential." His pulse quickened as he opened it, revealing a set of documents that immediately piqued his interest. There was a name, an address, and a photo of a man he had never seen before. The photo was grainy, taken from what appeared to be a security camera outside a nondescript building. But it was the location that caught his attention: a warehouse on the outskirts of town, just outside the reach of any official jurisdiction.

This was it. James felt it in his gut. He had stumbled upon a new lead, a thread that could finally unravel the web of deceit he had been fighting to untangle for months. His eyes darted back to the name on the file: Daniel Greene. The name was unfamiliar, but in this line of work, names could be false, and identities were as fluid as the shifting tides of power in the underworld.

He knew he couldn't waste any time. His instincts screamed that this was the break he had been waiting for. But he also knew he had to tread carefully. Whoever this Daniel Greene was, he was likely connected to something—or someone—far more dangerous. And if James played his cards wrong, this lead could vanish as quickly as it appeared.

• • • •

LATER THAT EVENING, James found himself standing outside the warehouse from the photo. It was an unremarkable building, the kind of place you'd pass without giving it a second thought. The air was cool, and the faint smell of rain lingered, though the storm that had passed through earlier in the day had left the streets wet and slick. As he stood there, he couldn't shake the feeling that he was being watched. The shadows seemed to stretch longer, darker, as if the city itself was trying to hide the secrets that lay within.

He approached cautiously, his every step muffled by the wet pavement. The entrance was a heavy steel door with no markings, no sign of life. James hesitated for a moment, listening for any sounds from inside. Silence. His hand hovered over the door, and with a steady breath, he pushed it open.

The warehouse was vast, its emptiness punctuated only by the distant hum of machinery and the occasional flicker of a failing fluorescent light. Crates and pallets were stacked high, casting ominous silhouettes against the walls. As he ventured deeper into the space, his heart pounded louder, the echo of each footstep merging with the tension that gnawed at him.

Then he saw it—an office in the far corner, barely visible behind a row of stacked boxes. The light inside was on, faint but steady, casting a warm glow through the grime-streaked windows. James moved closer, his hand instinctively hovering over the gun holstered at his side. He approached the door, hearing faint voices from within. Muffled. Heated.

He couldn't make out the words, but the urgency in the tone was unmistakable. He crouched low, pressing his ear to the cold metal door. His pulse raced as he strained to listen.

"...not enough time," one voice said, low and gravelly.

"We have to move faster. They're getting too close," another voice replied, sharper, more frantic.

James felt his adrenaline spike. He had to see who was inside. Slowly, he reached for the door handle, twisting it ever so slightly. The door creaked open, just enough for him to peer inside.

There, hunched over a desk cluttered with papers and maps, were two men. One was tall and broad, his back turned to James. The other, shorter and wiry, paced nervously, his hands fluttering as he spoke. The tension between them was palpable, and James quickly realized this wasn't just another run-of-the-mill meeting. These men were plotting something big.

He spotted a map pinned to the wall behind them. It was covered in red markings, circles, and lines connecting various points across the city. At the center of it all was the same warehouse James was standing in now. This was the hub, the nerve center of whatever operation they were running. He felt a surge of triumph. Finally, he had found something tangible, something real.

But before he could react, a floorboard beneath his foot creaked, the sound sharp in the silence. Both men froze, their heads snapping toward the door. James barely had time to pull back before the shorter man was at the door, yanking it open.

Their eyes locked.

For a split second, the world stood still.

Then everything exploded into motion.

The shorter man lunged at James, but he was ready. With a swift motion, he knocked the man's arm aside and shoved him back, slamming him against the wall. The taller man was on him next, swinging a fist that James narrowly dodged. The room was too small for a proper fight, the walls closing in as fists flew and furniture toppled.

James managed to land a solid punch to the taller man's jaw, sending him sprawling across the desk, but the shorter man recovered quickly, grabbing a lamp and swinging it wildly. James ducked just in time, the lamp shattering against the wall behind him.

He had to get out of there. This wasn't the time for a full confrontation. He needed more information before making his move. But as he backed toward the door, the shorter man grabbed something from the desk—papers, files, documents—and made a run for the exit on the other side of the room.

James bolted after him, but it was too late. The man disappeared into the maze of crates and pallets, and by the time James reached the other side of the warehouse, the sound of an engine roared to life, and a black sedan sped off into the night.

Breathing heavily, James stood in the now-silent warehouse, his heart pounding. The lead had been good, but it wasn't enough. Not yet. He needed to know more about Daniel Greene, about the operation they were running out of this place.

But he had a feeling this was only the beginning.

3. The Face Behind the Screen

The room was dimly lit, save for the flickering glow of the computer monitor that bathed everything in a cold, blue light. Alex leaned back in his chair, staring at the screen with a mixture of frustration and awe. For weeks, he had been chasing a ghost, a digital phantom who had been manipulating the flow of information with chilling precision. The trail had led him through layers of encryption, dark web forums, and buried online accounts. And now, after countless sleepless nights, he was closer than ever to uncovering the truth.

But what would he find on the other side of the screen? The question gnawed at him. For all his digging, the person behind the digital curtain had remained elusive, leaving breadcrumbs just out of reach, as though playing a game where the stakes were far higher than Alex had first realized. He could feel it now, that familiar tightness in his chest. This wasn't just a hacker or a whistleblower. No, this was something far bigger, someone far more dangerous. Someone who understood not just how to hide in the digital world, but how to control it.

Alex's fingers hovered over the keyboard, hesitant to press the next key, as if this one final stroke might unravel everything—or nothing. His mind flashed back to where it had all started, back when this was just a routine investigation. Back when he thought the crimes he was tracking were merely financial. Money laundering through complex web schemes, offshore accounts, shell companies—this was the bread and butter of his work as a cybercrime investigator. But now, things had shifted. There was more than money at play.

The initial lead had come from an anonymous tip, a vague whisper that something larger was afoot, something that threatened the balance of power far beyond what any one person could grasp.

It sounded like conspiracy nonsense at first, but as the pieces started falling into place, Alex knew he was dealing with someone who had mastered the art of staying hidden while pulling the strings of governments, corporations, and individuals alike.

His eyes scanned the lines of code once again, searching for the next clue. He had cracked through the firewall just a few hours earlier, breaking into a series of encrypted files that seemed to hold the answers he had been searching for. Names, dates, financial transactions—everything pointed toward one entity, one nameless, faceless organization that operated under the radar yet had its hands in every major scandal of the last decade. But none of the information revealed who was behind it. None of it gave him the face he needed.

The Face Behind the Screen. Alex had started thinking of the person that way weeks ago. Whoever they were, they were meticulous, leaving no trace behind. Alex had tracked hackers before, caught some of the most notorious cybercriminals in the world, but this—this was different. This person wasn't just a hacker. They were something else entirely. A manipulator. A puppet master. Someone who seemed to be able to predict every move Alex made before he made it.

He had tried everything—every trick in the book. He had traced IP addresses to obscure countries, followed money trails through untraceable offshore accounts, and even tried to bait the person into revealing themselves by planting false information. But each time, it was as though they knew. They always stayed one step ahead.

And now, here he was, staring at the last barrier between him and the truth. His fingers twitched, and then, with a deep breath, he pressed the key. The screen blinked once, then twice, before revealing a new file directory. His heart raced as he clicked through the folders, each one labeled in a cryptic manner. Finally, he found what he was looking for: a folder named simply "Truth."

With one more click, the contents of the folder loaded onto the screen, and Alex's breath caught in his throat. There it was. The face. Not a literal face, of course, but the digital fingerprint of the person behind the screen. For the first time, he could see patterns, habits, mistakes they had made along the way. It was subtle—so subtle that anyone less experienced would have missed it. But Alex was different. He had spent years learning how to read people through their digital presence, and now he could see it all.

He began piecing together the clues. The use of certain words in chat forums, the repetition of specific code styles, even the time zones in which this person worked—it all painted a picture. He wasn't just chasing a faceless entity anymore; he was chasing a real person. A human being with weaknesses, flaws, and a history.

But as he dug deeper, the picture that emerged wasn't comforting. This person wasn't just powerful—they were connected. Deeply. The files he had accessed revealed ties to some of the most influential people in the world. Politicians, business magnates, even law enforcement—many of them unwittingly entangled in the web this person had woven. And Alex knew, with a sinking feeling in his gut, that he was in over his head.

He thought back to the first time he had felt the pull of the digital world, back when he was just a kid, fascinated by computers and the possibilities they represented. Back then, hacking had been a game, a way to prove he was smarter than the system. But now, as he sat in his darkened apartment, he realized how much more was at stake. This wasn't just about proving his intelligence or catching a criminal. This was about survival—his own, and perhaps even the world's.

His thoughts were interrupted by the sound of a notification ping. He glanced at the screen. An email had appeared, and his blood ran cold. It was from the Face Behind the Screen.

"Nice try," it read. "But you're too late."

Alex's heart pounded as he read the words again. How? How could they know? He had covered his tracks meticulously, taken every precaution to remain anonymous. But somehow, they had found him. His mind raced as he considered his next move. Should he run? Should he try to fight back?

Before he could decide, another message appeared.

"You've been looking for me for a long time, haven't you? Well, now it's my turn."

Alex's fingers froze on the keyboard. It was a taunt, a game. This person wanted him to feel the same fear they had inflicted on so many others. But Alex wasn't going to back down. Not now. Not when he was so close. He had come too far, risked too much to let this slip through his fingers.

He quickly began typing a response, his fingers flying across the keyboard. He needed to gain control of the situation, to turn the tables on the person who had been playing him for weeks. He needed to show them that he wasn't afraid.

"You think you can intimidate me?" he typed. "I've seen your face. I know who you are."

He hit send, hoping the bluff would buy him some time. But the response came almost instantly.

"No," the message read. "You don't."

And then, just as quickly as they had appeared, the messages stopped. Alex stared at the screen, his mind racing. What did that mean? Was it another trick, another way to throw him off the trail? Or was there something he had missed?

He spent the next several hours combing through the files, searching for anything he might have overlooked. But the more he looked, the more he realized the truth: the Face Behind the Screen had always been one step ahead. And now, they had turned their gaze directly onto him.

As dawn broke and the first rays of sunlight crept through the blinds, Alex leaned back in his chair, exhaustion washing over him. He had come so close, but now it felt like he was further away than ever. The Face Behind the Screen had disappeared, leaving him with nothing but questions and a gnawing sense of dread.

He knew this wasn't over. Not by a long shot.

4. Chasing Shadows

The city was a maze of towering buildings and narrow streets, their walls casting long shadows that seemed to stretch endlessly into the night. Under the glow of streetlights, people moved like ghosts, their faces obscured by the darkness, their intentions hidden behind a veil of indifference. It was in these shadows that secrets thrived, growing in the cracks of forgotten alleys and echoing off the cobblestones that lined the narrow passages.

James Holt had always been drawn to the shadows. As a prosecutor, his job was to illuminate the darkest corners of the criminal underworld, but lately, he felt like he was chasing phantoms. Every lead seemed to evaporate just as he got close, every clue dissolving into nothingness the moment he thought he had a grasp on it. The case in front of him was no different—if anything, it was the most elusive yet.

Weeks earlier, the name "The Secret Hand" had appeared in an encrypted message intercepted by one of the few contacts James still trusted within the cyber division of law enforcement. It was a name that carried whispers of power, of unseen influence stretching beyond the borders of the city. There had been rumors for years—billion-dollar deals signed in back rooms, offshore accounts set up to funnel unimaginable wealth, political figures controlled like marionettes by invisible strings. But nothing tangible. No evidence, no witnesses, just shadows.

Now, those shadows seemed to be closing in on him. James had always prided himself on his methodical approach, never acting without certainty. But the deeper he dug, the more the lines between right and wrong blurred. What had started as an investigation into money laundering had spiraled into something far bigger, more insidious. Every connection he uncovered led to another, more complex, like a web with no end.

The latest lead had brought him here, to a derelict part of the city where the buildings loomed over the streets like sentinels guarding their secrets. He was meeting a man known only as "The Whisper," an informant who claimed to have inside knowledge of the organization pulling the strings. James didn't trust him—he didn't trust anyone anymore—but he had no choice. The pressure was mounting, the city was watching, and his reputation was on the line. He needed a breakthrough.

The alley was silent except for the distant hum of traffic. James leaned against the cold brick wall, his breath visible in the cool night air. His eyes scanned the street, his senses heightened. He'd been here too many times before, waiting in the dark for someone who might never show up. His patience was wearing thin.

The sound of footsteps approached, slow and deliberate, echoing off the buildings. James straightened, his hand instinctively moving toward the inside pocket of his coat where he kept his gun. He wasn't expecting trouble, but then again, he never did.

A figure emerged from the shadows, tall and thin, dressed in a long coat that flapped lightly in the breeze. The man's face was obscured by a hood, but his voice was unmistakable—low, raspy, like he'd spent a lifetime whispering in places where speaking aloud was too dangerous.

"You're alone," the man said, not a question but a statement.

James nodded. "For now."

The Whisper stepped closer, his movements slow, deliberate. "You're chasing ghosts, Holt. Shadows. Do you even know what you're after?"

"I know enough," James replied, his voice steady despite the doubt creeping into his mind. "I know that The Secret Hand is pulling the strings. I know they're behind the money laundering, the murders, the political corruption. I just need proof."

The Whisper laughed, a sound that sent a chill down James' spine. "Proof? You won't find proof. That's not how this works. They don't leave a trail, because they are the trail. Every lead you follow, every clue you think you've found, it's all part of their design. They want you to chase them. They want you to waste your time, your energy, until you have nothing left."

James clenched his jaw. "Then why are you here? Why reach out to me if you think it's all a waste?"

"Because," The Whisper said, stepping even closer, "there are some things that even they can't control. Loose ends. And loose ends are dangerous."

James narrowed his eyes, his instincts telling him that The Whisper was more than just a small-time informant. "What do you want?"

The Whisper hesitated, his hand disappearing into his coat before pulling out a small, unmarked envelope. "In here," he said quietly, "is something they don't want you to see. It's not the whole picture, but it's a start. Use it wisely. But remember, Holt—when you start chasing shadows, you might just become one."

Before James could respond, The Whisper turned and disappeared into the darkness, his footsteps fading until they were nothing but a distant echo. James stood there for a moment, the envelope heavy in his hand, his mind racing. He had been chasing shadows for so long, and now, he finally had something concrete.

He opened the envelope carefully, revealing a single piece of paper. At first glance, it seemed meaningless—a list of names, some familiar, most not. But as he studied it closer, he realized the significance. These weren't just names; they were connections, key players in the intricate web that The Secret Hand had woven across the city. Some were politicians, others were businessmen, and a few were names he had never expected to see on such a list—people he thought were clean, untouchable.

The realization hit him like a punch to the gut. This wasn't just about money or power. It was about control—control over everything, from the highest offices in government to the lowest street dealers. The Secret Hand wasn't just manipulating the system; they were the system.

For the first time in weeks, James felt a surge of adrenaline. He finally had something to work with, something that could unravel the entire operation. But with that realization came a wave of dread. If these people were as powerful as The Whisper suggested, then he was already in more danger than he had ever imagined.

James pocketed the list and started walking, his mind racing with plans, strategies, and contingencies. He knew he couldn't trust anyone, not even the people in his own office. This operation was bigger than anything he'd ever dealt with before, and the stakes were higher than he could have imagined.

As he walked deeper into the city, the shadows seemed to follow him, growing darker and more menacing with every step. He had always known that chasing shadows was dangerous, but now, he realized just how high the cost could be.

The streets were alive with the pulse of the city, but James felt strangely detached, as if he were walking through a dream. Faces blurred together, voices were muted, and the only sound that truly registered was the steady beat of his heart, hammering in his chest as the weight of what he had uncovered settled in.

The game had changed, and the shadows were closing in. But for the first time in a long time, James felt ready. He had spent his life chasing shadows, but now, he was ready to confront them.

5. Unraveling the Network

The deeper he delved into the case, the more intricate the web became. Every lead seemed to unravel not a single thread, but an entire tangle of connections that spanned cities, countries, and continents. What had begun as a local investigation into a series of suspicious financial transactions had now morphed into something far larger, far more sinister.

Jack Connolly, a seasoned prosecutor, had seen his fair share of corruption, but this—this was different. The money trail he was following wasn't just dirty; it was alive. It slithered through offshore accounts, shell companies, and charitable foundations like a snake in the grass, always shifting, always adapting. And no matter how many layers he peeled back, there was always another name, another front, another hidden hand pulling the strings.

It started small, almost innocuous—a routine audit by the government that flagged several wire transfers from a local real estate developer to an obscure bank in Cyprus. Jack's office was assigned the case, not because anyone thought it would amount to anything, but because no one else wanted to deal with it. The prosecutor's office was swamped with violent crimes, drug busts, and political scandals. A few dodgy financial transactions weren't high on anyone's priority list.

But Jack had a feeling about it. His instincts, honed over years of navigating the gray waters of corporate crime, told him there was more to the story. The real estate developer, Jason Whitman, was too small-time to be moving that kind of money. He built low-income housing projects and shopping plazas, the kind of developments that didn't generate the kind of capital being funneled overseas. Something didn't add up.

He started digging—first into Whitman's finances, then into his business associates. It wasn't long before Jack hit the first roadblock.

Whitman was a ghost. On paper, he existed—there were tax returns, corporate filings, contracts with city governments—but beyond that, there was nothing. No digital footprint, no media interviews, no social life to speak of. It was as if the man had gone out of his way to erase himself from the public record.

Jack's unease deepened when he met Whitman in person. The man was polite, well-spoken, and completely unremarkable. He answered every question with a calm, measured tone, offering just enough information to seem cooperative but not enough to be useful. Jack left the interview with a single, chilling thought: Whitman was exactly what he appeared to be— a puppet.

The first real breakthrough came when Jack got hold of Whitman's travel records. He had taken several trips to Dubai, the Cayman Islands, and Hong Kong over the last two years—locations notorious for their banking secrecy. These weren't the kinds of trips a small-time developer with limited cash flow should be making. Jack knew he was onto something big, but he had no idea how deep the rabbit hole would go.

That was when he brought in Maria Cortez, a forensic accountant with a reputation for being relentless. Maria was a former IRS agent who had transitioned into the private sector, working with government agencies to track down tax cheats and money launderers. Her expertise was exactly what Jack needed.

Within a week, Maria had cracked open the shell companies that Whitman had used to move his money. There were dozens of them, spread across multiple jurisdictions—Panama, the British Virgin Islands, Switzerland. Each company led to another, and another, until it became clear that Whitman was just a small cog in a much larger machine. The money he was funneling wasn't his own. It belonged to someone else, someone who was using Whitman as a front.

Maria's analysis revealed a network of transactions that led back to a central hub: a private equity firm in New York called Easton Capital. On the surface, Easton appeared legitimate, managing billions in assets for wealthy investors. But as Maria dug deeper, it became clear that Easton was at the center of the spider's web. It wasn't just a firm; it was a laundering operation, designed to take in illicit funds from around the world, clean them up, and redistribute them into the global economy.

Jack's mind raced as he realized the scope of what he was dealing with. Easton Capital wasn't just laundering drug money or tax evasion profits; they were cleaning up money for warlords, oligarchs, and arms dealers. The firm was quietly financing revolutions, corrupting governments, and fueling global chaos, all while keeping up the façade of a respectable Wall Street institution.

The more Jack learned, the more dangerous his position became. Whitman, who initially seemed like a low-level pawn, suddenly disappeared, leaving no trace behind. Jack suspected foul play, but without a body, it was impossible to prove. The deeper he pushed into the network, the more resistance he faced. Subtle threats began to appear—first in the form of cryptic emails, then in more overt ways. His car was broken into, his apartment ransacked. Nothing was taken, but the message was clear: stop digging.

But Jack wasn't the kind of man to back down. He doubled his efforts, enlisting Maria and a handful of trusted colleagues in the investigation. They worked in secret, careful not to tip their hand too early. Jack knew that if Easton Capital got wind of what they were up to, they'd either disappear or come after him with everything they had.

The next break came from an unexpected source—an anonymous whistleblower from within Easton Capital. The tipster, using the pseudonym "Orion," provided a treasure trove of documents that confirmed Jack's worst fears. Easton wasn't just laundering money; they were actively involved in the destabilization of governments. Their clients included dictators in Africa, drug cartels in Latin America, and even extremist groups in the Middle East.

The documents revealed that Easton had orchestrated coups, funded mercenaries, and bribed political leaders across the globe. And at the center of it all was a single figure: a woman known only as "The Architect." Her name appeared in several of the documents, always in connection with the most high-stakes operations. She was the one pulling the strings, the mastermind behind the chaos.

Jack couldn't shake the feeling that he was getting closer to something monumental, something that could bring down not just Easton Capital, but an entire global network of corruption. But the closer he got, the more isolated he became. His superiors at the prosecutor's office began to distance themselves from the investigation, citing "budget concerns" and "jurisdictional issues." Jack knew better. Someone high up was pulling the plug.

Undeterred, he pressed forward. Maria continued to work behind the scenes, tracing financial transactions and piecing together the puzzle. They were so close now, just one step away from exposing everything. But that step never came.

One morning, Jack arrived at the office to find Maria's desk empty. Her phone was off, and no one had heard from her since the previous night. Panic set in as Jack tried to contact her family and friends, but it was as if she had vanished into thin air. He knew what had happened—Maria had gotten too close to the truth, and now she was paying the price.

Rage and fear warred within him as Jack realized the full extent of the danger he was in. Whoever was behind Easton Capital—whoever "The Architect" was—had eyes everywhere. They knew his every move, and they weren't afraid to strike. Jack was running out of time, and the walls were closing in.

But he wasn't done yet. Maria's disappearance only fueled his resolve. He was going to bring them down, no matter the cost. He gathered the evidence they had so far—the whistleblower's documents, the financial records, the names of the shell companies—and prepared to go public. It was risky, but it was his only option. If he didn't act now, the network would bury the truth forever.

As Jack stood on the brink, ready to expose the conspiracy, he couldn't help but wonder if he had underestimated just how deep the network went.

6. Hidden Motives

It was a brisk evening when Ethan Graves first sensed the shift in the atmosphere. The streets, usually buzzing with the frenetic energy of the city, felt different tonight—quieter, almost expectant, as if the very air was holding its breath. His footsteps echoed sharply as he walked down the narrow alley, the weight of the day's revelations pressing on his chest. There were too many unanswered questions, and the closer he got to the truth, the more elusive it seemed to become. Every piece of evidence, every lead, felt like it was pointing to something bigger, something darker than he had anticipated. The deeper he dug, the more he realized that nothing—and no one—was what it seemed.

Ethan wasn't new to investigations; he had built a career out of unearthing the secrets people wanted to keep buried. But this case—this intricate, multilayered web of deceit—was different. It wasn't just about money laundering or the movement of illicit funds; there were personal vendettas at play, old grudges festering beneath the surface, and unseen forces pulling the strings in the background. The motives driving the key players weren't as straightforward as greed or power. No, there was something much more sinister lurking beneath the surface, something that Ethan couldn't quite put his finger on just yet.

It all began with a single, seemingly innocuous tip-off. A disgruntled employee from one of the shell companies had reached out, eager to offload information in exchange for a clean break. Ethan had taken the bait, thinking it would be a routine case of financial misconduct—maybe a few offshore accounts, a couple of falsified transactions. But as he started piecing together the puzzle, the picture that emerged was far more disturbing. The money was just the surface. Beneath it lay a complex network of alliances, betrayals, and vendettas stretching back decades, all linked by a shared past and a hidden agenda.

What unnerved him the most, however, was the realization that he was being watched. It wasn't paranoia—Ethan had learned to trust his instincts. Every step he took, every new lead he pursued, felt like it was anticipated. The more he tried to outrun it, the closer it came. Someone, somewhere, was always one step ahead, pulling strings he couldn't yet see.

Back at his apartment, Ethan spread the documents across his table, his eyes scanning the names and numbers, looking for a pattern. It wasn't just the money that connected these people—it was something deeper. Something personal. One name, in particular, kept appearing—Sophia Blackwood. She was elusive, always just out of reach, but there was no denying her central role in this twisted game. Ethan had heard whispers about her—an enigmatic woman with connections that spanned continents, known for her ability to manipulate people as easily as she did numbers. But no one seemed to know who she really was, or what she truly wanted. And that, more than anything, made her dangerous.

He couldn't shake the feeling that Sophia wasn't just another player in this game—she was the one pulling the strings, orchestrating events from the shadows. But why? What was her endgame? And why had she allowed Ethan to get this far without stepping in to stop him? These were the questions that kept him up at night, gnawing at the edges of his mind as he tried to make sense of the chaos.

The next morning, Ethan met with an old contact, a man who had once been deeply embedded in the criminal underworld but had since "retired" from the life. Over a cup of bitter coffee in a dingy diner, Ethan laid out what he had so far. The contact listened intently, nodding at intervals, but his expression remained guarded.

When Ethan finished, the man leaned back in his chair, his face shrouded in shadow.

"You're dealing with something much bigger than you realize," the contact said, his voice low and measured. "These people... they don't just move money. They move lives. Everything they do is calculated, every decision made with a purpose you won't understand until it's too late. You're chasing shadows, Graves. And those shadows? They're going to consume you if you're not careful."

Ethan bristled at the warning, but he knew better than to dismiss it outright. His contact had never been one for exaggeration, and the grimness in his voice sent a chill down Ethan's spine. "What can you tell me about Sophia Blackwood?" he asked, trying to steer the conversation back to the one name that seemed to hold the key to it all.

The contact hesitated, his eyes flickering with something Ethan couldn't quite read. Fear? Resignation? "Sophia's not someone you want to get too close to. She's a ghost. Appears when she needs to, disappears just as quickly. But make no mistake—everything she does, every move she makes, is deliberate. She's playing a long game, and she's been doing it for years."

Ethan frowned. "What's her motive?"

"That's the thing," the contact replied, leaning forward. "No one really knows. Some say it's power, others say it's revenge. But I've heard whispers that it's something else entirely—something personal. And that makes her more dangerous than anyone you've ever gone up against."

As Ethan left the diner, his mind raced with possibilities. If what his contact said was true, then Sophia wasn't just a manipulator—she was the architect of this entire operation, and her motives were buried so deeply in the past that unearthing them would be next to impossible. But Ethan knew he had to try. If he was going to take her down, he needed to understand what drove her—what had set her on this path of chaos and destruction.

Over the next few weeks, Ethan worked tirelessly, chasing down leads, interviewing anyone who had even the slightest connection to Sophia. But every time he thought he was getting close, the trail would go cold. It was as if she could sense when he was nearing the truth, and she would vanish, leaving him with nothing but fragments of information that led nowhere.

Then, one night, while reviewing an old case file, something clicked. It was a small detail, something he had overlooked before, but now it stood out like a beacon. A charity event, years ago. Sophia's name had appeared on the guest list, along with several other key players in this web of deceit. But there was one name on that list that caught Ethan's attention—a name he hadn't seen in years, but one that held a deep personal significance.

Marcus Graves. His father.

Ethan's pulse quickened as he stared at the name, the implications of it washing over him in waves. His father had died when Ethan was just a teenager, the victim of a tragic car accident. Or so he had always believed. But now, with this new information, he couldn't shake the feeling that there was more to the story. Had his father been involved in this shadowy world? And if so, what had been his role?

The realization hit Ethan like a freight train. This wasn't just about money or power. It was personal. Sophia had been targeting him from the very beginning, playing him like a pawn in her twisted game. And now, he was caught in the middle of it, with no way out.

As Ethan delved deeper into his father's past, he uncovered a series of events that painted a very different picture of the man he had idolized. Marcus had been involved in some shady dealings, working with the very people Ethan was now trying to take down. But why? And how had Sophia been connected to all of this?

The more Ethan learned, the more the pieces of the puzzle began to fall into place. His father's death hadn't been an accident—it had been orchestrated, a carefully planned event designed to silence him before he could expose the truth. And Sophia had been at the center of it all, pulling the strings from the shadows.

But why had she spared Ethan? Why had she allowed him to get this far?

The answer, when it finally came, was both devastating and liberating. Sophia hadn't spared him out of mercy or compassion—she had spared him because he was the final piece of her puzzle. She had been waiting for him to uncover the truth, waiting for him to see the full scope of her plan. And now that he had, she was ready to make her final move.

Ethan knew he was running out of time. If he didn't act quickly, Sophia would slip through his fingers once again, leaving behind nothing but chaos and destruction in her wake. But this time, he wasn't going to let her get away. This time, he was going to confront her, face to face, and bring her down once and for all.

The final showdown was inevitable.

Chapter 5: Layers of Deception

1. Unmasking the Victims

In the bustling city, shadows lurked in every corner, cloaked in secrets and lies. The vibrant streets, filled with laughter and life, hid an undercurrent of desperation that few could perceive. As the sun dipped below the horizon, the darkness enveloped the alleys where hope flickered like a dying ember. Here, the victims of a sinister game were often the unseen, their stories lost amid the noise of ambition and greed.

The prosecutor, weary yet determined, leaned over a desk cluttered with files, each one a testimony to the shattered lives that had crossed his path. He sifted through the documents, his brow furrowing as he read the accounts of those who had been swept into the chaos. These were not just statistics; they were real people, once full of dreams and aspirations, now reduced to mere casualties in a ruthless world.

There was Maria, a single mother whose hopes for a better life had been dashed by the machinations of a powerful organization. Her tale was a heartbreaking reminder of the collateral damage inflicted on the innocent. She had once worked multiple jobs, her nights filled with dreams of providing for her son, but the weight of debt and despair led her into the clutches of loan sharks. In a desperate attempt to escape, she had become entangled in a web of deceit that threatened to consume her.

Then there was Anton, a once-promising entrepreneur whose vision for a startup had attracted the attention of the wrong people. Lured by the promise of quick success, he found himself in a perilous alliance that spiraled out of control. With every compromise, every small betrayal of his values, he felt the grip of the organization tighten around him. The vibrant energy that had once fueled his ambitions faded, replaced by a suffocating sense of dread. His story echoed the plight of many who had believed they could play the game without understanding the stakes.

As the prosecutor connected the dots, a chilling pattern emerged. Each victim had been exploited not only for their vulnerabilities but also for their potential. The organization thrived on the desperation of others, turning dreams into nightmares. He noted how the powerful preyed upon the weak, crafting intricate schemes that left destruction in their wake. This unmasking of victims wasn't just an investigation; it was a mission to restore their dignity, to ensure their voices were heard.

Among the files was a photograph of a young girl, her smile radiant against the dark backdrop of her reality. Her name was Lena, and she had been a victim of human trafficking, lured by false promises of a better life. The prosecutor felt a pang of sorrow as he read her story—a tragic reminder that the innocence of youth was no shield against the evils of the world. Her resilience in the face of such horror became a beacon of hope for him, a testament to the strength of the human spirit even when battered by life's cruelties.

With each account, the prosecutor began to see the victims not as isolated cases but as a tapestry of interconnected lives. Their struggles, though unique, shared a common thread of exploitation. He realized that uncovering the truth was not just about seeking justice; it was about giving these individuals the recognition they deserved, the acknowledgment that their lives mattered.

The deeper he delved into their stories, the more determined he became. He was driven by a growing urgency to unearth the layers of deception that masked the true extent of the organization's reach. Each name he wrote down represented not just a victim but a call to action. He could not allow their suffering to be forgotten in the relentless march of time.

As days turned into weeks, he pieced together the puzzle, identifying key players and their methods. The victims began to transform from mere subjects of an investigation into allies in the fight for justice. Their testimonies, though painful, held the power to expose the organization's grip on the city.

The prosecutor organized meetings, bringing together those who had once felt isolated in their pain. In a small, dimly lit room, they shared their stories, their voices weaving a powerful narrative of resilience and defiance. Each testimony added depth to the understanding of how the organization operated, revealing its insidious tactics and the far-reaching consequences of its actions.

Through this process, the prosecutor became a conduit for their strength. He saw the fire rekindle in their eyes as they began to reclaim their narratives. Together, they were no longer victims; they were warriors united by a common goal. The organization had underestimated the resolve of those it had sought to break.

But the path to justice was fraught with peril. As the prosecutor delved deeper, he received threats, anonymous messages warning him to back off. The organization was watching, and they would not hesitate to silence anyone who dared to challenge their power. But he refused to be intimidated. The faces of the victims haunted him, their stories urging him forward.

In a pivotal moment, he decided to go public with the information he had gathered. He organized a press conference, inviting media outlets to hear the victims' stories firsthand. The room was filled with journalists and cameras, the atmosphere electric with anticipation. As he stood at the podium, he felt the weight of responsibility on his shoulders. This was more than just a press event; it was a chance to shine a light on the darkness that had engulfed so many lives.

One by one, the victims shared their experiences, their voices trembling but resolute. Maria spoke of her struggle to provide for her son, her words dripping with emotion as she described the fear that had gripped her life. Anton recounted the moment he realized he had lost control of his dreams, his voice steady as he spoke of the sacrifices he had made. Lena, with her newfound courage, detailed her harrowing journey from darkness into the light.

The impact was immediate. The public response was overwhelming, a surge of support flooding in from all corners of the city. People began to connect with the victims' stories, recognizing the shared humanity that transcended their circumstances. The prosecutor watched as hope flickered in the eyes of those who had once felt powerless, their pain transformed into a catalyst for change.

In the aftermath of the press conference, investigations gained momentum. Law enforcement agencies joined forces, fueled by public outrage and a commitment to dismantle the organization. The prosecutor found himself at the center of a movement, a rallying cry for justice echoing through the streets. As the tide turned, he could feel the weight of the victims' hopes resting on his shoulders.

But even in this moment of triumph, danger lurked. The organization, now exposed, would not go down without a fight. The prosecutor received cryptic warnings and sinister messages, each one a reminder of the stakes involved. He fortified his resolve, knowing that the battle ahead would require courage and cunning.

As the walls began to close in on the organization, the prosecutor felt a renewed sense of purpose. He understood that unmasking the victims was just the beginning; it was the first step in reclaiming their lives from the grasp of chaos. With every story shared, he was determined to forge a path toward justice that would resonate beyond the city limits, a legacy that would honor those who had suffered in silence.

In the end, the prosecutor realized that the true power lay not in revenge but in healing. By unmasking the victims, he had given them a voice, a chance to reclaim their narratives. Together, they were transforming their pain into a force for change, weaving a tapestry of resilience that would echo through the corridors of time. Their stories would not be forgotten; they would serve as a beacon of hope for generations to come, a reminder that even in the face of chaos, the human spirit could rise above and reclaim its dignity.

2. Ties That Bind

The air was thick with tension as Detective Elena Hart sat across from her informant in a dimly lit diner on the outskirts of the city. The flickering neon lights outside cast eerie shadows on the cracked vinyl booths, and the smell of stale coffee lingered in the air. She could feel the weight of the secrets swirling between them, and she knew that uncovering the truth would not only test her resolve but also threaten the fragile connections that tethered her to those she loved.

Elena had spent years piecing together a labyrinthine puzzle of corruption and deceit that snaked its way through the very heart of the city. As a dedicated prosecutor, she believed in the law, yet every day she found herself navigating a treacherous web where the line between right and wrong blurred into a haze of gray. The criminal underworld was more than just a collection of villains; it was a system, one built on fear, loyalty, and an intricate network of ties that bound its players together.

"Listen, Elena," her informant whispered, glancing around as if the walls themselves had ears. "What I'm about to tell you could change everything. But you need to understand the stakes. These people don't play games. They play for keeps."

She leaned in closer, her heart racing. "I need names. I need connections. Who's behind this?"

He took a deep breath, his eyes darting nervously. "It all leads back to the Marcelli family. They've been in the game for decades, and they know how to cover their tracks. But there's one thing you should know: they're not just a crime family. They're also tied to politicians, law enforcement... even judges."

Elena's mind raced. The Marcellis were known for their ruthlessness, but the extent of their influence was staggering. If she could untangle their web, she might just have a chance to bring them down. But the deeper she dug, the more dangerous it became.

As the weeks passed, she began to notice the subtle signs of a growing threat. Friends turned into shadows, and alliances began to fracture. A colleague she had trusted suddenly became distant, whispering behind closed doors. The pressure was mounting, and Elena knew that the ties she thought were strong were beginning to fray.

In a world where loyalty was currency, she had to decide who she could trust. Each encounter left her more isolated, questioning the very foundations of her relationships. She started to see her colleagues through a different lens—who was truly on her side, and who was simply playing a role in the game?

One evening, while reviewing files in her cramped office, she received an anonymous tip about a meeting happening that night. The address was a nondescript warehouse on the outskirts of town, a place she recognized as a Marcelli front for laundering money. With adrenaline coursing through her veins, she made her way there, heart pounding with the thrill of the chase.

Inside, the air was thick with anticipation. Elena peered through the cracks in the door, her breath catching in her throat as she recognized several figures engaged in a heated discussion. Among them stood Victor Marcelli, the youngest heir to the notorious crime family, flanked by enforcers who looked like they meant business.

As she strained to hear their conversation, snippets of information began to fall into place. They were discussing an upcoming shipment, one that could shift the power dynamics in the city. Elena's mind raced. This was the break she needed, a chance to gather evidence that could bring them to their knees.

Just then, her phone buzzed—a text from an unknown number. "Get out now. They're onto you." Panic gripped her, but she couldn't leave empty-handed. She shifted her focus back to the conversation, her instincts driving her to stay.

Suddenly, the door burst open, and she barely had time to react. The enforcers moved with deadly precision, fanning out to secure the area. Heart racing, she ducked behind a stack of crates, adrenaline surging as she weighed her options. She had to find a way to escape but knew she couldn't leave without evidence.

Elena's thoughts were a whirlwind as she navigated through the shadows of the warehouse. She remembered the phrase that had guided her through years of perilous investigations: "The truth is a powerful ally." With that in mind, she reached for her phone, desperately snapping pictures of the meeting. Each click felt like a lifeline, a reminder that she wasn't alone in this fight.

But her moment of triumph was short-lived. Just as she was about to slip away, a firm hand gripped her shoulder, spinning her around. It was one of the enforcers, his eyes cold and unyielding.

"Thought you could play spy, huh?" he sneered, tightening his grip.

In that moment, Elena realized how easily her world could unravel. The ties she had forged over the years—trust, loyalty, and friendships—felt like shackles, binding her to a fate she desperately wanted to escape. But she refused to give in. With a surge of strength, she fought back, her instincts kicking in as she elbowed him in the stomach and bolted for the exit.

The sounds of chaos erupted behind her as she dashed through the dimly lit corridors. Her heart raced with every step, the echoes of her pursuers ringing in her ears. She could feel the weight of the evidence in her pocket, the proof she needed to expose the Marcelli empire.

As she burst out into the cool night air, the world around her seemed to come alive. She ran toward her car, the adrenaline coursing through her veins. With each stride, she thought of the ties that bound her to the people she loved, the sacrifices she was willing to make to protect them.

Back in the safety of her car, she took a moment to catch her breath, the weight of the night crashing over her. She knew she had to be smarter, faster, and more vigilant. The fight was far from over, but she had taken the first step toward unraveling the complex tapestry of deceit that surrounded her.

In the days that followed, the tension continued to mount. Elena found herself questioning everything. With each new piece of evidence, she became increasingly aware of the precarious nature of her alliances. Friends became foes, and trust seemed like a distant memory.

Determined to forge a path forward, she began reaching out to those who still believed in her cause. Each conversation revealed new layers of corruption, the ties that bound the city's power players tightening around her. Yet with each revelation, she felt the shadows grow deeper, whispering doubts about her choices and the people around her.

But Elena was resolute. She had come too far to turn back now. As the investigation reached a fever pitch, she realized that the ties that bind were also the ties that could be severed. In a world where loyalty was tested at every turn, she was prepared to do whatever it took to expose the truth, even if it meant standing alone.

The journey ahead would be fraught with peril, but she was no longer just a pawn in their game. She was ready to become the player, ready to sever the ties that bound her to a life of fear and uncertainty. And as she prepared for the battles to come, she steeled herself with the knowledge that the strongest ties of all were those forged through truth and resilience.

3. The Unseen Puppeteer

In the dimly lit backroom of a forgotten bar, a single overhead light flickered, casting shadows that danced along the cracked walls. A group of men sat huddled around a table, their voices low, conspiratorial. Each one had a story, a connection to the sprawling web of power and deceit that entwined their lives. But one man, sitting silently in the corner, observed intently, his presence almost ghostly.

Victor had always been a ghost in the world of crime—never quite seen, yet always felt. His fingers were entwined in every major deal that transpired in the city, yet he remained an enigma, a puppeteer pulling the strings from the shadows. His reputation was built on whispers, on rumors that slithered through the underbelly of society. He didn't need to flaunt power; it was inherent in his silence, in the way people shied away from discussing him in open air. Victor knew the art of invisibility.

As the men at the table plotted their next move against a rival gang, they remained blissfully unaware of the eyes watching them. They spoke of blood, of revenge, unaware that Victor had already anticipated their every thought, their every desire. He had been the one to set the game in motion, creating conflicts that would serve his own interests. The chaos that would ensue was merely a prelude to his ultimate play—a move that would shift the balance of power in the city.

Across town, in a high-rise office that overlooked the chaos below, a different kind of player moved. Caroline, a young attorney with a fierce sense of justice, had started to unravel a case that seemed simple at first but grew tangled in layers of corruption. Every lead she followed brought her closer to Victor, the unseen puppeteer, though she was yet unaware of his presence. For Caroline, justice was a calling, a mission that consumed her every waking moment. She meticulously combed through documents, interviewed witnesses, and pieced together a narrative that seemed to escape everyone else.

Yet, with each step she took, Victor's influence loomed like a shadow. He had planted seeds of doubt, misdirection, and fear among those who might help her. Witnesses went missing, evidence vanished, and every door she knocked on seemed to lead to a brick wall. It was as if the city itself conspired against her, urging her to retreat, to abandon the fight. But Caroline was stubborn, driven by a need to expose the truth, no matter how deeply it was buried.

As the weeks passed, the tension in the city escalated. The rival gang grew more aggressive, sensing weakness among their adversaries, while Victor quietly orchestrated their downfall. He fed information to both sides, ensuring that their conflicts would spiral out of control, leading to bloodshed that would ultimately serve his purpose. The streets echoed with violence, the air thick with the scent of fear and uncertainty.

Caroline, however, was undeterred. In her mind, every obstacle was a challenge to be overcome. One evening, while sifting through a pile of files in her cramped office, she stumbled upon a connection—a series of transactions that linked prominent figures in the city to the very criminal activities she was investigating. It was a breakthrough, but the realization came with a chilling thought: if Victor was behind it all, then exposing him would mean stepping into a labyrinth from which few emerged unscathed.

That night, she lay awake, contemplating her next move. The weight of the truth pressed down on her, a heavy burden she felt unprepared to carry. But the thought of inaction gnawed at her. In a world where the unseen could manipulate lives without consequence, she knew she had to fight back. She needed allies, people who could stand beside her in the face of danger. But who could she trust when trust itself was a commodity in short supply?

The following days were a blur of meetings and late-night strategy sessions. Caroline sought out fellow lawyers, community leaders, anyone who might be willing to join her cause. Each conversation was fraught with tension; she could sense the fear in their voices as they weighed the risks of opposing the unseen puppeteer. Yet, as she laid out the evidence she had gathered, a flicker of hope ignited in their eyes. Together, they began to form a plan—a coalition to confront the corruption that had suffocated their city for far too long.

Unbeknownst to them, Victor was watching, his keen intuition sensing a shift in the air. The pieces on his chessboard were moving differently, and for the first time in a long while, he felt a flicker of uncertainty. His control, so meticulously crafted over the years, was being challenged. He leaned back in his chair, contemplating his next move. The game was about to become far more interesting.

With each passing day, the coalition grew stronger, emboldened by the knowledge that they were not alone in their fight. Caroline led the charge, organizing rallies and community meetings, rallying the citizens to stand against the tide of fear that had washed over them for too long. They demanded accountability from their leaders, transparency in their justice system, and an end to the corruption that had seeped into every crevice of their lives.

As the movement gained momentum, Victor's grip began to slip. The city, once a playground for his schemes, was awakening to the truth. It was becoming increasingly difficult for him to remain in the shadows as the spotlight turned towards him. Yet, Victor was not one to back down easily. He thrived in chaos and had a talent for manipulating situations to his advantage. He needed to regain control before the coalition could gather enough strength to dismantle his empire.

Late one night, as Caroline reviewed her notes in the office, the phone rang, shattering the silence. The voice on the other end was shaky, a former associate of Victor's seeking protection in exchange for information. Caroline listened intently, her heart racing. The details he provided were explosive, revealing the intricate network of corruption that had long kept Victor in power. But there was a catch—meeting him would mean stepping into a dangerous game.

After a brief deliberation, Caroline decided she had no choice. The risk was worth the potential reward. The next day, she arranged to meet the informant in a secluded location, a park that had seen better days. As she approached, the weight of anticipation pressed heavily on her. Would this man truly have the answers she sought, or was it merely another trap laid by the unseen puppeteer?

The meeting unfolded in hushed tones, each word hanging in the air like a fragile promise. The informant spoke of hidden accounts, names of powerful allies, and a plan Victor had been hatching to eliminate any threats to his empire. Caroline listened, her mind racing with the implications. If she could piece together this puzzle, she could expose Victor and his web of deceit once and for all.

Yet, as the informant leaned closer, his voice dropping to a whisper, Caroline felt a chill crawl up her spine. "He's always watching, you know," he cautioned, glancing over his shoulder as if expecting shadows to materialize around them. "Don't trust anyone. Not even me."

His warning echoed in her mind as she left the park, the weight of her mission heavier than ever. She returned to her office, heart pounding, fingers trembling as she typed out a detailed report, piecing together the fragments of truth she had gathered.

But Victor was already several steps ahead. He had received word of her meeting and understood the threat she posed. The unseen puppeteer was not one to be underestimated, and he was ready to remind everyone why.

As Caroline and her coalition prepared to confront the shadows that loomed over their lives, the stage was set for a clash that would determine the fate of the city. The battle between light and dark was imminent, and with each passing moment, the stakes grew higher. Would the truth finally emerge, or would the unseen puppeteer continue to pull the strings, shrouded in darkness?

The fight for justice had only just begun, and in the intricate dance of power, every move mattered. The city held its breath, awaiting the outcome of a game that had been played for too long, teetering on the edge of chaos.

4. Turning Points

The air in the office was thick with tension, punctuated only by the rhythmic clicking of the keyboard. David stared at the screen, the glow illuminating the lines of text that detailed a web of corruption and deceit. He had always believed in justice, but the deeper he delved into this case, the more it felt like he was staring into the abyss. Each piece of evidence revealed not just the extent of the criminal organization but also the complicity of those who were supposed to uphold the law.

His phone buzzed, breaking his concentration. It was a message from Lisa, his informant, a woman with a past as tangled as the case they were embroiled in. She had become an unexpected ally, offering insights that only someone on the inside could provide. But he also knew she was walking a tightrope, balancing her loyalty to him with the risks that came from her connections.

"David, meet me at the café on Fifth. We need to talk. It's urgent."

His stomach tightened at the urgency in her message. He grabbed his jacket and left the office, the city bustling around him, oblivious to the storm brewing in the shadows. As he walked, he reflected on the turning points that had led him here. It started innocently enough, a routine case that had spiraled into a full-fledged investigation, revealing layers of deception he had never imagined.

The café was dimly lit, a refuge from the harshness of the street. Lisa was already there, her eyes darting nervously. He took a seat across from her, studying her expression. "What's going on?" he asked, leaning in.

"I've uncovered something," she whispered, glancing around as if the walls had ears. "You need to understand the depth of this.

It's bigger than we thought. There are people involved who could destroy us both."

David felt a chill run down his spine. He had always suspected that the organization had deeper roots, but the implications of her words sent a ripple of fear through him. "What do you mean?"

She took a deep breath, steadying herself. "Remember the names we came across? They're not just players in this game. They're linked to political figures, even within the police department. They've built a fortress around themselves."

His mind raced. "So, we're dealing with corruption at the highest levels?"

"Exactly," she replied, her voice barely above a whisper. "And they won't hesitate to silence anyone who threatens their empire."

As he processed her words, David felt a weight settle on his shoulders. The idea of facing not just criminals but also those sworn to protect the law was daunting. Yet, there was no turning back. The scales of justice had tipped too far, and he couldn't abandon the fight.

They spent the next hour poring over documents and making plans, the stakes rising with every revelation. Lisa's insights painted a picture of a vast network, a secret hand orchestrating events from the shadows. David knew they had to act swiftly, but the fear of retaliation loomed over them like a dark cloud.

When they finally emerged from the café, David's mind was spinning. He felt a mixture of adrenaline and dread as he realized that they had crossed a threshold. There was no going back; their lives were irrevocably changed.

Days turned into weeks as they worked tirelessly, gathering evidence and building their case. Each lead uncovered new connections, each interview revealing more about the organization's reach. David found himself in a constant state of alert, always looking over his shoulder, always aware that danger lurked just beyond the periphery.

Then came the moment he had dreaded yet anticipated: a breakthrough. An anonymous tip pointed them to a meeting scheduled at an abandoned warehouse on the outskirts of the city. It was a gathering of key players in the organization, and they had to seize the opportunity to gather hard evidence.

As David and Lisa prepared for the operation, he felt a surge of determination. This was their chance to expose the truth. They devised a plan, enlisting a small team of trusted colleagues who shared their commitment to justice. But as they approached the warehouse, a nagging doubt crept into David's mind. What if they were walking into a trap?

The air was heavy with tension as they positioned themselves around the warehouse, each member of the team knowing the stakes. They had only one shot at this, and failure was not an option. David glanced at Lisa, who nodded, her resolve mirroring his own. They would see this through together.

As the meeting commenced inside, David's heart raced. They could hear snippets of conversation through the cracked walls, the tone of voices growing increasingly animated. He signaled for silence, the group holding their breath as they waited for the right moment to make their move.

Suddenly, the atmosphere shifted. Raised voices turned into heated arguments, and David caught the phrase "loose ends" from within. A cold sweat broke out on his forehead as he realized the true danger of their mission. The meeting was not just about business; it was a reckoning.

In that instant, the turning point they had been building towards unfolded. David's instincts kicked in. "We have to go in now!" he urged the team. They burst through the doors, adrenaline fueling their movements. What lay ahead was chaos, a confrontation that would determine their fates and the outcome of the investigation.

The scene inside was frenetic. Tables overturned, papers flying, the air thick with tension as those gathered realized their meeting had been compromised. David and Lisa shouted commands, their voices cutting through the confusion as they fought to gain control.

But amidst the chaos, David locked eyes with one of the leaders, a man he had only seen in photographs. The glint of recognition ignited a fire within him. This was the man behind the curtain, the orchestrator of the chaos they had uncovered.

"Freeze!" David shouted, aiming his weapon with unwavering resolve. But in that moment, the warehouse erupted into chaos, and the world he thought he knew crumbled around him.

The turning points in their investigation had led them to this decisive moment, a culmination of risks taken, alliances forged, and a relentless pursuit of justice. As the dust settled, David understood that there was no going back; they had crossed the line into a world of danger that would challenge everything they believed in.

In the aftermath, as they regrouped and assessed the damage, David realized that they had ignited a spark. The investigation was far from over, and the ramifications of their actions would echo long after that day. But one thing was certain: they were no longer mere players in a game—they had become a force to be reckoned with.

The turning points had shaped their journey, but it was just the beginning. David felt a renewed sense of purpose as they prepared for the battles ahead, knowing that the ultimate fight for truth and justice was still to come.

5. Secrets and Lies

In the heart of the city, where shadows danced between towering skyscrapers, secrets lay buried beneath the surface, waiting to be uncovered. For years, the whispers of betrayal echoed through the narrow alleys, intertwining the lives of those who dared to tread too close to the truth. The air was thick with tension, a palpable reminder that in this world, trust was a luxury few could afford.

As the rain began to fall, slicking the streets in a glossy sheen, prosecutor Alex Mercer felt the weight of the impending storm—not just in the weather, but in the looming investigation that threatened to unravel everything he believed. The case of the decade had landed on his desk, a labyrinthine web of corruption and deceit that stretched far beyond the city's borders. It was a case that involved powerful figures, hidden agendas, and a clandestine organization whose reach seemed infinite.

Alex's mind raced with the implications of what lay ahead. He had spent countless nights poring over documents, chasing leads that often turned into dead ends. The deeper he dug, the more he realized that the very foundation of the city was built on lies. Promises made in the shadows had led to a flourishing underworld, one where money flowed freely, and morality was a mere afterthought.

His thoughts drifted to the victims—ordinary citizens caught in the crossfire of a war they never chose. Each name on the list of the fallen resonated with him, each story echoing in the recesses of his mind. The police reports painted a grim picture: families shattered, lives irrevocably altered. But it wasn't just the victims that haunted him; it was the realization that those in power wielded their influence like a weapon, silencing dissent and manipulating the truth to serve their ends.

He glanced at his notes, a chaotic amalgamation of connections and theories. Names like Derek Calhoun, a real estate mogul with a penchant for shady deals, and Veronica Stein, a politician whose promises were as empty as her campaign slogans. Their lives were intertwined in a complex dance of ambition and greed, each step calculated to stay one step ahead of the law.

Yet, the more he scrutinized their paths, the more he sensed an unseen hand guiding their movements. It was as if they were players on a chessboard, their every move dictated by an unseen puppeteer. Who could it be? Alex couldn't shake the feeling that there was a mastermind lurking in the shadows, orchestrating the chaos for their own gain.

Determined to uncover the truth, Alex enlisted the help of an old friend, a seasoned investigator named Rachel, whose instincts were sharp as a razor. Their partnership had been forged in the fires of previous cases, and he trusted her to see the patterns he might overlook. Together, they began to piece together the fragments of a much larger picture.

Their first lead took them to a dimly lit bar on the outskirts of town, a place where the air was thick with smoke and the walls seemed to absorb the secrets shared within. Here, the clientele was a mix of lost souls and desperate characters, each with their own stories to tell. As they settled into a booth, the dim light flickering overhead, Rachel slid a folder across the table.

"Here's what we have on Calhoun," she said, her voice barely above a whisper. "But I have a feeling he's just the tip of the iceberg."

The folder contained photographs, transaction records, and snippets of conversations captured by informants. One particular note caught Alex's eye—a reference to a "Secret Hand," an entity that operated behind the scenes, manipulating the fates of those too weak or too corrupt to resist. It sent a chill down his spine.

"Do you think this is just a rumor?" he asked, his brow furrowing.

"Rumors often have a kernel of truth," Rachel replied, her expression serious. "But if this 'Secret Hand' exists, we need to tread carefully. They could be the reason so many people are terrified to speak out."

As they delved deeper into their investigation, they uncovered a network of shell companies, offshore accounts, and a dizzying array of connections that linked the city's elite to organized crime. Each lead felt like a step further into the abyss, where every answer only led to more questions. Who were the true architects of this chaos?

Days turned into weeks, and the pressure mounted. Alex found himself unable to sleep, his mind racing with the implications of their findings. Each evening, he returned home, haunted by the faces of the victims and the shadows that loomed over the city. The lies he uncovered weighed heavily on his conscience, and he questioned how he could possibly dismantle such a deeply entrenched system.

One evening, as he sat in his office reviewing case files, his phone buzzed with a message that turned his world upside down. It was from Rachel: "Meet me at the usual place. Urgent." The urgency in her text sent alarm bells ringing. He grabbed his coat and headed out into the night, the rain still falling, a rhythmic reminder of the storm brewing around them.

At the bar, Rachel was already seated, her expression grave. "I spoke to someone," she said, glancing around as if expecting eavesdroppers. "They know about the 'Secret Hand'—and they're scared."

"What did they say?" Alex leaned in, his heart racing.

"There's a meeting happening tonight, a gathering of the city's most influential figures. They're discussing how to handle the growing scrutiny," she replied, her voice low. "If we could just get a glimpse into that meeting..."

Alex's mind raced with possibilities. This could be the breakthrough they needed. But the stakes were higher than ever, and they had to move swiftly. As they plotted their course, the reality of what lay ahead settled in. They were no longer just prosecutors chasing justice; they were now players in a dangerous game where the odds were stacked against them.

With every passing moment, the city seemed to pulse with anticipation, the lies festering beneath the surface. In the shadows, the 'Secret Hand' continued to pull the strings, but Alex and Rachel were determined to shine a light on the truth, no matter the cost. Their journey had only just begun, and the secrets and lies that bound them would either break them or lead them to the ultimate revelation.

6. A Dangerous Revelation

As the rain poured down relentlessly, the city felt more like a trapped beast than a thriving metropolis. Neon lights flickered in the murky night, illuminating the alleyways where secrets festered and shadows whispered. Prosecutor Alex Carter leaned against the cold brick wall, his mind racing with the implications of what he had just uncovered. The lead he had been pursuing for weeks had finally cracked open, revealing a web of deceit that stretched far beyond anything he could have imagined.

The meeting with his informant had been tense. In the dimly lit café, the man had spoken in hushed tones, glancing over his shoulder as if the walls themselves had ears. "You're getting too close, Alex," he had warned, his voice a low rasp. "They don't take kindly to curiosity. You need to back off." But backing off was never an option for Alex. He was driven by a need for justice that sometimes felt like an addiction.

Now, as he stood in the rain, the weight of the revelation pressed heavily on his chest. The underground network he was unraveling was more than just a money-laundering operation; it was a labyrinthine enterprise involving high-profile politicians and influential business tycoons. Their names were etched in the margins of the files he had gathered, connected by a delicate thread of corruption that wove through the very fabric of the city's governance. The truth was like a double-edged sword, capable of cutting through the veil of power but also threatening to sever the ties he held dear.

He turned sharply, the water splashing around his feet, and made his way to the car parked a few blocks away. The weight of the files felt almost comforting in his hands, a tangible representation of his journey into darkness. As he drove through the rain-soaked streets, his mind drifted to the faces behind the names in the files—people he had once admired, leaders who had promised change. It was a sobering thought, realizing that the very pillars of society could be crumbling under the weight of their own greed.

Arriving at his modest apartment, he felt a familiar sense of isolation wash over him. The walls were adorned with case files and photographs, reminders of the lives he was fighting to protect. He dropped the files onto the kitchen table, each one a small testament to the injustices he had witnessed. As he pored over the documents, a sense of urgency began to pulse through him. Time was not on his side.

The first name that jumped out at him was Victor Antonov, a businessman with a philanthropic image that masked a more sinister reality. His investments spanned multiple sectors, from real estate to technology, but it was the money trail leading back to a series of offshore accounts that had caught Alex's eye. Each transaction was a breadcrumb leading deeper into the woods of financial malfeasance.

Flipping through the pages, he found photographs from a gala event—a charity fundraiser that had been nothing more than a front for laundering money. Smiling faces, clinking glasses, the façade of civility. But behind that glittering veneer lay a truth darker than the night outside. Alex knew that the more he dug, the more dangerous his pursuit would become.

That night, he decided to pay a visit to an old friend—Detective Mia Thompson, who had a reputation for navigating the murky waters of organized crime. She had a way of making the impossible seem achievable, and Alex hoped that her insight could illuminate the path ahead. As he arrived at her precinct, he was greeted by the bustling sounds of officers working diligently, the air thick with the scent of burnt coffee and determination.

Mia was in the back, poring over case files that seemed to blur into one another. When she looked up and saw Alex, her expression shifted from surprise to concern. "You're in deep, aren't you?" she asked, motioning for him to sit.

"Deeper than I thought," he admitted, pushing the files across the table toward her. As she began to skim through them, her brow furrowed, and the gravity of the situation settled in. "This isn't just a money-laundering operation, is it? There's a whole network here."

"Exactly. And they won't hesitate to protect their interests," Alex replied, leaning in closer. "I'm worried about the lengths they'll go to keep this under wraps."

Mia nodded, her eyes narrowing in thought. "If what you're saying is true, we're not just looking at financial crimes. This could tie into something much larger—political corruption, possibly even racketeering."

Alex felt a chill run down his spine. He had considered the implications but had hoped they were exaggerated. "We need to move quickly. If we don't act now, this could disappear into the shadows."

The two of them began strategizing, mapping out their next steps. It was clear they would need more evidence to take on such powerful adversaries. As the hours slipped away, they poured over the files, exchanging ideas and piecing together the fragmented puzzle of corruption that enveloped the city.

By dawn, a plan had formed. They would reach out to other contacts—people who had been affected by Antonov's machinations. If they could gather testimonies, they might be able to create a case strong enough to withstand the inevitable pushback. Alex felt a renewed sense of purpose coursing through him.

But the danger was palpable. As they prepared to leave the precinct, a figure caught his eye—a man lurking just outside the entrance, watching them intently. His heart raced as he exchanged glances with Mia. They had been followed.

The adrenaline surged as they rushed to their cars, but Alex couldn't shake the feeling that they were already too late. The man had seen them, and with that knowledge, he was now a player in their deadly game. The revelation had unleashed a torrent of danger, and as they drove away, the weight of it settled heavily in Alex's gut. The truth was out there, but so were the forces determined to bury it.

Over the next few days, they worked tirelessly, gathering testimonies and compiling evidence. Each new piece of information seemed to shine a light on the hidden depths of corruption that plagued the city. But with every advancement, the threats grew closer.

Late one night, as Alex returned home, he found his apartment had been ransacked. Papers were strewn across the floor, and the files he had worked so hard to compile were missing. Panic surged through him. He knew they were onto him, and the urgency to act intensified.

He called Mia immediately. "We need to meet. They've found us."

As he sped through the rain-soaked streets toward their rendezvous point, the gravity of their situation loomed larger than ever. It wasn't just his career on the line; it was his life. The revelation had set off a chain reaction, and the consequences would ripple through their lives in ways they couldn't yet fathom.

Mia was already waiting when he arrived, her expression grave. "I've got some leads, but we need to be careful. This isn't just about Antonov anymore. We've stirred the hornet's nest."

Together, they strategized their next move. With the walls closing in, they needed to strike before the shadowy figures lurking in the periphery snuffed out their light for good. The game had changed, and now it was a race against time to reveal the truth before it was swallowed by the chaos they had uncovered.

As dawn broke, they felt the weight of their choices pressing down on them. The city around them was a labyrinth of danger and deceit, but within it lay the hope of justice. They would navigate the shadows, risking everything for the revelation that could change their lives—and the lives of countless others—forever.

Chapter 6: The Enigmatic Woman

1. The First Encounter

In the dim light of the bar, shadows danced across the faces of the patrons, a tapestry of secrets and whispers. The air was thick with the scent of aged whiskey and desperation, an intoxicating blend that drew in those seeking solace or distraction. At the far end, beneath a flickering neon sign that buzzed like a disturbed hornet, sat Alex, nursing a drink that had long since lost its chill. He wasn't here for pleasure; he was on a mission.

Tonight, he was waiting for a woman known only as Mira. Her name had surfaced in hushed conversations, often accompanied by a shroud of intrigue and danger. Rumors painted her as both a victim and a mastermind, a woman who could navigate the murky waters of the city's underbelly with grace and cunning. As he glanced at his watch, impatience gnawed at him. Time was a luxury he could no longer afford.

The bar's entrance swung open, a gust of cold air preceding her arrival. Mira stepped in, her silhouette striking against the dim light, a vision of poise and confidence. Her coat, a sleek black, clung to her figure, and her eyes—sharp and calculating—scanned the room. The moment their gazes met, an electric charge filled the air, a silent acknowledgment of the game they were about to play.

She approached, her heels clicking rhythmically against the wooden floor, each step echoing like a heartbeat in the silence that surrounded them. Alex straightened in his seat, trying to appear composed despite the turmoil brewing inside. She slid into the booth opposite him, a sly smile curving her lips.

"Alex, I presume?" she said, her voice smooth as silk, laced with a hint of amusement. "I've heard a lot about you."

"Likewise," he replied, carefully measuring his words. "I'm hoping you can help me with something."

"Help is a broad term," she said, her eyes glinting. "What exactly are you looking for?"

He leaned in closer, lowering his voice to a whisper. "I need information about the Syndicate—specifically, their operations and anyone involved in their money laundering schemes."

Mira raised an eyebrow, intrigued yet cautious. "That's dangerous territory. You know what they say about curiosity, don't you?"

"Curiosity killed the cat, but satisfaction brought it back," he quipped, attempting to inject levity into the tense atmosphere. Yet, her expression remained serious.

"I can get you information, but it won't come cheap," she warned, her gaze unwavering. "And once you step into this world, there's no turning back."

He nodded, acutely aware of the weight of her words. The deeper he delved, the more perilous his situation would become. But the truth was like a siren's call, impossible to resist. "I'm willing to take that risk."

Mira studied him for a moment, as if gauging the sincerity of his resolve. "Fine. Meet me tomorrow night at the docks. Midnight. There's someone you need to meet—a source who can provide you with the details you seek."

"Who is it?" he asked, curiosity piqued.

"A ghost," she replied cryptically. "A man who knows more than he should. But be careful; he's not the only one watching."

With that, she stood up, slipping a card across the table before turning to leave. "Remember, Alex, the shadows have eyes. Stay alert."

As she walked away, he couldn't shake the feeling that this encounter was just the beginning of a treacherous journey. He picked up the card, running his fingers over the embossed lettering. It bore her name and a number, but it was the message scrawled on the back that caught his eye: "Trust no one."

The night dragged on, but Alex's mind raced with thoughts of Mira and the implications of her words. The city was a labyrinth of deceit, and he had willingly entered its depths. He finished his drink, the warmth of the whiskey no longer providing comfort. Instead, it heightened his senses, sharpening his focus as he prepared for the meeting at the docks.

The following night, he arrived early, the salty breeze whipping through the air as he stood at the edge of the dock. Shadows loomed large, the silhouettes of ships creaking gently in the water. His heart raced with anticipation and fear—what would he uncover tonight?

As midnight approached, the atmosphere thickened with tension. The moonlight cast a silver sheen on the water, illuminating the way for the shadows lurking beneath. Suddenly, a figure emerged from the darkness—a man dressed in a worn leather jacket, his face obscured by the brim of a hat. He moved with a purposeful gait, each step deliberate and confident.

"Alex?" the man asked, his voice low and gravelly. "Mira sent me."

"Yeah, I'm Alex," he replied, attempting to mask his unease. "Are you the source?"

The man chuckled softly, a sound devoid of warmth. "I know things. But knowledge comes at a price. What are you willing to give?"

"I need information about the Syndicate—who's involved, where the money's going," Alex said, cutting to the chase. "I'm willing to do whatever it takes."

"Be careful what you wish for," the man warned, stepping closer, his expression unreadable. "The deeper you go, the more you'll lose."

"Just tell me what you know," Alex urged, desperation creeping into his voice.

The man paused, glancing around as if ensuring they weren't being watched. "They operate from the shadows, using fronts to hide their tracks. But there's a woman at the heart of it—Mira knows her too. She's the one pulling the strings."

Alex felt a chill run down his spine. "What's her connection?"

"She's a ghost, just like me. But don't underestimate her; she's more powerful than you realize," the man warned, his tone grave. "Trust her at your own peril."

With that, he slipped a folded piece of paper into Alex's hand. "This will help you. But remember, in this game, nothing is as it seems. Watch your back."

Before Alex could respond, the man melted back into the shadows, leaving him alone with the weight of the revelations. He unfolded the paper, revealing a list of names, addresses, and a network that stretched far beyond what he had imagined. The Syndicate was larger and more insidious than he had anticipated, its roots entwined within the very fabric of the city.

He stood there, the dock's cool breeze wrapping around him, feeling both exhilarated and terrified. The first encounter had opened a door, and he was now standing at the threshold of a world where trust was a luxury and every decision could cost him everything. As he made his way back through the night, one thought consumed him: this was only the beginning.

2. Charms and Deceit

In the dimly lit corner of a high-end bar, where shadows danced across polished mahogany, Clara sat with an effortless grace. The soft jazz floated through the air, a perfect accompaniment to the murmur of well-dressed patrons engaged in their own clandestine conversations. She sipped her bourbon, the amber liquid catching the light, while her piercing green eyes scanned the room, alert yet seemingly relaxed. Clara was not just another face in the crowd; she was a master of illusions, a connoisseur of charms, and a woman whose secrets ran as deep as the whiskey in her glass.

Across the bar, a man in a tailored suit caught her attention. He was handsome in a rugged way, with dark hair that fell just above his piercing blue eyes. His demeanor radiated confidence, and he seemed to hold an air of mystery that intrigued Clara. As he approached, she felt a familiar thrill. This was the game she played best—drawing in unsuspecting souls, weaving her web of deceit. The man slid onto the stool beside her, flashing a charming smile that revealed a hint of mischief.

"Is this seat taken?" he asked, his voice smooth like the whiskey Clara enjoyed.

She turned to him, arching an eyebrow. "Only if you can keep up with the conversation."

He laughed, a sound that mingled effortlessly with the music. "I'm up for the challenge. I'm Ethan, by the way."

"Clara," she replied, extending her hand. Their fingers brushed, and a flicker of electricity passed between them. She noted the slight tension in his grip—a sign of someone accustomed to control. It piqued her curiosity.

As they exchanged pleasantries, Clara couldn't help but observe the subtle shifts in his expressions. His charm was evident, but there was an underlying wariness, as if he was weighing her every word.

This only added to her intrigue. It wasn't uncommon for her to attract attention, but she relished the challenge of uncovering the layers beneath the charm.

"So, what brings you here?" Clara asked, tilting her head slightly, her voice laced with curiosity. "This doesn't seem like your usual haunt."

Ethan leaned in closer, lowering his voice. "Just passing through on business. But I'm starting to think this place is more interesting than my meetings."

"Business, huh?" Clara replied, feigning innocence. "What kind of business?"

"Let's just say it involves some high stakes." His gaze locked onto hers, and she felt the heat of his intensity. "What about you?"

"Just enjoying a night out," she said with a nonchalant shrug. But internally, Clara was calculating. High stakes often meant trouble, and trouble was exactly what she thrived on.

As the conversation flowed, Clara expertly wove her stories, each carefully crafted to spark his interest while hiding the truth. She was no stranger to deceit; her life was built on a foundation of lies and half-truths. Every detail was a brushstroke on the canvas of her persona—a cocktail of charm and intrigue. The more she revealed, the deeper Ethan seemed to fall under her spell.

"You're quite the enigma," he remarked, his eyes narrowing slightly as he studied her. "I can't quite figure you out."

"Good," Clara replied with a smirk. "If you could, it would make things boring."

Ethan's smile faded for a moment, replaced by a look of contemplation. "Boredom can be dangerous, you know. It makes people do reckless things."

"Like what?" Clara asked, genuinely intrigued.

"Like taking risks they shouldn't," he said, his tone dropping. "Or trusting the wrong people."

The weight of his words lingered in the air between them, a palpable tension that seemed to electrify the space. Clara leaned back, contemplating his insight. Trust was a fragile thing, and in her world, it was a currency more valuable than gold. The right deception could open doors or close them forever.

"Tell me," Clara began, her voice laced with playful curiosity, "what's the most reckless thing you've ever done?"

Ethan paused, his gaze drifting as he pondered the question. "I once found myself involved in a high-stakes poker game with some unsavory characters. The kind of people who don't take losing lightly."

Clara leaned in, her interest piqued. "And what happened?"

"I lost," he admitted, a hint of a grin on his lips. "And I walked away with a broken wrist and a reminder that some games are better left unplayed."

"Lesson learned, then," she said, her heart racing at the thrill of their exchange. It was this adrenaline—the sense of danger—that drew her to men like Ethan. They were complex, layered, and often hiding their own secrets beneath the charm.

The evening wore on, drinks flowing and laughter ringing out, but beneath the surface, a silent dance of deception was unfolding. Clara knew Ethan was probing, searching for the truth behind her carefully curated facade. She had to be cautious; charm was a double-edged sword, and the moment she revealed too much, she risked losing her advantage.

As the clock approached midnight, Ethan leaned in closer, his voice barely above a whisper. "You're not like anyone I've met before, Clara. There's something about you."

"Is that good or bad?" she asked, a teasing smile playing on her lips.

"Good, I think," he replied, his eyes sparkling with mischief. "But I can't shake the feeling that you're hiding something."

Clara's heart raced at his observation. She had always been adept at concealing her true self, but something about Ethan felt different. The challenge of maintaining her charm while dancing on the edge of truth was exhilarating, and she found herself drawn to him in a way she hadn't anticipated.

"Perhaps I am," she said, a playful glint in her eye. "But then again, everyone has secrets. It's what makes us interesting."

Ethan raised his glass, a silent toast to the game they were playing. "To secrets then, and the stories they tell."

"To secrets," Clara echoed, their glasses clinking together. The night held promise, the thrill of the unknown tantalizing both of them. Little did they know, the shadows of their pasts were about to collide in ways they couldn't imagine.

As they shared stories and laughter, Clara felt the weight of her own secrets pressing down on her. The line between charm and deceit blurred further, and she knew she had to tread carefully. With each passing moment, the stakes grew higher, and the allure of danger wrapped around them like a silken thread.

In that dimly lit bar, amid the flickering lights and swirling smoke, Clara embraced the chaos of her life. The dance of charm and deceit was one she knew well, but with Ethan, it felt different—charged with a tension that left her breathless. As the night unfolded, she couldn't shake the feeling that their paths were intertwined, and the secrets they carried would soon lead them down a road neither of them was prepared to travel.

When the clock struck one, Clara glanced at Ethan, his expression shifting to one of resolve. "Let's get out of here," he said, his tone leaving no room for argument.

"Where to?" she asked, intrigued.

"Somewhere we can talk without the noise," he replied, a hint of urgency in his voice.

She nodded, her heart racing as they slipped out of the bar, leaving the world behind. The night air was cool, a refreshing contrast to the warmth of their earlier exchange. They walked in silence for a moment, the city lights casting a soft glow around them.

As they turned a corner, Clara couldn't help but feel the weight of the night pressing down on her. This was where the real game began—the world outside was fraught with danger, and she was stepping deeper into the shadows. But with Ethan by her side, the thrill of uncertainty surged within her.

"Tell me about the stakes," Clara urged, glancing sideways at him. "What's really going on?"

Ethan hesitated, the charm slipping momentarily from his facade. "I can't give you all the details yet, but trust me, it involves people who will do anything to protect their interests. And those interests are worth billions."

"Billions," she repeated, intrigued. "What kind of interests are we talking about?"

"Money, power, influence," he replied, his voice low. "And some very dangerous players. It's a tangled web, and I'm right in the middle of it."

Clara's heart raced. She thrived on chaos, and the prospect of being entangled in a high-stakes game was intoxicating. But she also knew the risks. The more she delved into Ethan's world, the more exposed she would become.

"Why me?" she asked, her curiosity piqued. "What makes you think I can help?"

"Because you're not afraid to play the game," he said, his gaze unwavering. "You've navigated these waters before. And I sense you want to know the truth, just as I do."

She felt a flicker of connection, a shared understanding that transcended the surface. Clara had always been a seeker of truth, even when it meant wading through deception. The stakes had just risen significantly, and she was drawn in like a moth to a flame.

As they reached a quiet alley, Ethan turned to her, his expression serious. "I need someone I can trust, Clara. And trust is a rare commodity in my world."

Clara's heart raced, the thrill of the unknown coursing through her veins. She had always been a master of deception, but this was different. She felt the weight of his gaze, and for the first time in a long while, she found herself

considering the possibility of vulnerability.

"I'll help," she said, surprising herself with the conviction in her voice. "But understand this—trust is earned, not given freely."

Ethan nodded, a flicker of respect in his eyes. "I wouldn't have it any other way."

And with that, the dance of charm and deceit took on a new intensity. The night was still young, and the shadows were only beginning to reveal their secrets. Clara felt a rush of excitement, a sense that her life was about to take an unexpected turn.

Together, they stepped into the darkness, ready to confront the chaos that awaited them. In that moment, Clara knew one thing for certain: the allure of danger was irresistible, and the game had only just begun.

3. The Power of Manipulation

In the dimly lit backroom of a nondescript café, the air buzzed with an electric tension that seemed almost palpable. At a corner table, Lila sat with her coffee growing cold, her gaze fixed on the door as if waiting for someone—or something—to appear. She had always known the art of manipulation was a powerful weapon, one that could shape destinies and rewrite narratives. Today, she would have to wield it carefully, like a surgeon with a scalpel, if she wanted to navigate the treacherous waters of the criminal underworld.

Across the table, a figure emerged from the shadows. Ethan was a man who wore confidence like a tailored suit, each gesture deliberate, each word laced with intent. They had met several times before, but this meeting felt different. This was not merely a business transaction; it was a dance of power, where the stakes were higher than ever. "You know why I'm here," he said, his voice low and steady.

"Information is a currency more valuable than gold," Lila replied, a sly smile creeping across her lips. "And you're here to buy."

Ethan leaned in closer, his eyes narrowing. "But it's not just about money, is it? It's about control. You have something I need, and I know you'll use it to your advantage." His words hung in the air like a challenge.

Lila chuckled softly. "Control is an illusion, Ethan. Everyone thinks they hold the reins, but the truth is far more complex. You see, the real power lies in understanding how to pull the strings without being seen. It's about knowing what makes people tick—what fears drive them, what desires compel them."

As she spoke, she could see the flicker of interest in his eyes. The game was afoot. "You're right, of course," he admitted. "But you must understand, I'm not the only player at this table. There are others who would pay handsomely for the same information. Those who are far less forgiving."

Lila's heart raced at the implication. The world they inhabited was filled with shadows and whispers, a realm where alliances shifted like sand. "Then perhaps we should establish a partnership," she proposed, her voice smooth as silk. "I have no intention of becoming collateral damage in this game. We could achieve great things together."

"Trust is a fragile thing in our world," Ethan replied, his tone turning cautious. "You may be skilled in manipulation, but I've seen friendships dissolve into ash when the stakes are raised. What guarantees do I have that you won't turn on me?"

"Guarantees are for the naïve," Lila countered. "But mutual benefit is a powerful motivator. If we work together, we can not only survive but thrive. I know secrets about our competitors that could give us the upper hand. They underestimate you—and me. That's where our strength lies."

Their eyes locked, and Lila could feel the weight of unspoken possibilities filling the space between them. This was the heart of manipulation—the ability to create an illusion that masked one's true intentions. Ethan leaned back, considering her words, and in that moment, she sensed a shift in the dynamics of power.

"The other players won't sit idly by," he warned. "If we proceed, it will be a calculated risk. You'll need to prove your loyalty, and I'll have to ensure you don't double-cross me."

"Then let's make the first move," she replied, her heart pounding with anticipation. "We begin by sowing discord among our rivals. A little chaos can go a long way in establishing dominance."

As they hatched their plan, Lila knew the game was just beginning. The art of manipulation required not only a keen understanding of human psychology but also the courage to act decisively when the moment was right. She felt a thrill run through her—this was the life she craved, a world where she could play the puppeteer and dance on the strings of fate.

Days turned into weeks as Lila and Ethan orchestrated their strategy, sowing seeds of doubt and mistrust among their competitors. With each whisper and rumor, they carefully dismantled alliances and friendships, transforming the landscape of the criminal underworld. It was a delicate operation, but Lila thrived in the chaos.

One night, as they convened in a dimly lit warehouse, she could see the fruits of their labor. Rivals who once stood united were now fractured, their once-strong bonds weakened by suspicion. Lila reveled in the power they wielded, realizing that manipulation was not merely a means to an end—it was an art form, a symphony of strategy and psychological insight.

Yet, with every ascent came the inevitable fall, and Lila couldn't shake the feeling that their growing influence was drawing unwanted attention. It wasn't long before the murmur of danger crept into their conversations, and she began to question whether they had underestimated the depths of their adversaries.

"You're playing a dangerous game," Ethan cautioned one evening as they pored over their next moves. "Our actions have consequences, and those we've wronged won't forget easily. We need to prepare for retaliation."

Lila nodded, but a flicker of doubt stirred within her. "We can't let fear dictate our strategy. We've come too far to back down now. If we act swiftly and decisively, we can stay one step ahead."

As the tension escalated, Lila found herself reflecting on the nature of manipulation. It was a double-edged sword—while it could be wielded to achieve greatness, it also had the power to cut deep, leaving scars that were difficult to heal. She had become embroiled in a world where trust was a rare commodity, and every alliance was fraught with peril.

In the days that followed, they intensified their efforts, ensuring that their rivals remained off-balance. But just as they seemed to be gaining the upper hand, a new player emerged—a mysterious figure whose reputation for ruthlessness preceded them. Whispers of their involvement sent ripples of fear through the community, and Lila felt the ground shift beneath her.

The new player was a master of manipulation in their own right, known for their ability to exploit weaknesses and turn allies against one another. Lila realized they were no longer just battling rival factions; they were in a high-stakes chess game where every piece could be sacrificed to achieve victory.

"Who is this new player?" Ethan asked, his expression darkening. "We need to know what we're up against."

Lila took a deep breath, steeling herself for the revelation. "I've heard whispers. They call them 'The Broker.' Rumor has it they control an extensive network of informants and hold leverage over key figures in the city. They thrive on chaos, and they won't hesitate to use it to their advantage."

"Then we need to make our move first," Ethan said, his voice resolute. "If we can expose them before they strike, we might regain control of the narrative."

Lila's heart raced at the thought. They had come too far to let fear dictate their actions. The power of manipulation lay not only in the ability to deceive but in the courage to confront the shadows head-on. As she and Ethan crafted their plan to unveil The Broker, she knew they were venturing deeper into the labyrinth of power, where every decision could lead to liberation or destruction.

The night before their confrontation, Lila couldn't sleep. She sat in her dimly lit apartment, the city's lights twinkling like distant stars outside her window. Her thoughts raced, reflecting on the path that had brought her to this moment. She was no longer just a player in this game; she was a force to be reckoned with, a woman who had learned to wield manipulation like a sword.

As dawn broke, she felt an exhilarating rush of determination. Today would mark a turning point—an opportunity to reclaim not just her narrative, but the very essence of her identity. Manipulation was not merely a tool; it was her lifeblood, the fuel that propelled her forward.

The confrontation with The Broker was set to take place in an abandoned warehouse on the outskirts of the city—a fitting backdrop for the chaos that awaited them. As Lila and Ethan arrived, they were met with an eerie silence, a prelude to the storm that was about to unfold.

"Stay sharp," Ethan whispered, his eyes scanning the shadows. "We don't know what to expect."

Lila nodded, her heart pounding with anticipation. They stepped into the dim light, ready to face whatever came next. The power of manipulation would be their greatest ally, but it was the courage to confront the darkness that would ultimately determine their fate. In this world of chaos and deception, only the bold would emerge victorious.

4. A Game of Intellect

It was a quiet evening in the city, the kind where the bustle of everyday life seemed to taper off into a distant hum. In the dimly lit office of Adrian Stark, the walls were lined with books on philosophy, history, and crime. A large window overlooked the city, its flickering lights twinkling like stars in the distance, each one representing a life tangled in the web of the world's complexities. Stark sat at his desk, leaning back in his chair, his hands steepled beneath his chin as he considered the latest development in his investigation.

The woman had appeared out of nowhere—well, not exactly nowhere. She was there, but always on the periphery, always one step ahead. A whisper in the wind, a shadow that moved just out of sight. No one knew her name, and that's what intrigued Stark the most. How could someone so powerful, so deeply embedded in the city's underworld, maintain such an air of mystery?

Adrian wasn't the kind of man who was easily impressed. He had dealt with criminals, politicians, and the occasional genius with delusions of grandeur. But this was different. There was something methodical, almost surgical, about the way she operated. Every move calculated, every action planned several steps ahead. She was playing a game, a game of intellect, and he was just now beginning to understand the rules.

It had started with a seemingly small lead—a name on a financial document that should never have been there. From there, the trail wound through offshore accounts, shell companies, and a network so intricate it would have taken anyone else months, maybe years, to untangle. But Stark was different. His mind worked like a chessboard, every piece in motion, every possibility considered. He lived for puzzles like this.

As he sifted through the layers of deceit, he couldn't help but feel a grudging respect for her. She was brilliant, no doubt about it. But in every game, there must be a winner and a loser, and Stark had no intention of playing second fiddle.

He leaned forward, pulling a dossier from the edge of his desk, the papers rustling softly in the silence. Her picture was there—grainy, captured by a security camera at some event downtown. The details were vague: a slender figure in a dark dress, her face obscured by the tilt of her head. No name, no clear identity, but her presence was unmistakable. Adrian had seen enough to recognize a player when he saw one. She was playing with the same level of precision he prided himself on, and he was eager to meet her on the board.

The first move had already been made—he just hadn't realized it at the time. That name on the document, the faint breadcrumb leading him deeper into the labyrinth. She wanted him to follow, but why? Was it arrogance? A desire for recognition from someone she considered her intellectual equal? Or was it something more sinister, a trap designed to ensnare him in her web?

Adrian's mind raced through the possibilities, but he didn't have enough information yet. He needed to see more, to understand the full scope of what she was orchestrating. This wasn't just about money or power. There was something personal in her actions, a challenge issued to him specifically. He felt it in the way the pieces moved across the board.

The phone rang, cutting through his thoughts. He picked it up, his voice measured. "Stark."

"Adrian, it's Julia. I've got something for you."

Julia was one of his most reliable contacts, an investigative journalist with a penchant for uncovering things people would rather keep buried. She had her own way of playing the game, often dancing on the line between legality and the forbidden.

"What do you have?" Adrian asked, already knowing it was going to be something useful.

"It's her," Julia said, and Stark's pulse quickened slightly. "There's a connection. A foundation—looks legitimate on the surface, but it's tied to a series of donations to political campaigns, all through a shell company. She's pulling the strings, Adrian."

"Are you sure it's her?" He needed more than hunches now. Certainty was the currency in this game.

"Positive. I followed the money trail, and it all leads back to her. I'm sending you the files now."

The line went dead, and within moments, his computer chimed with the incoming data. Adrian opened the files, his eyes scanning the information with rapid precision. Julia had been right—there it was, a web of transactions, donations, and accounts that all pointed back to one central figure. She was manipulating the system, controlling everything from the shadows. The magnitude of it all was staggering.

Stark sat back, absorbing the gravity of the situation. She was playing on a level most people couldn't even comprehend. The complexity of her operation was astounding, yet it was her audacity that impressed him most. She wasn't just after money or power—she was after control. Total control of the game, of the city, of the very fabric that held everything together.

But there was something else. A clue hidden deep within the data, something that sent a chill down Stark's spine. A pattern emerged, one so subtle it would have been missed by anyone else. She wasn't just controlling events—she was predicting them. Somehow, she was always ahead, not by chance, but by design. It was as if she knew what moves he would make before he even made them.

For the first time in years, Adrian felt a pang of uncertainty. He wasn't used to playing against an opponent who seemed to be as sharp as he was. Every step he took, she had already accounted for.

Every decision, every action—it was as if she had been watching him for far longer than he had been aware of her.

He closed the file, his mind churning with new possibilities. This wasn't just a game of intellect—it was a war of minds, a battle for supremacy in a world where the stakes couldn't be higher. She had made her move, and now it was his turn. But he had to be careful, methodical. One wrong step and the entire board could collapse beneath him.

The city outside continued its steady hum, oblivious to the high-stakes battle unfolding in the shadows. Adrian knew he couldn't afford to lose focus. She was watching, waiting for him to slip. But Stark had been in this game far too long to let someone else dictate the terms. He would find her, unravel her schemes, and bring her world crashing down.

The question was: Could he do it before she made her next move?

The silence of the night crept into the room as Stark stood from his desk, his mind racing with possibilities. He needed to reach out to his contacts, to gather more intel, but this time he would tread carefully. She had shown her hand, but only just enough to taunt him, to keep him chasing. He wouldn't let her lead him blindly into a trap.

As he stepped out into the night, the cool air hit his face, sharp and bracing. The city stretched before him, a labyrinth of secrets and lies. Somewhere in the darkness, she was out there, waiting, plotting. But Adrian Stark wasn't just any player. He was a master in his own right, and if she wanted to play, he was ready.

This game of intellect was just beginning.

5. Secrets in Her Eyes

It was her eyes that first caught his attention—deep, impenetrable, and unsettling. They had a way of pulling you in, making you feel like you were just a step away from discovering something profound, something hidden. For someone like Michael Donovan, a seasoned prosecutor who had spent years staring down hardened criminals, her gaze was something he couldn't quite figure out. It wasn't fear or guilt, but there was something behind those eyes—something that made him uneasy.

She sat across from him, poised and calm, her hands resting lightly on the arms of the chair. Her name was Elena Volkov, a woman with a mysterious background and a reputation that whispered more than it screamed. Everyone who knew of her spoke in half-finished sentences, as if afraid that finishing the thought would make it real, or perhaps, they simply didn't have the full story themselves.

"You seem distracted, Mr. Donovan," Elena said, her voice smooth, almost playful. "Is there something on your mind?"

Michael blinked, quickly masking his thoughts with the practiced neutrality of a man who had spent his life concealing emotions in the courtroom. "No, just thinking," he replied, his tone steady. But he wasn't just thinking. He was analyzing, studying every minute detail about her—the way she held herself, the subtle arch of her brow, the slight curve of her lips. People like Elena were dangerous not because they were overtly threatening but because they were unreadable. And that made them impossible to trust.

He leaned back, feigning casualness. "Why don't you tell me why we're here, Ms. Volkov?"

Elena smiled, a slow, deliberate smile that didn't quite reach her eyes. "I think you already know why we're here," she said softly. "But if you'd prefer, I can start from the beginning."

Her accent was faint, just a hint of something Eastern European that danced around the edges of her words. It gave her an air of exoticism, adding to the allure that surrounded her. Michael had dealt with his fair share of manipulative people, but Elena wasn't like the others. She didn't need to push or pull to get what she wanted. She simply existed, and people bent to her will, often without realizing it.

"I'm listening," Michael said, careful to keep his gaze locked on hers. It was a small power move, an attempt to gain some sort of advantage in a situation where he felt completely out of control.

Elena leaned forward slightly, her eyes never leaving his. "There are things happening in this city, things that are much bigger than you or I. And while you believe you're chasing after criminals, I assure you that the real danger is far more elusive." She paused, letting her words sink in before continuing. "I can help you, Mr. Donovan. But only if you're willing to accept that not everything is as black and white as you'd like to think."

Michael's stomach tightened. He had heard similar promises before—people claiming they had the key to unlock some larger conspiracy, offering their help in exchange for leniency. It almost never led anywhere. But with Elena, something felt different. He couldn't place it, but it was there, lurking beneath the surface.

"I don't need your help," Michael said flatly. "What I need are answers."

Elena laughed, a light, musical sound that seemed almost out of place in the sterile room they occupied. "Oh, Michael," she said, using his first name as if they were old friends. "Answers are overrated. What you need is understanding. And that... that is something I can give you."

There was a weight to her words that made Michael pause. It wasn't that she was trying to be dramatic or cryptic, but rather that she genuinely believed what she was saying. For a moment, Michael considered the possibility that maybe she wasn't playing a game—that maybe, just maybe, she was offering him a piece of the truth.

But then he remembered who he was dealing with.

Elena Volkov wasn't just any informant. She was a key player in the very organization Michael had spent years trying to dismantle. The Volkov family, infamous in their circles, had built an empire on secrecy, deception, and violence. They had ties to nearly every major criminal operation in the region, and yet, somehow, they had managed to stay largely untouchable. It was as if they operated in the shadows, always one step ahead of the law.

And now here she was, sitting across from him, offering him understanding. It was almost laughable.

"I'm not interested in your understanding," Michael said, his voice hardening. "I'm interested in facts. In crimes. In the people responsible for them."

Elena's smile faded slightly, though the intensity in her eyes remained. "And that's where you and I differ, Mr. Donovan. You see the world in terms of right and wrong, guilty and innocent. But in my world, those lines are blurred. The people you're after aren't the ones pulling the strings. They're just pawns in a much larger game."

She leaned back in her chair, her gaze never wavering. "The real question is, are you willing to learn the rules of that game? Or are you content to keep chasing shadows?"

Michael stared at her, trying to gauge whether she was feeding him a carefully crafted line or if there was something more to her words. It was hard to tell. Elena was a master of subtlety, and he knew better than to take anything she said at face value.

But her eyes... there was something in them, something that made him doubt his own instincts.

"I'll play along," Michael said after a long pause. "For now."

Elena's smile returned, though this time it felt more like a victory. "Good," she said softly. "Because once you start, there's no turning back."

• • • •

THE NEXT FEW DAYS WERE a blur of half-truths, cryptic messages, and late-night meetings in darkened corners of the city. Michael had agreed to follow the trail Elena was offering, but every step forward felt like walking deeper into a labyrinth with no clear way out.

Elena was always just out of reach—never giving him more than a fragment of information at a time, always leaving him wanting more. It was infuriating, and yet Michael found himself drawn further into her web. Every clue she provided led him to a dead end, but at the same time, it opened up new avenues of investigation. It was as if she were leading him in circles, but each circle was larger than the last, bringing him closer to something... something he couldn't yet define.

One night, after a particularly frustrating meeting, Michael found himself staring at a photograph of Elena. It was an old image, taken years ago, but her eyes were just as haunting in the picture as they were in real life. There was a sadness there, a depth that hinted at untold stories.

Who was she, really? He had tried to dig into her background, but every record, every piece of information he found seemed deliberately vague, as if someone had gone to great lengths to erase her history. All he knew for certain was that Elena Volkov was not who she appeared to be.

The next morning, Michael received a message. It was from an unknown number, but he didn't need to ask who it was from. The text was short and to the point: "Meet me at the docks. Midnight."

Michael knew it was risky—walking into a situation where he had no control—but he had no choice. Elena had him on a string, and no matter how much he tried to fight it, he couldn't cut himself free.

When he arrived at the docks, the night was quiet, save for the occasional sound of water lapping against the wooden beams. Elena stood at the edge of the pier, her silhouette barely visible in the dim light of a nearby streetlamp.

"You came," she said as he approached, her voice carrying across the still water.

"I didn't have a choice," Michael replied, his tone clipped.

Elena turned to face him, her eyes catching the faint light. There it was again—that unreadable expression that sent a shiver down his spine.

"I'm going to show you something," she said, her voice low. "But you need to promise me one thing."

"What?"

"No matter what happens next, you won't try to stop it."

Michael's heart skipped a beat. "What are you talking about?"

Elena stepped closer, her gaze locking onto his. "There are forces at play here, Michael, forces you can't even begin to understand. If you try to interfere, you'll only make things worse—for both of us."

Michael wanted to argue, to demand answers, but the look in her eyes silenced him. There was something raw, almost desperate, in her expression—something he hadn't seen before.

"Elena, what's going on?" he asked, his voice softer now, less accusatory.

She shook her head, turning away from him. "You'll find out soon enough," she said quietly. "But for now, you need to trust me."

Michael hesitated, torn between his instinct to take control and the gnawing feeling that Elena was right—that there were forces beyond his comprehension at work here.

"Alright," he said finally. "I'll trust you."

Elena didn't respond, but as they stood there, side by side, staring out at the dark water, Michael felt the weight of her secrets pressing down on him. Whatever game she was playing, it was only just beginning—and he was already too deep to back out now.

6. A Sinister Proposition

The night hung heavy in the air, thick with anticipation and the kind of unease that only comes when you know something is about to happen, but not what. It had been days since the last real break in the case, and every lead felt like a dead end. The city buzzed quietly beneath the prosecutor's feet as he sat in his office, staring at the same set of documents he'd been poring over for hours. His coffee had gone cold, and the hum of the fluorescent lights above him only added to the growing tension that curled like smoke in the back of his mind.

The phone on his desk rang, breaking the silence with an abruptness that made him jump. He wasn't used to being startled. His hand moved instinctively, answering the call before his mind had fully caught up.

"Yes?"

There was a pause, a silence so thick it felt purposeful. Then, a voice, calm, almost too smooth.

"I hear you're looking for answers, Mr. Sandler."

David Sandler. Prosecutor. A man who had seen it all, or so he thought. But this voice—it wasn't familiar, yet it carried the weight of someone who knew things. Dangerous things.

"And who might you be?" Sandler asked, his tone betraying none of the sudden quickening of his pulse.

"Someone who can give you what you're looking for. But only if you're willing to take a leap of faith."

Sandler's fingers tightened around the phone. "I don't work in the shadows," he said, his voice low but steady. "If you've got information, bring it forward, and we'll deal with it legally."

The laugh on the other end of the line was soft but mocking, like a parent humoring a child. "Legally? That's rich, coming from someone chasing shadows themselves. You're up against forces bigger than you can imagine, Mr. Sandler. You really think the law is going to help you here?"

Sandler leaned back in his chair, eyes narrowing. He had been in this game long enough to recognize a setup when he saw one. But something about this caller, something in the way they spoke, made him hesitate.

"I'm listening," Sandler said, finally.

"I thought you might be." The voice was silk now, slipping through the phone like it belonged there, like it had been waiting for this moment. "There's a woman—let's call her 'The Lady in Red.' She's not just another piece in this puzzle you're trying to solve, Mr. Sandler. She's the hand that moves the pieces."

Sandler's breath caught in his throat. He had heard whispers of her, a name spoken in dark corners, always with fear. A woman who was said to control the strings of the city's underworld with a grace and ruthlessness that left no room for error. But until now, she had been nothing more than a rumor, a ghost.

"I can lead you to her," the voice continued. "But it won't be easy. And it won't be clean. You'll have to make a choice, Sandler. A choice between what's right and what's necessary."

Sandler stood, pacing now, the phone still pressed to his ear. His mind raced, considering the options. He had been at this too long to not know the cost of shortcuts. They always came back to haunt you. But the idea of finally putting an end to this—the chance to bring down The Lady in Red—was too tempting to dismiss outright.

"What's the catch?" he asked, his voice quiet, almost defeated.

"No catch. Just a proposition. You follow the trail I give you, and when the time comes, you'll know what to do. It's that simple."

Sandler's mind flashed to the images of victims, families torn apart by the kind of violence that made headlines for a day and scars for a lifetime. He thought of the cases that had gone cold, the witnesses too scared to speak, the threats that had silenced even the bravest. And then he thought of her—the elusive woman at the heart of it all, a phantom who controlled the chaos with a smile and a shrug.

"If I do this," Sandler said slowly, "there's no turning back, is there?"

The voice was silent for a moment, as if considering. Then it answered, "No, Mr. Sandler. There's not."

The line went dead.

Sandler stood in the quiet of his office, the weight of the call hanging heavy in the air. He knew better than to trust faceless voices, but something about this one—something about the promise of finally getting close to the woman he had been chasing for so long—made him want to believe.

• • • •

THE FOLLOWING DAYS were a blur of half-answers and cryptic clues, each one more maddening than the last. But slowly, the pieces started to fall into place. A name here, a location there. Nothing concrete, but enough to keep him moving forward.

It wasn't until the third night after the call that things took a darker turn.

Sandler was sitting in his car, parked outside a dilapidated warehouse on the outskirts of the city. The tip had come anonymously, but the location matched a pattern he had been following for weeks. This was where the money changed hands, where deals were made, and where people disappeared.

He watched the warehouse from a distance, his fingers drumming nervously on the steering wheel. There was no sign of movement, no indication that anything was happening inside. But he knew better than to trust appearances.

He was about to step out of the car when his phone buzzed. A single text message.

"Turn back now, or face the consequences."

Sandler's heart raced as he stared at the screen. He had expected threats, of course, but this was different. This felt personal.

He looked up at the warehouse again, the shadows inside seeming to move, to shift. He couldn't shake the feeling that he was being watched.

Taking a deep breath, he opened the door and stepped out into the cool night air. He wasn't turning back. Not now.

• • • •

INSIDE THE WAREHOUSE, the air was thick with the smell of oil and metal, a reminder of the building's former life as a manufacturing plant. Now, it was empty, abandoned except for the faint echo of his footsteps on the concrete floor.

Sandler moved carefully, his eyes scanning the darkness for any sign of life. He had been here before—in places like this, where danger lurked just out of sight, waiting for the right moment to strike.

And then he saw her.

She was standing near the far wall, bathed in the pale light of a single flickering bulb. Her red dress clung to her figure, elegant and sharp against the grimy backdrop of the warehouse. She was taller than he had imagined, her presence commanding, her eyes locked on him with a gaze that was both curious and predatory.

"The Lady in Red," he whispered, more to himself than to her.

She smiled, a slow, deliberate curl of her lips. "Mr. Sandler," she said, her voice smooth and melodic. "I've been expecting you."

Sandler's heart pounded in his chest, but he forced himself to remain calm. "You know why I'm here."

"Of course I do," she replied, stepping closer. "You've been following my breadcrumbs for some time now. But tell me, Mr. Sandler, do you really think you're ready for what comes next?"

He didn't answer, and she laughed softly, the sound sending a chill down his spine.

"You're a smart man," she continued. "Smarter than most of the men who have come before you. But intelligence only gets you so far in this game. At some point, you have to decide—how far are you willing to go?"

Sandler's jaw tightened. "I'm willing to do what it takes to stop you."

She raised an eyebrow, her smile widening. "Is that so? And what if stopping me means becoming something you've spent your whole life fighting against?"

She stepped closer again, so close now that he could see the faint glint of something sharp in her eyes. "You see, Mr. Sandler, you and I aren't so different. We both want control. We both want justice. The only difference is, I'm willing to do whatever it takes to get it. Are you?"

Sandler felt the weight of her words press down on him, the truth of them sinking in like a knife. He had always prided himself on being a man of principles, a man who stood for what was right. But now, standing in front of this woman, this force of nature, he couldn't help but wonder—was he really any different?

Before he could respond, she spoke again, her voice low and dangerous. "Here's my proposition, Mr. Sandler. You walk away from this, right now. Forget about me, forget about all of this, and I'll let you live your life in peace. Or," she paused, letting the silence stretch between them, "you continue down this path, and I promise you, it won't end well for either of us."

Sandler stared at her, his mind racing. The weight of the decision pressed down on him, a choice between light and darkness, between who he was and who he might become.

Finally, he spoke, his voice steady but soft. "I can't walk away."

She nodded, as if she had expected his answer. "Then I suppose we'll see just how far you're willing to go, Mr. Sandler."

With that, she turned and walked away, her red dress disappearing into the shadows, leaving him alone in the empty warehouse, with the weight of his decision hanging heavy in the air.

Chapter 7: Fractured Loyalties

1. Friends Turned Foes

There's a strange and unsettling moment in life when someone you once called a friend becomes something else entirely. You don't notice it at first; it's a slow change, like a ship gradually drifting off course. But one day, you find yourself looking across the table at someone whose eyes you used to trust and realize they're no longer the same person. Or perhaps it's you who has changed. Either way, the bond between you is now a fragile thread, ready to snap under the weight of betrayal, suspicion, and lies.

For Daniel, the shift began subtly. He had known Alexei for over a decade, their friendship born in the rough alleys of a city that devoured the weak. They weren't just friends—they were brothers-in-arms, both fighting their way out of the shadows of crime and into positions of influence. They had sworn to each other, on countless occasions, that no matter what happened, they would remain loyal, that nothing could break the bond forged in the fires of their shared struggles. But that was before. Before money. Before power. Before the stakes became so high that trust was a luxury neither could afford.

It started with the smallest of things—a missed meeting here, a vague answer there. Alexei, always the more charismatic and ambitious of the two, had started keeping secrets. He was meeting with people behind closed doors, people Daniel didn't recognize. When Daniel pressed him, Alexei brushed it off with a laugh, saying, "You worry too much, brother. It's just business." But Daniel had been in the game long enough to know when business was about to turn deadly.

The first real crack appeared on a cold November night. Daniel was at a bar, nursing a drink and watching the rain beat against the windows. His phone buzzed. It was a message from someone on the inside, someone who had been feeding him small but valuable pieces of information for years. "You need to know," the message read. "Alexei is talking to them."

Them. The ones who controlled the city from the shadows. The ones Daniel and Alexei had both sworn to avoid at all costs. They were ruthless, unstoppable. Once they had their hooks in you, there was no getting free. Alexei knew this as well as Daniel did. So why would he be talking to them? What could they possibly offer him that was worth the risk?

Daniel's mind raced as he tried to make sense of it all. Was Alexei planning something? Was he setting up a deal without telling him? Or worse, was he cutting him out completely? The thought of betrayal twisted in Daniel's gut like a knife. He couldn't confront Alexei outright, not without proof. He needed to play it smart, figure out what was really going on before making any moves.

Over the next few weeks, Daniel kept a closer eye on Alexei. He started noticing things he hadn't before—the way Alexei would glance over his shoulder in meetings, as if expecting someone to be watching, the whispered phone calls that ended abruptly when Daniel entered the room. It was clear now: Alexei was hiding something big. And whatever it was, it wasn't good.

One evening, after another fruitless meeting where Alexei dodged his questions, Daniel decided to follow him. It wasn't something he wanted to do, but he had no other choice. If Alexei had crossed a line, Daniel needed to know. He needed to understand why, and more importantly, he needed to decide what he was going to do about it.

Alexei left the meeting early, claiming he had another appointment. Daniel waited a few minutes before slipping out and trailing him through the winding streets. He kept his distance, staying in the shadows, just like they used to when they were kids running from trouble. But this time, it wasn't trouble they were running from. It was each other.

Alexei led him to an upscale restaurant on the other side of town, the kind of place where deals were made, the kind of place you didn't go unless you had something important to discuss. Daniel watched from across the street as Alexei entered the restaurant and was quickly ushered to a private room in the back. For a moment, Daniel hesitated. Did he really want to know what was happening behind those doors? Once he crossed this line, there was no going back.

But he had to. He had to know the truth, no matter how much it hurt.

Inside, the restaurant was dimly lit, with soft jazz playing in the background. The waitstaff moved about quietly, unobtrusive, as if they had seen it all before. Daniel moved quickly and quietly toward the back, slipping past the bar and into the hallway where the private rooms were located. He stopped outside the door where Alexei had disappeared and listened.

He could hear voices—Alexei's, and another man's, deeper, more authoritative. Daniel recognized it instantly. It was Mikhail, one of the key players in the city's underworld, a man who wielded power like a weapon. Daniel's heart sank. This was worse than he thought.

"You're making the right decision," Mikhail was saying. "With our resources and your connections, we can control everything. But you need to leave the past behind. That includes him."

"I know," Alexei replied, his voice lower, almost hesitant. "It's just... we've been through a lot together. He's like a brother."

"A brother?" Mikhail's laugh was cold, hollow. "Brothers are a liability. In this business, loyalty only goes so far. You want power? You want the money? Then you cut ties. Clean. He won't see it coming."

Daniel's blood ran cold. So this was it. Alexei was planning to betray him. After everything they had been through, all the promises, all the fights they had survived together, it came down to this—money and power. Alexei was willing to throw it all away for a seat at the table with the city's most dangerous men.

For a moment, Daniel considered bursting in, confronting Alexei right then and there. But he stopped himself. Mikhail was right about one thing—Alexei wouldn't see it coming. And that was Daniel's only advantage now. He couldn't let his emotions get the better of him. If he wanted to survive, if he wanted to take down Mikhail and the rest of them, he needed to play this carefully.

The next few days were a blur of planning and paranoia. Daniel knew he had to act fast, but he couldn't tip his hand too soon. Alexei was still pretending everything was normal, still smiling and laughing like they were on the same side. But Daniel could see the cracks now—the way Alexei avoided eye contact, the slight tension in his voice when he spoke.

The hardest part was pretending. Pretending he didn't know. Pretending he wasn't already making moves to protect himself. He called in every favor he was owed, setting up safeguards, gathering evidence. If Alexei wanted to play dirty, Daniel was going to beat him at his own game.

Then, finally, the moment came.

It was a rainy night, just like the night Daniel had first learned of Alexei's betrayal. They were supposed to meet at their usual spot, an old bar they had been going to for years. Daniel arrived early, his mind racing through all the possible outcomes. Would Alexei try to kill him? Would he make one last plea for forgiveness? Or would he simply walk away, leaving their friendship in ruins?

Alexei arrived a few minutes late, drenched from the rain but smiling as if nothing had changed. "Sorry I'm late," he said, shaking the water from his jacket. "Got caught up in something."

Daniel forced a smile. "No worries. What's going on?"

They ordered drinks, exchanged pleasantries, but the tension was palpable. Daniel could feel the weight of everything unspoken between them, hanging in the air like a storm about to break.

Finally, Alexei leaned in, his expression serious. "There's something we need to talk about."

Daniel nodded, his heart pounding in his chest. "Yeah. There is."

For a moment, they stared at each other, the silence stretching between them. And then, just as Alexei opened his mouth to speak, Daniel's phone buzzed on the table. He glanced down, and his blood ran cold.

It was a message from one of his sources. A single line that changed everything.

"They're coming for you."

In that instant, Daniel knew. Alexei hadn't come here to talk. He had come to finish it.

2. The Cost of Betrayal

Betrayal is an act often committed in whispers, a knife slipped into the back under the cloak of friendship or loyalty. But the cost of betrayal? That is something that lingers long after the act itself. It seeps into the lives of those affected, warping their perceptions, hardening their hearts, and leaving behind scars that never fully heal.

For Ethan, the day of betrayal didn't arrive with a bang or a confrontation. No, it crept up quietly, disguising itself in the mundane routine of life. Ethan had always trusted Jacob, his childhood friend and closest confidant, with his deepest secrets. They had grown up together, fought their battles together, and shared dreams of a future free from the chaos that surrounded them. But life, as it often does, took unexpected turns.

The signs were there, in hindsight. Jacob's sudden absences, his vague explanations, and the way his eyes seemed to dart away when certain topics were brought up. But Ethan, blinded by trust, had refused to see it. To him, Jacob was still the boy who had stood by his side in countless schoolyard fights, the man who had helped him bury their mutual demons beneath layers of bravado and shared memories. But as Ethan would soon learn, trust can be the most dangerous of illusions.

It started with a deal. A simple business transaction that Jacob had insisted would be a game-changer for both of them. Ethan, always cautious, had his doubts, but Jacob's enthusiasm was contagious. He spoke of offshore accounts, of money laundering schemes that would funnel millions into their pockets without a trace. Ethan hesitated. He had always walked the line between legality and crime, but this felt different. The stakes were higher, the risks more pronounced.

Yet, in the end, it wasn't the potential rewards that convinced him, but Jacob's unwavering belief that they could pull it off. "Trust me," Jacob had said, his voice steady, his eyes meeting Ethan's with a sincerity that was impossible to ignore. And trust him Ethan did.

For months, the plan seemed to be working flawlessly. The money flowed in from accounts scattered across the globe, from countries Ethan had only ever heard about in passing. It was easy—too easy. But the ease lulled him into a false sense of security. He stopped asking questions, stopped wondering where the money was really coming from, and began to enjoy the fruits of their labor. Luxury cars, expensive dinners, vacations that took them to the most exclusive destinations on Earth—it all seemed within their grasp.

Then, one cold autumn evening, everything came crashing down. It began with a phone call—an anonymous tip that left Ethan's blood running cold. "They're onto you," the voice on the other end had said, a low, gravelly whisper that carried with it the weight of impending doom. At first, Ethan had dismissed it as a prank, a scare tactic meant to rattle him. But as the days passed, the warning signs became impossible to ignore.

The authorities were closing in, and it was only a matter of time before they would come knocking on his door. Panic set in, but through it all, Ethan clung to the belief that Jacob would have an answer, a plan to get them out of the mess they had created. After all, Jacob had always been the one with the solutions, the one who could talk his way out of any situation.

But when Ethan confronted him, Jacob was nowhere to be found.

The realization hit him like a freight train. Jacob had disappeared, leaving behind nothing but empty promises and a trail of deceit that led directly back to Ethan. As the walls of his life closed in around him, Ethan was left with only one question: Why? Why had Jacob betrayed him, after everything they had been through together?

The answer, as it turned out, was simple—greed. Jacob had taken the money, all of it, and vanished into the night without so much as a goodbye. The millions they had funneled into their accounts, the offshore holdings, the carefully crafted network of shell companies—it was all gone. And with it, any hope Ethan had of walking away unscathed.

The cost of Jacob's betrayal was far greater than the loss of money. It was the loss of trust, the shattering of a bond that had once seemed unbreakable. Ethan found himself standing on the edge of a precipice, his life in ruins, with nowhere to turn. The authorities were closing in fast, and he knew it was only a matter of time before they caught up with him.

Desperation breeds reckless decisions, and Ethan was no exception. With his back against the wall, he turned to the only option he had left—revenge. If Jacob thought he could walk away from this unscathed, he was sorely mistaken. Ethan would find him, no matter how far he had run, no matter how well he had covered his tracks.

The hunt for Jacob became an obsession, consuming Ethan's every waking moment. He scoured the globe, following every lead, every rumor, every whisper of Jacob's whereabouts. But the deeper he delved, the more he realized just how elaborate Jacob's betrayal had been. This wasn't just a simple double-cross—Jacob had been planning this for years. Every move he had made, every conversation they had shared, had been part of a larger scheme to cut Ethan out and take everything for himself.

And the worst part? Ethan wasn't the only one. As he dug deeper, he discovered that Jacob had betrayed countless others along the way, leaving a trail of ruined lives and broken promises in his wake. He had built an empire on lies and deceit, and now Ethan was determined to bring it all crashing down.

But vengeance, as Ethan would soon learn, comes at a price. As he closed in on Jacob, he began to lose sight of who he had once been. The lines between right and wrong blurred, and he found himself making choices that would have horrified the man he used to be. In his quest for retribution, Ethan became the very thing he had once despised—a man willing to do whatever it took to win, no matter the cost.

The final confrontation came not with a bang, but with a whisper. Ethan found Jacob in a small, remote village halfway around the world, living under an assumed name, far from the life of luxury he had once enjoyed. The years of running had taken their toll—Jacob was a shadow of the man he had once been. But even in his diminished state, there was still a glimmer of the cunning, manipulative man who had orchestrated Ethan's downfall.

Ethan stood over him, gun in hand, the weight of years of betrayal pressing down on him. But as he looked into Jacob's eyes, he realized something unexpected. Killing Jacob wouldn't bring back what he had lost. It wouldn't restore the trust that had been shattered, or the friendships that had been destroyed. The cost of betrayal was too high, and Ethan had already paid more than enough.

In the end, Ethan walked away, leaving Jacob to face the consequences of his actions alone. Revenge, he realized, wasn't the answer. It never had been. The true cost of betrayal wasn't in the loss of money or power—it was in the loss of self. And Ethan, for all the mistakes he had made, wasn't willing to lose himself any further.

The road ahead would be long, and the scars of Jacob's betrayal would never fully heal. But as Ethan walked away from the past, he knew that he had taken the first step toward reclaiming his life, and in doing so, he had found something far more valuable than the millions they had once pursued—peace.

3. A Race Against Time

The city was suffocating under the weight of its secrets. Dark alleys, neon lights flickering on the edges of shadowy streets, and whispers that followed the unwary. In the heart of this chaos, Jacob Hale could feel the clock ticking. Every second mattered now. He had been chasing leads for weeks, his investigation into the sprawling web of corruption growing more convoluted with every discovery, but today was different. Today, he wasn't just chasing a case—he was racing against time to prevent a catastrophe.

Jacob had never been one to panic, even under pressure, but something about this case was different. It wasn't just the magnitude of the conspiracy he was uncovering, nor the sheer scale of the power involved. It was the realization that at any moment, the entire operation could collapse, burying him and everything he'd worked for under the rubble. His hands trembled slightly as he adjusted his wristwatch, a habit he'd picked up in the field—a futile attempt to control time, even when it seemed to slip through his fingers.

The information he had uncovered led him to an unsettling conclusion: the key to the entire operation was hidden in plain sight, masquerading as an innocuous company in the financial district. On the surface, it was just another corporate entity, but Jacob knew better. It was the beating heart of the empire that had caused so much devastation, a façade for a network of criminal enterprises that spanned continents. The clock was ticking, and if he didn't act now, they would slip away—again.

Jacob's footsteps echoed in the empty hallway of his office, the only sound breaking the oppressive silence. His mind raced as he reviewed the plan. He had exactly twelve hours before the transfer—a massive, untraceable sum of money would disappear into the labyrinth of offshore accounts, funding operations he could only begin to imagine. He couldn't let that happen. But he was running out of time, and the odds were against him.

The phone on his desk buzzed, breaking his concentration. He reached for it without looking at the caller ID, already knowing who it was.

"Jacob, we've got a problem," said a voice on the other end. It was Lisa, his most trusted ally in this entire operation. Her voice was strained, barely concealing the tension she was under. "They've changed the schedule. The transfer is happening in six hours, not twelve."

Jacob froze, his mind spinning. Six hours. That wasn't enough time. "What do you mean they've changed it? How is that even possible?"

"Something spooked them. I think they're onto you. They've been moving assets all day, trying to cover their tracks. If we don't stop this now, we're going to lose everything."

He swore under his breath, the weight of the situation crashing down on him. He had planned for this, of course—he had contingencies for everything—but this was different. They were moving faster than he'd anticipated, and now he had to act with even more urgency.

"Okay, listen," he said, trying to keep his voice steady. "We need to regroup. I'll meet you at the safe house in twenty minutes. We'll figure out a way to stop this."

"Jacob, there's something else," Lisa's voice trembled. "We've been compromised. Someone inside our circle is feeding them information. I don't know who we can trust anymore."

The revelation hit him like a punch to the gut. He had suspected as much for weeks, but hearing it confirmed made everything worse. Now, not only was he racing against time to stop the transfer, but he was also facing betrayal from someone within his own team.

"I'll be there soon," he said, hanging up before she could say more. He couldn't afford to dwell on it now. There would be time for that later—if they survived this.

He grabbed his jacket, slipping a small revolver into the inner pocket. He wasn't the type to carry a gun unless absolutely necessary, but tonight felt different. Tonight, he wasn't sure who he'd be facing, or whether he'd make it out alive.

The streets were eerily quiet as he made his way to the safe house, his senses on high alert. Every shadow seemed to hide a potential threat, every passing car a possible tail. He had been in this game long enough to know when the walls were closing in, and right now, they were closing in fast.

The safe house was an unremarkable building on the outskirts of the city, tucked away in a rundown neighborhood where no one asked questions. As Jacob approached, he could see Lisa waiting for him by the door, her face pale and drawn. She looked up as he approached, her eyes wide with fear.

"We don't have much time," she said as soon as he reached her. "I've been monitoring their communications. They're moving faster than we thought."

Jacob nodded, his mind already racing through the possibilities. "We need to cut them off before they make the transfer. If we can intercept their signal, we can disrupt the entire operation."

Lisa hesitated, her eyes darting nervously around the empty street. "There's something else. I found out who's been feeding them information."

Jacob's heart skipped a beat. "Who?"

"It's Daniels."

The name hit him like a physical blow. Daniels had been his partner for years, someone he had trusted implicitly. The betrayal stung, but there was no time to process it now. "Are you sure?"

Lisa nodded, her expression grim. "I intercepted a message. He's been working with them for months."

Jacob clenched his fists, his mind racing. Daniels had access to everything—their plans, their contacts, their safe houses. He could have sabotaged the entire operation without them even knowing.

"We'll deal with Daniels later," he said, his voice hard. "Right now, we need to stop that transfer."

They moved quickly, heading to the nondescript van parked a few blocks away. Inside, it was filled with surveillance equipment, monitors displaying real-time feeds from around the city. Lisa slid into the driver's seat, her fingers flying across the keyboard as she pulled up the coordinates they needed.

"We've only got one shot at this," she said, her voice tight with concentration. "If we miss the signal, the transfer goes through and we're done."

Jacob nodded, his eyes fixed on the screen. The seconds ticked by, each one feeling like an eternity. He could feel the weight of the situation pressing down on him, the knowledge that one wrong move could cost them everything.

"There," Lisa said suddenly, her voice sharp. "I've got the signal. It's coming from the financial district."

Jacob's heart pounded in his chest. "Let's move."

They sped through the city, the streets blurring past in a haze of lights and shadows. Time was running out, and the closer they got to their target, the more he could feel the tension building.

As they approached the gleaming tower at the center of the financial district, Jacob's phone buzzed. He glanced at the screen and saw a message from an unknown number: "You're too late."

His blood ran cold.

4. The Breaking Point

The room was suffocating, the dim light casting long shadows across the cracked walls. Jake leaned against the table, his knuckles white as he gripped the edges, trying to steady himself. He had reached his breaking point, and there was no going back now. The weight of everything—the lies, the betrayals, the violence—pressed down on him like an unbearable force. He had always thought of himself as unshakable, someone who could weather any storm, but this was different. This storm was inside him, and it was tearing him apart.

It had been weeks since the investigation had begun to spiral out of control, and every day felt like a battle against forces he couldn't fully understand. The deeper he dug, the more tangled the web became. What had started as a straightforward case had morphed into something far more sinister, and Jake found himself caught in the crosshairs. Every step forward revealed more questions than answers, and with each revelation, he felt the ground beneath him crumble a little more.

He closed his eyes, trying to block out the chaos swirling in his mind. But it was no use. The faces of those he had trusted, now revealed as enemies, flashed before him. The cold realization that he had been used, manipulated, gnawed at his insides. He had always prided himself on his instincts, but they had failed him when it mattered most. And now, he was paying the price.

The worst part was the isolation. Jake had always been a lone wolf, but this was different. This was isolation not by choice, but by necessity. He couldn't trust anyone anymore. Every ally had turned into a potential threat, every friend a possible foe. The lines between right and wrong, good and evil, had blurred beyond recognition. In a world where everyone had their own agenda, how could he ever be sure who was on his side?

The case had started small, a simple investigation into financial discrepancies within a local business. But the more Jake had dug, the more he realized that this was just the tip of the iceberg. What lay beneath was an intricate network of corruption, power, and greed that stretched far beyond the city limits. Billion-dollar deals were being made in the shadows, and those who controlled the flow of money had their hands in every dirty corner of society. It wasn't just about money; it was about control. And those in control were willing to go to any lengths to protect their empire.

Jake had always known the game was rigged, that the rich and powerful played by different rules. But he had never seen it up close like this. He had never realized just how deep the rot went. Now that he was in the middle of it, he felt like he was drowning in a sea of deceit, struggling to keep his head above water. Every time he thought he had a lead, it would slip through his fingers like sand. Every time he thought he was close to a breakthrough, something—or someone—would get in his way.

He had tried to play it smart, to stay one step ahead, but it was becoming clear that he was outmatched. The people he was up against weren't just powerful; they were untouchable. They operated in the shadows, pulling strings from behind the scenes, making sure that no one could trace anything back to them. They had built their empire on lies and blood, and they were experts at covering their tracks.

But Jake couldn't walk away. Not now. He had come too far, uncovered too much. He had seen firsthand the destruction these people caused, the lives they ruined for their own gain. He had made a promise to himself that he would see this through, no matter the cost. But now, standing on the edge of the abyss, he was starting to wonder if the cost was too high.

His thoughts drifted to Rachel. She had warned him, told him that this case would be different, that it would consume him if he let it. But Jake, ever the stubborn idealist, had ignored her warnings. He had believed that he could handle it, that he could take down the people responsible and still come out the other side unscathed. But Rachel had been right. He wasn't unscathed. He was barely holding on.

He hadn't seen her in weeks, not since the night they had argued about his obsession with the case. She had begged him to let it go, to walk away while he still could. But he had pushed her away, convinced that she didn't understand. Now, he realized that she had understood better than he had. She had seen the toll it was taking on him, the way it was eating away at him from the inside. But by the time he had realized it, it was too late. She was gone, and he was left alone with the wreckage of his choices.

The door to the room creaked open, and Jake's eyes snapped open. Standing in the doorway was David, his once-loyal partner, now the embodiment of betrayal. The sight of him stirred something deep within Jake, a mixture of rage and despair that threatened to overwhelm him.

"You look like hell," David said, his voice calm, almost mocking.

Jake said nothing, his jaw clenched so tight he thought it might shatter. He had trusted David, leaned on him when things had gotten tough. And all along, David had been feeding information to the very people they were supposed to be taking down. It was a betrayal that cut deeper than any wound.

David stepped further into the room, his eyes cold and calculating. "You should have listened when I told you to back off. This was never your fight, Jake. You were always in over your head."

Jake's pulse quickened, the anger boiling over. "You think you're so smart, don't you? Playing both sides, selling out everyone who ever cared about you. But you're just another pawn, David. And when they're done with you, they'll throw you to the wolves, just like everyone else."

David smirked, shaking his head. "You still don't get it, do you? This isn't about sides. It's about survival. And in this world, the only way to survive is to make sure you're on the winning team."

Jake pushed himself away from the table, the tension in the air thick enough to cut with a knife. "I'd rather die standing up than live on my knees, selling out everything I believe in."

David's eyes darkened. "That's the problem with you, Jake. You still think this is about right and wrong. But there's no room for idealists in this game. The world doesn't care about your morals. It cares about power. And the people who have it will always win."

For a moment, the two men stood in silence, the weight of everything unsaid hanging between them. Jake could feel his heart pounding in his chest, the adrenaline coursing through his veins. This was it. The breaking point. The moment where everything would either come crashing down or he would finally find a way to fight back.

But he wasn't sure he had anything left to fight with.

5. Lines Drawn in the Sand

The day started like any other. The air was thick with the scent of the city—exhaust, sweat, and the lingering trace of last night's rain. But today was different. There was a charge in the atmosphere, something invisible but palpable, like the city itself was holding its breath, waiting for the inevitable confrontation.

Detective Michael Carver leaned against the cold stone of the precinct steps, a cigarette dangling from his lips, barely touched. His eyes, hidden behind dark sunglasses, scanned the street, though his mind was elsewhere. There were always choices, decisions that changed the course of everything, and today was one of those days. Somewhere, lines had been drawn. Some visible, others not, but all unshakably real.

He was waiting for a call. Not just any call, but the one that would mark the beginning of the end. The investigation had dragged on for months, pulling him deeper into a world he barely recognized anymore—a labyrinth of lies, power, and corruption so vast it felt infinite. And yet, here he was, standing on the edge of it all, knowing that whatever came next would change his life forever. That was the thing about lines—they weren't just drawn in the sand. They were carved into the people who dared to cross them.

The phone buzzed in his pocket, snapping him out of his thoughts. He took one last drag from the cigarette before flicking it into the gutter and pulling out his phone. The name on the screen sent a jolt of adrenaline through his veins: Marcus Voss.

Voss wasn't just any informant. He was deep in the game, so deeply embedded that sometimes Carver wasn't sure which side he was really on. But Voss had something, something big, and Carver had no choice but to listen.

"Talk to me," Carver said, keeping his voice low.

"They're meeting tonight," Voss's voice crackled through the line, barely audible over the city noise.

Carver's heart raced. "Where?"

"The warehouse by the docks. Midnight. You didn't hear it from me."

The line went dead, and for a moment, Carver just stood there, letting the words sink in. This was it. This was the moment they had been waiting for. After months of chasing shadows, the players were finally stepping into the light.

Carver had been tracking the organization for longer than he cared to admit. It was a network, intricate and dangerous, with tendrils stretching from the lowest rungs of the underworld to the highest offices in the city. Politicians, businessmen, enforcers—they were all part of the same machine, fueling chaos for their own gain. And at the heart of it all was a woman. A woman so elusive, so powerful, that no one knew her true name, only her title: The Queen.

He knew tonight would be his one shot at bringing the operation down. But in his gut, he felt something more—this wasn't just about justice anymore. There was a personal edge to it now, a line he hadn't realized he'd crossed until it was too late.

• • • •

BY THE TIME CARVER arrived at the docks, the sun had dipped below the horizon, casting long shadows across the abandoned streets. The warehouse loomed ahead, a hulking mass of rusted metal and cracked concrete. It looked like a place where bad things happened, and tonight would be no exception.

He parked his car a few blocks away and approached on foot, keeping to the shadows. His heart thudded in his chest, his senses heightened. Every noise—every creak, every footstep—seemed amplified in the stillness of the night. He wasn't sure if it was paranoia or just instinct, but something told him he wasn't alone.

Inside the warehouse, voices echoed through the empty space, bouncing off the walls like whispers carried on the wind. Carver crouched behind a stack of crates, straining to hear. He couldn't make out the words, but the tone was clear—business. The kind of business that ended with bodies and blood.

He peered around the corner and saw them: a group of men standing in a loose circle, their faces obscured by the dim light. At the center of the group was a figure that made Carver's blood run cold. She was tall, elegant, with a grace that seemed out of place in this grimy setting. Even from a distance, Carver could feel her presence, a quiet power that radiated from her like heat off asphalt.

The Queen.

He had heard stories about her, but nothing had prepared him for this. She wasn't just another player in the game. She was the game.

Carver's hand tightened around the grip of his gun. He could take the shot right now, end it all in a single moment. But something held him back. Maybe it was fear, maybe it was doubt. Or maybe it was something deeper, something darker. He realized then that this wasn't just about catching the criminals. This was about survival—his own, and everyone else's.

As he watched, one of the men stepped forward, holding a briefcase. He opened it, revealing stacks of cash, neatly arranged, like a silent testament to the corruption that had infected every corner of the city.

The Queen smiled, a small, knowing smile, and nodded. The deal was done.

Carver's mind raced. He had to act, and fast. But just as he was about to move, a hand clamped down on his shoulder, and he froze.

"Easy, Detective," a voice whispered in his ear. "Wouldn't want to get ahead of yourself."

Carver spun around, his gun already drawn, but the man behind him was faster. A gloved hand knocked the weapon from his grip, sending it skittering across the floor. Carver barely had time to register the blow before a fist connected with his stomach, doubling him over in pain.

"Did you really think you could just walk in here and take them down?" the man sneered, his voice low and mocking.

Carver gasped for breath, his vision swimming. He had been careless, too focused on the prize to notice the danger lurking in the shadows. But it wasn't over yet. Not by a long shot.

With a grunt of effort, he surged forward, driving his shoulder into the man's chest. They tumbled to the ground, fists flying in a brutal, desperate struggle. Carver's mind was a blur of pain and adrenaline, but through the chaos, one thought burned bright: He had to survive. He had to finish this.

Finally, with a well-placed punch, Carver managed to knock the man out cold. He staggered to his feet, wiping blood from his mouth, and glanced back toward the center of the warehouse. The Queen was gone.

• • • •

CARVER SAT IN HIS CAR, staring out at the empty street. The night had been a disaster. He had been so close, closer than he'd ever been, and yet he had nothing to show for it. The Queen had slipped through his fingers like sand, and now he was left with nothing but questions and regrets.

But he knew one thing for sure: the lines had been drawn, and there was no going back.

6. Trust No One

Trust. It's a simple word, yet one of the most complex ideas in human relationships. At its core, trust is a fragile thing — one wrong move, and it shatters into a thousand irreparable pieces. For Ethan, this truth had never been clearer than in the past few months. He had learned that lesson the hard way, over and over, until the word itself seemed like an illusion, a distant concept that no longer had meaning in his world.

He stood in front of the grimy window of his apartment, watching the rain trickle down the glass like tears. The city outside was alive with its usual hum — the noise of cars, distant voices, the occasional siren. But it felt detached, almost unreal, like a world he no longer belonged to. Ethan had once trusted the system, believed in the black-and-white nature of justice and law, in right and wrong. Now, all of that seemed like a naive dream.

It wasn't one thing that had shattered his trust. It was a series of events, small at first, and then bigger, snowballing into a truth he couldn't ignore. In his line of work as a prosecutor, he had seen the worst of humanity — the lies, the betrayals, the cold-hearted manipulation — but he had never expected it to touch him personally. He had always believed that as long as he stayed on the right side of the law, did his job, and kept his moral compass intact, he would be safe.

That illusion was gone now.

It started with a case. A simple one, really. At least, that's what it appeared to be on the surface. A mid-level accountant involved in a money-laundering scheme for one of the city's notorious crime syndicates. Ethan had prosecuted hundreds like it before. But there was something off about this one — a gnawing feeling in the pit of his stomach that told him this wasn't just another routine case.

As he delved deeper, the threads began to unravel. One piece of information led to another, until he was no longer sure where the trail would end. It was then that he realized he was dealing with something far more dangerous than he had anticipated. The deeper he went, the more tangled the web became. What seemed like a small operation turned out to be part of a larger, more sinister network — one that reached into places he had never imagined.

Ethan's first instinct was to turn to the people he trusted. His colleagues, his boss, even a few old friends from law school. But each time he reached out, he found doors closing in his face. People who once had his back suddenly became distant, vague in their responses, unwilling to help. Some even seemed afraid to be seen talking to him. That was when he knew he had stepped into something far bigger than he had anticipated.

He began to question everything — the case, the people around him, even his own instincts. The fear crept in slowly, like a shadow at the edges of his mind, and before long, it consumed him. Who could he trust? Who was playing him? The paranoia was suffocating, and Ethan found himself constantly looking over his shoulder, waiting for the other shoe to drop.

The final blow came when he received an anonymous tip, leading him to a meeting with someone who claimed to have information that would blow the case wide open. He was cautious, of course. He had learned the hard way not to trust anyone without evidence, but desperation clouded his judgment. He had been chasing leads for weeks, and this was the first concrete piece of information he had come across in days.

The meeting was set in a dimly lit bar on the outskirts of town, a place where anonymity was the norm and questions weren't asked. Ethan sat in a booth in the corner, nursing a drink, his eyes scanning the room for his contact. When the man finally arrived, Ethan felt a chill run down his spine. There was something unsettling about him

— the way he moved, the way his eyes darted around the room, as if he were being followed.

The man slid into the booth across from Ethan, his face partially obscured by the low lighting. He spoke in a low, hurried voice, as if every word he said carried the weight of a thousand secrets. He gave Ethan a name — a name that sent shockwaves through his entire being. It was someone he knew, someone he had worked with, someone he had trusted.

At first, Ethan couldn't believe it. There had to be some mistake. But the man laid out the evidence, piece by piece, and slowly, the horrifying truth began to take shape. The person he had trusted most had been playing him all along, feeding him misinformation, leading him down false paths, and all the while, working for the very people Ethan was trying to bring down.

It was like the ground had fallen out from under him. Everything he thought he knew, every relationship he had built, every decision he had made — it all crumbled in an instant. He wanted to scream, to lash out, to confront the traitor, but he knew that would be foolish. He had to play it smart. He had to pretend he didn't know, keep his cards close to his chest, and wait for the right moment to strike.

From that point on, Ethan moved through his days in a haze of suspicion. Every conversation felt like a game, every glance was filled with hidden meaning. He no longer trusted anyone — not his colleagues, not his friends, not even himself. He had been played once, and he wouldn't let it happen again.

As the days turned into weeks, Ethan became more isolated. The few people he had left in his life drifted away, sensing the change in him, but not understanding the reasons behind it. He couldn't explain it to them, couldn't risk letting them in on what he knew. The stakes were too high, and the web of deceit was too tangled. He was on his own now.

The paranoia grew worse with each passing day. Ethan began to question his own actions, his own memories. Was he seeing things that weren't there? Was he reading too much into every little detail? Or was the world around him truly as treacherous as it seemed? He didn't know anymore. The lines between truth and lies had blurred, and he was trapped in the middle, unable to find his way out.

There were moments when he considered walking away from it all — leaving the case, leaving the city, starting fresh somewhere far away where no one knew him. But he couldn't. Not now. He was too deep, and the truth, no matter how painful, was too important. Someone had to be held accountable, and if no one else was willing to do it, Ethan would.

But to get there, he had to be careful. He had to play the game just as well as those who had deceived him. He had to lie, manipulate, and deceive — the very things he had once fought against. It was a bitter pill to swallow, but there was no other way. In this world, the rules were different. The good guys didn't always win, and trust was a luxury he could no longer afford.

In the end, it all came down to one thing: survival. Ethan had to survive long enough to expose the truth, and to do that, he had to become someone else. He had to let go of the person he once was — the man who believed in justice, who believed in the system, who believed in people. That man was dead now, replaced by someone colder, harder, and far more cynical.

The transformation wasn't easy, but it was necessary. Every day, Ethan reminded himself that this was the only way. He couldn't trust anyone, not even himself. He had to rely on facts, on evidence, on things that couldn't be twisted or manipulated. Everything else was noise, distractions designed to lead him astray.

And so, he moved forward, step by step, always watching, always waiting, always questioning. The paranoia never left him, but it became a part of him, like a second skin. He learned to live with it, to embrace it even. It kept him sharp, kept him focused, and most importantly, it kept him alive.

Trust no one. It was a simple rule, but one that Ethan would carry with him for the rest of his life. In a world where everyone had an agenda, where lies were currency and deception was the norm, it was the only way to survive.

And survive he would.

Chapter 8: The Chase Intensifies

1. Close Calls

Sweat trickled down the side of his face as his hands tightened around the steering wheel. The engine hummed beneath him, a low and constant vibration that matched the pounding in his chest. He checked the rearview mirror again, but nothing had changed. The dark sedan tailing him remained at a steady distance, neither closing in nor falling back. It was a professional's move—keeping close enough to remind him he wasn't alone, but far enough to avoid suspicion. They wanted him to know they were there, yet give him just enough room to breathe. Whoever they were, they weren't amateurs.

His mind raced as the streetlights cast long, distorted shadows on the damp asphalt. Every instinct told him to floor the gas pedal, but logic held him back. Running would only accelerate the inevitable. They'd be ready for that. This wasn't the first time he'd been followed, but this time felt different. There was a cold precision to it. These weren't low-level thugs trying to shake him down for a quick score. These people were after something bigger—information, leverage, maybe even his life.

The city seemed quieter than usual tonight. The hum of the engine was almost the only sound, interrupted only by the occasional passing car or the distant wail of a siren. He turned onto a side street, narrower and less crowded, but still the sedan followed. His pulse quickened. He was running out of options.

It wasn't supposed to be like this. Not now. Not after everything. He'd played the game as carefully as anyone could, hiding in plain sight, never drawing attention. But somehow, somewhere, he'd made a mistake, and now they were closing in.

Another turn. A wrong one. His gut sank as the street dead-ended into an alley. Trapped. He slammed the brakes, tires screeching, and the car jolted to a halt. For a moment, there was silence, as if the whole city was holding its breath. He glanced at the sedan—it had stopped too, the headlights casting a long shadow across the brick walls surrounding him. There was nowhere to run. The adrenaline surged through his veins, and his hand instinctively reached for the glove compartment, where he kept his gun. Not that it would make much of a difference. He was outnumbered and outplayed, but something in him refused to surrender without a fight.

He waited, expecting the doors of the sedan to open, for someone to step out and approach him, guns drawn, ready to finish this once and for all. But nothing happened. The seconds ticked by, each one stretching longer than the last. He squinted through the windshield, trying to make out any movement. Was this some kind of sick game? Were they waiting for him to make the first move?

Just then, the radio crackled. A voice, low and urgent, cut through the silence. "Don't move." It wasn't coming from his car, but from somewhere nearby. His heart skipped a beat. How long had they been watching? His eyes darted around the alley, looking for hidden cameras, for the source of the voice. He was trapped in more ways than one.

"Get out of the car, slowly," the voice commanded. His fingers itched to grab the gun, to fight back, but he knew it was useless. Whoever they were, they had the upper hand. He opened the door and stepped out into the cold night air, his muscles tense, every nerve on edge.

The sedan's engine revved, and suddenly, it sped away, disappearing into the night. He blinked, stunned. They were gone. What the hell was going on?

Before he could process it, footsteps echoed behind him. He spun around, but it was too late. A figure emerged from the shadows, dressed in black, their face hidden under a hood. He barely had time to react before they were on him. A hand grabbed his arm, twisting it painfully behind his back, while the other pressed something cold and metallic against his temple.

"You're in deep now," a voice hissed in his ear. It was a woman's voice, smooth and calm, almost too calm for the situation. "But this isn't your time to die. Not yet."

He tried to pull away, but the grip tightened. "Who are you? What do you want?"

"That's not important right now," she replied. "What matters is that you're going to listen, and you're going to listen carefully. You've made some powerful enemies, and they're getting impatient. Tonight was a warning. The next time, you won't be so lucky."

His mind raced, trying to piece together the puzzle. "Why are you telling me this? If they want me dead, why not just do it now?"

She let out a quiet laugh, her breath warm against his skin. "You still don't get it, do you? You're valuable—alive. Dead men can't talk, and you, my friend, have a lot to say."

The pressure on his arm eased slightly, and he took the opportunity to twist free, spinning around to face her. But before he could get a good look, she stepped back into the shadows, her face obscured once more.

"You think you can just disappear?" he called after her, his voice a mix of anger and desperation. "You think you can toy with me?"

But she was already gone, vanished as quickly as she had appeared. The alley was silent again, the only sound his own ragged breathing.

He stood there for a moment, trying to steady himself, his heart still racing. This wasn't over, not by a long shot. Whoever these people were, they were playing a game far beyond his understanding, and he was stuck right in the middle of it. He had to figure out what they wanted before it was too late.

Back in the car, his hands shook as he started the engine. The sedan was gone, the woman was gone, but the feeling of being hunted lingered. He pulled out of the alley, merging back into the quiet city streets, his mind whirling with questions. Who were they? What did they want from him? And most importantly—how long could he keep running before they finally caught up?

The city unfolded before him, a labyrinth of streets, buildings, and secrets. As he drove, he couldn't shake the sensation that he was being watched, that every turn brought him closer to another near miss, another close call. It was only a matter of time before the next one wouldn't be so close.

• • • •

THE NEXT FEW DAYS PASSED in a blur, each one more paranoid than the last. He felt their presence everywhere—on the streets, in the crowded cafes, even in the quiet of his apartment. Every phone call, every glance from a stranger, felt like a potential threat. Sleep came in short, restless bursts, interrupted by nightmares of dark figures and cold metal against his skin.

He couldn't live like this forever. Something had to give.

Late one evening, as he sat in the dim light of his kitchen, staring at the nearly empty bottle of whiskey in front of him, his phone buzzed. He picked it up, expecting another anonymous message or cryptic threat, but this time it was different. A name flashed across the screen—an old contact, someone he hadn't spoken to in years.

He hesitated for a moment before answering.

"Still alive, huh?" The voice on the other end was gruff, familiar. "I figured they'd have gotten to you by now."

"Close," he replied, his voice rough from lack of sleep. "Too close."

"I heard," the contact said. "That's why I'm calling. You're playing a dangerous game, my friend. And I don't think you realize just how high the stakes are."

"I didn't ask for this," he said, running a hand through his hair. "I don't even know what 'this' is."

There was a pause on the other end, then a sigh. "It's bigger than you. Bigger than all of us. You need to get out while you still can."

He clenched his jaw. "I don't run."

"Then you'll die." The words hung heavy in the air. "You think you're in control, but you're not. They've been watching you, studying you. You've had some close calls, but your luck's running out."

He leaned back in his chair, closing his eyes. "What do you suggest?"

"Disappear. Change your name, your face, everything. Walk away before they take away the choice."

For a moment, he considered it. The idea of leaving everything behind, starting fresh, was tempting. But he couldn't. Not now. Not with so many unanswered questions.

"I can't," he said finally.

"Then I hope you've made peace with your fate," the contact replied, his voice laced with resignation. "Because it's coming for you."

The line went dead, and he was left alone in the dim light, the bottle of whiskey staring back at him.

2. Secrets Revealed

The room was dimly lit, with heavy velvet curtains pulled halfway shut, allowing only thin rays of light to filter through the dust that hung in the air. It had been years since anyone had disturbed this place. The once-grand library now felt like a tomb, and as Daniel stood in the middle of the room, he could feel the weight of history pressing down on him. There was an uneasiness here, as if the walls themselves whispered secrets, begging to be uncovered, yet threatening anyone foolish enough to try.

Daniel's fingers trembled slightly as he reached for the old wooden box on the desk. It was the key. He knew it. The box had been passed down through generations, hidden, protected. People had died because of it. His mother had warned him never to touch it, never to ask questions about the family's past. But now, with her gone and the truth gnawing at his soul, he had no choice. He had to know.

The box creaked as he opened it, the sound cutting through the stillness like a blade. Inside, a bundle of yellowed papers tied together with a faded red ribbon. He undid the knot carefully, as if he were handling something sacred, and began to read.

The first document was a letter, dated nearly fifty years ago. It was written in hurried, almost frantic handwriting, addressed to someone named Marcello. Daniel had never heard of this man, but the tone of the letter was unmistakably urgent.

"The money is safe for now, but they are getting closer. I fear the day will come when we can no longer hide in the shadows. There are too many watching. Too many who know. If this letter finds you, remember the plan. No one must know the full extent of the operation. Not even your closest allies."

Daniel's heart raced as he scanned the page. The operation. Could this be the secret his family had guarded for so long? The money, the hidden fortunes—the very lifeblood of their power and influence. He had always known there was more to his family's wealth than they let on, but he had never imagined it went this deep. His father's cold detachment, his mother's cryptic warnings—everything started to make sense.

But the letter was just the beginning. Beneath it lay another set of documents, these typed and official-looking. Bank records. Transactions. Offshore accounts. A tangled web of financial dealings that spanned the globe. The sums were staggering, the names involved even more so. High-ranking politicians, business tycoons, members of royalty—people who should have been above suspicion were listed here, all connected by the invisible threads of money and power.

Daniel's pulse quickened as he read further. There, among the signatures and stamps of approval, was a name he knew all too well. His own father. His name appeared again and again, authorizing transfers, overseeing deposits, his initials scrawled in the margins of deals that stretched back decades. The man Daniel had idolized as a child, who had instilled in him the values of honesty and integrity, was at the center of a sprawling criminal enterprise.

He felt sick, the bile rising in his throat as the weight of the revelation crushed down on him. He had spent his life believing in the righteousness of his family, in their legitimacy and respectability. They were pillars of the community, leaders. But this—this was something else. They weren't just part of the corruption. They were the architects of it.

His hands trembled as he turned the last few pages, revealing a set of coded messages. At first, they appeared as random sequences of letters and numbers, but then he noticed a pattern, a rhythm to the characters. His father had always been methodical, precise. Daniel remembered the cryptography books that lined his father's office, the puzzles he would challenge him with as a child. This was no random string of information—it was a code. And his father had left it here, waiting to be found.

Why now? Why had his father, a man who had concealed so much, left this trail for him to follow? Was it a warning, a challenge, or something else entirely? Daniel's mind raced as he pieced together the fragments of information. The deeper he dug, the clearer the picture became. The criminal empire his family had built was not just about money—it was about control. They had pulled the strings of governments, influenced elections, toppled regimes, all while hiding behind the facade of legitimacy.

He took a step back from the desk, the pages still spread out before him. The room felt colder now, the air heavy with the weight of what he had uncovered. Every instinct told him to stop, to walk away before it was too late. But something inside him wouldn't let go. He had to know the full extent of the truth, no matter how dark, no matter how dangerous.

There was a sudden noise from behind him—the sound of footsteps. Daniel spun around, his heart pounding in his chest. He wasn't alone.

From the shadows, a figure emerged. It was a woman, tall and elegant, with an air of confidence that unnerved him. She stepped forward, her eyes fixed on the papers scattered across the desk. She didn't need to say a word. Daniel knew who she was.

"You've found it," she said, her voice smooth, almost soothing. "I was wondering how long it would take."

Daniel swallowed hard, trying to mask the fear rising within him. "Who are you?"

She smiled, but it didn't reach her eyes. "I'm someone who knows far more about your family than you ever will."

The weight of her words hung in the air between them, thick with implication. Daniel realized in that moment that whatever he thought he knew, whatever secrets he had uncovered, there was more. Much more.

The woman circled the desk, her fingers brushing lightly over the documents as she spoke. "Your father was a brilliant man. Ruthless, yes, but brilliant. He understood the world in ways most people never could. He knew that power wasn't something you were given. It was something you took."

Daniel's throat tightened. "And you? What's your role in all of this?"

Her smile widened. "Let's just say I'm the one who made sure it all ran smoothly."

His mind raced, trying to process the implications. "You were part of the operation?"

"I was the operation," she corrected, her tone sharp. "Your father may have built the foundation, but I was the one who ensured it flourished."

Daniel's pulse pounded in his ears. This woman, whoever she was, had been pulling the strings all along. The hidden billions, the corruption, the chaos—it all traced back to her.

"You must have questions," she said, her voice softening again. "But I'll warn you, some things are better left in the dark."

He stared at her, his mind torn between the desire for answers and the fear of what they might be. The secrets of his family had already shaken him to his core. How much more could he take?

But she didn't wait for his response. She leaned closer, her voice barely a whisper. "The truth, Daniel, is a dangerous thing. It can set you free, or it can destroy you. And right now, you're standing on the edge."

His breath caught in his throat as the weight of her words sank in. He was on the precipice of something far bigger than he had ever imagined. The secrets he had uncovered were only the beginning, and the path ahead was fraught with peril.

But there was no turning back now.

The woman straightened, her gaze piercing. "Choose wisely, Daniel. Once you step into the shadows, there's no going back."

With that, she turned and disappeared into the darkness, leaving him alone with the truth he had sought for so long—and the chilling realization that he was now a part of the very world he had uncovered. The secrets had been revealed, but the cost of knowing them had only just begun to unfold.

3. The Final Piece of the Puzzle

It was late in the evening when the weight of the investigation truly settled on him. The dim light of the lamp cast long shadows across the papers strewn about his desk, each one a fragment of a much larger story—a story that had haunted him for months. Names, dates, financial records, all of them seemed to float just out of reach, each clue promising answers but delivering only more questions. He rubbed his temples, trying to fend off the fatigue that crept into his bones, the type of exhaustion that came not from lack of sleep but from carrying too many unsolved mysteries.

The prosecutor leaned back in his chair, staring at the corkboard on the wall where he had pinned every critical piece of the investigation. Red strings crisscrossed the board like the web of a particularly meticulous spider. At the center of it all was the woman who had evaded him for so long, a phantom in every sense of the word. She was the puppeteer behind the criminal empire, but the evidence linking her to the crimes had always been circumstantial. She was careful, elusive, and maddeningly good at covering her tracks.

But tonight, something felt different. He could sense it, a shift in the air, the sensation of being on the verge of discovering the final piece of the puzzle. It wasn't a hunch or a fleeting instinct—it was the culmination of months of painstaking work. Every dead-end, every misleading clue, had led him to this point. And now, as he sifted through the remaining files, the last unanswered questions seemed to form a picture, albeit faint and incomplete.

His phone buzzed on the desk, a brief distraction from his thoughts. A message popped up on the screen: We need to meet. Urgent. It was from one of his most trusted informants, a man who had spent years embedded deep within the criminal underworld. The prosecutor knew this wasn't just another false lead. When this informant said something was urgent, it meant he had something big—something that could blow the case wide open.

Within half an hour, he was driving through the rain-soaked streets of the city, the windshield wipers rhythmically slapping away the downpour. The location for the meeting was a grimy, out-of-the-way diner on the edge of town, the kind of place where no one asked questions and the regulars knew better than to listen too closely to conversations in the back booths.

As he stepped inside, the bell above the door jingled weakly, and he spotted his informant already seated in a corner, a cup of coffee steaming in front of him. The man was jittery, his eyes darting around the room as if he expected trouble to walk in at any moment. The prosecutor slid into the booth across from him, his heart pounding with the weight of anticipation.

"You're cutting it close," the informant said in a low voice, barely glancing up.

"I came as fast as I could," the prosecutor replied. "What do you have for me?"

The informant leaned forward, lowering his voice even further. "I've been hearing things—rumblings from the higher-ups. The woman, the one you've been chasing, she's getting nervous. Word on the street is, she's tying up loose ends, getting ready to disappear."

The prosecutor's pulse quickened. "She knows we're closing in."

"Yeah, but it's more than that. She's preparing for something big, something that'll make it impossible for you to touch her. Once she makes her move, she'll be untouchable."

The prosecutor leaned in closer, his voice a harsh whisper. "What move?"

The informant shook his head. "I don't know the specifics, but I heard one name. A location, actually. It's where she's planning to finalize everything."

"What's the name?"

For a moment, the informant hesitated, as if weighing the consequences of saying the next word aloud. Finally, he leaned in, his eyes locking with the prosecutor's.

"Zeta."

The prosecutor sat back, his mind racing. He had heard that name before—a whisper among whispers, a code word mentioned in passing by those deep inside the criminal network. But no one had ever been able to explain what Zeta was. Some said it was a person, others thought it was a place. A few even speculated it was the name of a shadow organization, a power even darker than the one he was chasing.

The informant glanced at his watch, clearly anxious. "I've said all I can. You need to move fast."

Before the prosecutor could respond, the informant was already getting up, slipping out the door and disappearing into the rain-soaked night. He watched him go, feeling the cold grip of urgency close around his heart. There was no time to waste.

Back in his office, the prosecutor threw himself into his files, searching for any mention of Zeta that might have slipped through the cracks. He was looking for a needle in a haystack, but there was no turning back now. He was too close.

Hours passed, the night dragging on as the city outside his window seemed to grow quieter, as if holding its breath. Then, in a file marked as unimportant, he found it—buried in a footnote from an old witness statement, a single word: Zeta. It was connected to an abandoned warehouse on the outskirts of town, a place that had once been a hub for illicit activity before it fell into disuse. And now, it seemed, it was about to become the epicenter of everything.

The next morning, just before dawn, he stood outside the warehouse, watching as a few early rays of light struggled to break through the overcast sky. The building looked decrepit, long forgotten by anyone who didn't know what to look for. But to him, it was alive with danger, humming with the unseen energy of secrets waiting to be uncovered.

He had come alone. Bringing a team would have drawn too much attention, and he couldn't risk tipping her off before he had what he needed. His mind raced as he approached the door, every instinct on high alert. This was it—the final piece of the puzzle.

The warehouse was dark, the air thick with dust and the lingering smell of mildew. His footsteps echoed off the concrete floor as he moved deeper into the building, every shadow feeling like it could hold a hidden threat. And then he heard it—a faint rustling sound coming from one of the rooms in the back.

He crept closer, his hand instinctively moving to the gun at his side. As he peered around the corner, he saw her. She was standing by a table, her back to him, meticulously arranging a series of documents and hard drives. It was the first time he had seen her in person, and for a moment, he was struck by how ordinary she looked—nothing like the powerful mastermind he had built up in his mind.

But he knew better than to underestimate her. She had slipped through his fingers too many times before, always one step ahead. This time, though, he had her. The final piece of the puzzle had fallen into place, and there was no escape.

He stepped into the room, his voice cutting through the silence. "It's over."

She didn't turn around right away, but when she finally did, her expression was calm, almost amused. "Is it?"

The prosecutor kept his gun trained on her, but even as he did, a flicker of doubt crept into his mind. She was too calm, too collected. And then, in one swift motion, she knocked the table over, sending papers and hard drives flying. He lunged forward, but it was too late. She bolted for the door, disappearing into the labyrinth of the warehouse.

For the next agonizing hour, he hunted her through the maze of corridors and storage rooms, the sound of their footsteps echoing off the walls. Every time he thought he had her cornered, she slipped away again, like a ghost vanishing into the shadows.

Finally, they found themselves back where they started, in the main room of the warehouse. She stood near the exit, breathing hard but still defiant. "You'll never catch me," she said, her voice steady despite the adrenaline coursing through her veins.

The prosecutor leveled his gun at her. "This ends now."

For a long moment, they stared at each other, neither willing to back down. And then, with a small, almost imperceptible smile, she reached into her pocket and pressed a button on a small device.

There was a deafening explosion, and the world went dark.

4. A Desperate Flight

The night was suffocating, cloaked in thick clouds that blanketed the sky, blotting out the moonlight. Every step echoed louder than it should have, and the only thing more oppressive than the darkness was the fear that gnawed at the edges of reason. Ava's heart raced in time with her footsteps, each beat a frantic reminder that she was running out of time. Her breath, shallow and ragged, was the only sound she could focus on as she darted through the narrow alleys of the city.

Her mind churned with a thousand possibilities, but none offered a way out. Every corner felt like a trap, every shadow a threat. The weight of what she'd uncovered was unbearable, the kind of truth that could get you killed just for knowing it. And now, they were after her. She had seen the message, deciphered the code, and followed the trail — a trail that led her straight into the labyrinth of lies and deception. But with each step forward, the walls closed in tighter, and the stakes rose higher.

The envelope she carried felt heavier with every stride. Inside were documents that could bring down powerful people, expose the hidden network operating under the cover of legality, and ruin lives built on corruption. She clutched it to her chest, a lifeline she couldn't afford to lose.

It wasn't supposed to be like this. Ava had thought she could outsmart them, move quietly enough not to be noticed. But she had underestimated their reach, their resources. The chase had begun the moment she crossed a line she didn't even know existed. Now, she was in their sights, and they wouldn't stop until they had her cornered.

Her only hope was to reach the safe house before they did. It was the last place she could think of, the only sanctuary left in a world where friends had become enemies and allies were few. She knew the route by heart; it was imprinted in her mind after months of preparation. But preparation meant nothing when you were being hunted.

The streets were eerily empty, as if the city itself was holding its breath, waiting for what would come next. Ava felt exposed, as if unseen eyes were watching her every move, calculating her next step. The paranoia was suffocating, but she couldn't afford to stop. Not now.

Her phone buzzed in her pocket, a sharp reminder that she wasn't alone. With shaking hands, she pulled it out and glanced at the screen. A single message blinked up at her: "They're closer than you think."

Panic surged through her veins like fire. She turned left, ducking into an alleyway that smelled of decay and old rain. Her mind raced as she tried to make sense of who could have sent the message. There were only a handful of people who knew where she was, but trust was a luxury she could no longer afford.

The alley opened up into a wide street, and she slowed her pace, scanning the area for any sign of a tail. She couldn't shake the feeling that something was wrong, that she was being funneled somewhere — like prey driven into a snare.

Suddenly, a pair of headlights appeared at the end of the street, cutting through the fog of darkness like twin beacons. The car moved slowly, deliberately, as if its driver knew exactly what they were looking for. Ava's blood ran cold. She turned on her heel and sprinted down the nearest side street, her pulse thundering in her ears. She could hear the engine roar to life behind her, the tires screeching as they gave chase.

The city blurred around her as she ran, her legs burning with the effort of keeping her pace. She knew she couldn't outrun them forever, but there was no other choice. They were closing in, and every second mattered.

Ava's mind darted to the plan she had rehearsed countless times in her head. The safe house was still miles away, hidden in the industrial district on the outskirts of the city. But she had to shake them first. She veered off into a park, the towering trees offering some semblance of cover as she zigzagged through the dark paths.

She didn't look back, but she could hear the car slowing down behind her, the soft hum of its engine like a predator stalking its prey. Ava pushed herself harder, her lungs burning with the cold air, her muscles screaming for relief. But relief was a luxury she couldn't afford.

Ahead, she saw a small footbridge leading over a canal. The water below was sluggish, reflecting the dim glow of distant streetlights. She didn't think, didn't hesitate. Without breaking stride, she vaulted over the low railing and plunged into the freezing water.

The shock hit her like a punch to the gut, stealing the air from her lungs as she sank beneath the surface. For a moment, everything was silent — the world above muted by the water, the chaos of her flight reduced to a cold, dark stillness. She kicked hard, forcing herself upward until her head broke the surface and she gasped for breath.

The car screeched to a halt on the bridge above, its headlights cutting through the fog but failing to pierce the water's depths. Ava swam to the side of the canal, pulling herself out with trembling arms. She was soaked and shivering, but alive.

The car lingered for a moment longer before its headlights winked out, and the night swallowed it whole. Ava stayed crouched in the shadows, her breath ragged as she waited for the sound of the engine to fade into the distance. They would circle back soon, she knew. They wouldn't give up that easily.

With shaking hands, she pulled her phone from her pocket and checked the time. She had less than an hour to reach the safe house before her window of escape closed for good. The documents in her possession were too valuable to lose, and the people chasing her were too dangerous to face without backup.

The only person she could trust now was herself.

Ava moved cautiously through the empty streets, her clothes clinging to her skin, her heart still racing from the close call. She knew they would be waiting for her at every turn, but she also knew the city better than they did. Every alley, every shortcut, every hidden corner — this was her territory. And if she was careful, she could still make it out alive.

The industrial district loomed ahead, a maze of warehouses and abandoned factories. The safe house was hidden in one of the old buildings, its entrance concealed behind a rusting door that looked like it hadn't been opened in decades. She had to get there, had to disappear before they found her again.

As she approached the district, Ava's phone buzzed again. This time, it was a different message: "They know where you're going. Run."

Her heart skipped a beat, but she didn't slow down. She couldn't. There was no time to second-guess, no time to wonder who was sending these cryptic warnings. She had to move, had to keep going.

The warehouse was just ahead, its hulking silhouette barely visible in the fog. Ava sprinted the last few steps and slipped through a narrow gap in the fence. The building loomed above her, a massive structure that seemed to pulse with an eerie, silent energy.

She found the door, hidden just as she remembered, and forced it open with a creak that echoed through the empty space. Inside, the air was thick with dust, the smell of rust and decay hanging heavy in the air. Ava moved quickly, her footsteps muffled by the layers of grime and debris that covered the floor.

The safe house was in the basement, accessible through a hidden stairwell at the back of the building. Ava found it without trouble, her memory guiding her through the darkness. She descended the stairs two at a time, her breath coming in short, sharp bursts as she reached the bottom.

The room was small and windowless, the kind of place that no one would think to look. Ava locked the door behind her and leaned against it, her body trembling with exhaustion and fear. She had made it.

But she knew the fight wasn't over yet. The documents were still in her possession, and the people chasing her would stop at nothing to get them back.

5. Confrontation in the Shadows

The air was thick with tension as Michael stood in the alley, his breath clouding in the cold night. The only sound was the distant hum of the city and the occasional drip of water from the rusting gutters above. He checked his watch, feeling the weight of time pressing down on him, but the waiting was part of the plan. It always was.

He didn't trust this meeting. Something about it felt wrong, like a trap waiting to spring, but he had no choice. Too many doors had been slammed shut in his face over the past few weeks, and the deeper he went into this case, the more he realized how little control he had. Everything—every lead, every whisper—seemed to point toward a singular force lurking just out of sight. The Secret Hand, they called it, and tonight was supposed to be his first real encounter.

A shadow moved at the far end of the alley, barely perceptible in the dim light. Michael's instincts flared, but he stayed still, not giving anything away. His hand hovered near his coat pocket, where a small revolver waited. He hated carrying a gun, but in his line of work, especially with the people he was dealing with now, it had become a necessary evil. He hadn't fired it in years, but tonight... tonight, he might not have a choice.

"You're late," a voice said, low and gravelly, coming from the shadows ahead. Michael couldn't see the man's face clearly, but he recognized the silhouette. It was Riker, one of the many informants who had slipped through the cracks of the underworld and found themselves on both sides of the law. Riker was a middleman, a broker of secrets, and a man who seemed to thrive in the murk of moral ambiguity.

"I don't have time for games, Riker," Michael replied, his voice steady despite the pounding in his chest. "You said you had something on them. I want it now."

Riker stepped forward, the dim light from the street lamp casting a harsh glow on his scarred face. He looked different from the last time Michael had seen him. There was a nervous energy about him now, a twitch in his eye that wasn't there before. Something had changed, and Michael could sense it.

"The Hand doesn't play by your rules, man," Riker said, lighting a cigarette with shaky fingers. "You think you're chasing ghosts? Nah. They're real. And they're watching everything."

Michael frowned, feeling the cold grip of paranoia tighten around him. He had heard the rumors—whispers about an organization that controlled everything from the shadows. Politicians, corporations, even law enforcement were supposedly under their thumb. But so far, all he had were fragmented pieces of a puzzle that refused to come together.

"Give me something concrete, Riker," Michael said, his patience wearing thin. "Names, locations, anything I can use. I didn't come here to listen to ghost stories."

Riker blew out a cloud of smoke, his eyes darting nervously around the alley as if he expected someone to be lurking in every corner. "Concrete, huh?" He reached into his coat and pulled out a worn envelope, yellowed with age and crumpled at the edges. "This is all I got. Don't ask where I got it, but it's real. And dangerous."

Michael took the envelope, feeling the weight of it in his hands. It was heavier than he expected, filled with something more than just paper. He hesitated for a moment, then opened it. Inside were photographs, black and white, grainy but clear enough to see the faces of men he recognized—powerful men. Politicians, business magnates, even a few faces from the police force.

"You've got to be kidding me," Michael muttered, flipping through the pictures. "These people... they're untouchable."

"Not if you know where to look," Riker replied, his voice low. "Not if you know how to hit them where it hurts."

Michael's mind raced as he processed the information. If these photos were real, if they could be traced back to the Secret Hand, it could blow the whole thing wide open. But that was a big "if," and he wasn't sure how much he trusted Riker—or the evidence in his hands.

"Why are you giving me this?" Michael asked, narrowing his eyes at the informant. "What's in it for you?"

Riker chuckled, a sound that was more hollow than amused. "Survival, man. You think I want to end up like the others? The Hand doesn't leave loose ends. I'm already dead, just trying to buy myself a little more time."

Michael pocketed the envelope, his mind racing with possibilities. He knew he couldn't trust Riker, not fully, but right now, this was the closest he'd come to getting a real lead on the Secret Hand. He'd have to tread carefully, though. One wrong move, and he could end up like all the others who'd tried to take them down—erased, forgotten, just another casualty in a war fought in the shadows.

"You're walking a dangerous line, Riker," Michael said, turning to leave the alley. "You better hope you're not playing me."

Riker didn't respond, just took another drag of his cigarette and melted back into the darkness.

As Michael walked away, he couldn't shake the feeling that this was only the beginning of something far worse than he had imagined. The Secret Hand was no ordinary criminal organization. They were patient, meticulous, and ruthless. And now, they knew that someone was coming for them.

• • • •

THE CITY LOOMED LARGE as Michael drove through the empty streets, the envelope burning a hole in his pocket. His thoughts were a whirlwind of questions, suspicions, and fear. He needed to be smart about this, and more importantly, he needed help.

He parked outside his apartment, taking a moment to steady himself before heading inside. The weight of the case was pressing down on him harder than ever, but he couldn't afford to crack. Not yet. Not when he was so close.

As he stepped through the door, the faint sound of movement caught his attention. He froze, his hand instinctively reaching for his gun. The apartment was dark, but he knew it well enough to sense when something was off. Someone was here.

"Who's there?" he called out, his voice sharp in the silence.

There was no response, just the faint creak of floorboards from the living room. Michael moved slowly, carefully, his gun drawn as he rounded the corner.

A figure stood in the middle of the room, their back to him, gazing out the window. The dim light from the street outside cast a long shadow across the floor.

"Turn around," Michael ordered, his finger hovering over the trigger.

The figure obeyed, turning slowly to face him. It was a woman, tall and poised, with an air of calm confidence that sent a shiver down Michael's spine. She didn't look surprised to see him. In fact, it was almost as if she had been waiting for him.

"Who are you?" Michael demanded, keeping his gun trained on her.

The woman smiled, a cold, calculated smile that didn't reach her eyes. "I think you already know," she said, her voice smooth as silk.

Michael's grip tightened on the gun. "You're one of them, aren't you? The Hand."

She tilted her head slightly, as if amused by his accusation. "I prefer to think of myself as a facilitator," she replied. "Someone who ensures that things run smoothly, without interference."

"Why are you here?" Michael asked, his heart pounding in his chest. He knew he was in over his head now, but there was no turning back.

The woman took a step forward, her eyes never leaving his. "I'm here to offer you a choice, Michael," she said, her tone almost sympathetic. "You can walk away from this. Forget everything you've seen, everything you've heard. Live your life in peace."

"And if I don't?" Michael asked, though he already knew the answer.

The woman's smile faded. "Then you'll die, like the others."

For a moment, Michael considered it. Walking away, leaving this nightmare behind, living a quiet life. But deep down, he knew he couldn't. Not after everything he had uncovered. Not with the truth so close, just out of reach.

"I'm not walking away," he said, his voice steady despite the fear clawing at him.

The woman sighed, as if disappointed but not surprised. "I thought you might say that."

Before Michael could react, she moved. Faster than he expected, faster than he could follow. Her hand shot out, knocking the gun from his grip, and in an instant, she had him pinned against the wall, her strength far greater than her slim frame suggested.

"You should have taken the offer," she whispered in his ear, her breath cold against his skin.

Michael struggled, but it was no use. She had him, and he knew it.

6. The Tipping Point

It was the kind of night that weighed heavily on the city, where even the streetlights seemed reluctant to pierce the darkness. The oppressive heat clung to the air, making every breath feel labored. From his vantage point high above, Marcus could see the city's veins of neon lights snaking through the grid of streets, but even the city's usual hum seemed muted. Tonight, something was different. Something was about to give.

He paced the length of the room, his mind running through the events of the past weeks. The investigation had reached a crucial point, but it wasn't the breakthroughs that worried him. It was everything that lay beneath the surface. The quiet looks exchanged in courtrooms, the odd phone calls that ended just as he picked up, the way his colleagues had suddenly stopped meeting his eyes in the hallway. Marcus had been in this business long enough to recognize the signs. The web was tightening around him, and soon, there would be no escape.

Tonight, he needed clarity. The boardroom had been his sanctuary, a place to think without the distractions of the outside world. It was strange to think how quickly everything had escalated. Just months ago, he had been a rising star, one of the youngest prosecutors in the city's history to be handed such a high-profile case. But as the pieces of the puzzle began to fit together, Marcus realized he wasn't just dealing with an ordinary crime syndicate. He had stumbled onto something far larger, something deeply ingrained in the city's very structure. The people he was going up against weren't just criminals—they were powerful, untouchable. And they were watching his every move.

A soft knock at the door pulled him out of his thoughts. His assistant, Rebecca, stepped into the room, her face pale. She held a small envelope in her hand.

"This just arrived," she said, her voice barely above a whisper. "There was no return address. I thought you should see it immediately."

Marcus took the envelope from her and nodded. "Thank you, Rebecca," he said. She hesitated for a moment, as if wanting to say something more, but then thought better of it and left him alone again.

The envelope was plain, unmarked. His name was written in a neat, almost mechanical script. It felt cold in his hand, like it carried more than just paper inside. Carefully, he slid his thumb along the edge, opening it with a sense of foreboding. Inside was a single sheet of paper, folded once. The message was short:

"You're running out of time. Walk away, or everything you know will come crashing down."

No signature. No hint of who had sent it. But Marcus didn't need one. He knew. He could feel their presence in the words, the subtle threat. The tipping point had been reached. He was no longer chasing shadows—now, they were chasing him.

He placed the note on the table and leaned back in his chair, staring at the ceiling. There were only two options left: walk away, as the note suggested, or push forward, knowing full well what the cost might be. But could he walk away? Could he leave this unfinished, knowing what was at stake?

His phone buzzed on the table, pulling him from his reverie. It was Rebecca again.

"You need to see this," she said, her voice trembling.

Marcus hurried to the monitors. A live feed from the courthouse was streaming across the screen. What he saw made his blood run cold. The courtroom was in chaos. Someone had set off a bomb, and the scene was nothing short of carnage. People were screaming, running for cover. Smoke billowed out of the shattered windows. In the distance, the sound of sirens wailed as emergency vehicles rushed to the scene.

This was no accident. It was a message. The Syndicate was done with subtle threats. They were making their move, and they wanted him to know they were serious.

His mind raced. He had no choice now. He had to act quickly, but every step had to be calculated. One wrong move, and it could all come crashing down—not just for him, but for everyone he cared about. He grabbed his coat and headed for the door, his heart pounding in his chest. The game had changed, and it was no longer about catching criminals. It was about survival.

As he drove through the city streets, his thoughts turned to the others—his team, his allies, and the few he still trusted. He needed to get them all together, to regroup before the Syndicate could strike again. But there was something else gnawing at the back of his mind, something darker. The note. Whoever had sent it wasn't just warning him—they were giving him an out. A way to escape. But why?

He knew too much now. The Syndicate had been careful, keeping their operations hidden beneath layers of legitimate businesses, political connections, and shell companies. But Marcus had found the cracks. He had followed the money trail, traced the bribes, and now he was close to pulling back the curtain on the entire operation. That's why they were getting desperate. That's why they were making mistakes.

As he parked outside the old warehouse where they were meeting, Marcus felt the weight of the decision pressing down on him. The tipping point. He had to choose—push forward and risk everything, or walk away and let the Syndicate continue their reign unchecked.

The warehouse door creaked as he stepped inside. The others were already there—Rebecca, Daniel, and Michael, his closest confidants. They looked up at him, their faces a mixture of fear and determination.

"What's the plan?" Daniel asked.

Marcus looked around the room. This was it. There was no going back. He took a deep breath and spoke, his voice steady.

"We're going to finish this," he said. "No matter what it takes."

The next hours were a blur of strategy, phone calls, and hastily drawn maps. They needed to strike fast, hit the Syndicate where it hurt the most. But there was a problem. Every move they made seemed to be anticipated, every plan met with resistance. It was as if the Syndicate was always one step ahead. And then it hit him—the leak. Someone on the inside was feeding them information.

"Someone's been playing both sides," Marcus said, his eyes narrowing. "We have a mole."

The room fell silent. Trust was already in short supply, and now, it was crumbling even further. But there was no time to dwell on it. They had to move.

Hours later, as the sun began to rise, Marcus found himself standing on the rooftop of a high-rise building, overlooking the city once again. It was quiet, almost peaceful, but he knew the chaos that was brewing beneath the surface. The Syndicate was out there, watching, waiting.

He took a deep breath. The tipping point had been reached, but the scales hadn't yet fallen. The next move would determine everything—his fate, the fate of his team, and the future of the city. There was no margin for error.

As the first light of dawn touched the horizon, Marcus knew there was no turning back. The battle had begun, and it wouldn't end until one side was destroyed. The city, the power, the billions—it was all on the line now.

Chapter 9: Truth and Consequences

1. The Unraveling

It all started with a single thread. A detail so small that, at first glance, no one could have noticed it. The case that had been dominating the headlines for months was reaching a stalemate. The press had grown impatient, and the public was demanding answers. Yet, for all the noise and pressure, nothing seemed to break. Investigations were underway, files were piling up on desks, and prosecutors were doing their best to present a compelling case. But for every question that found an answer, two more would arise, casting a deeper shadow over the entire situation.

In the quiet of his office, David Lawson, the lead prosecutor, sat behind his desk, pouring over the endless stacks of papers and digital files. His eyes had grown tired of the repetition of names, dates, and meaningless transactions. The web was there, tangled in front of him, but no matter how hard he tried to pull at the threads, nothing gave. It was as if the truth were buried beneath layers of misdirection, cloaked in a fog of deception that kept everyone chasing their tails.

That was, until the name resurfaced: Alexandra Laurent. She had been mentioned early on, in passing, during a witness deposition, and then seemed to disappear into the background noise. She wasn't a primary suspect, nor did she appear in any of the financial records or police files that David had reviewed over the past months. But there was something about the way her name was mentioned — as though everyone was deliberately trying to avoid saying it again. It was a whisper in a room full of shouting, subtle yet unnerving.

David leaned back in his chair and stared at the name, now circled in red ink at the top of his notes. "Alexandra Laurent," he muttered to himself. He couldn't shake the feeling that there was more to her than met the eye. He tapped the pen against his desk, trying to connect the dots. Who was she really? And why had she slipped through the cracks of the investigation?

After several hours of sifting through files, David stumbled upon an old article about Alexandra. It was an innocuous piece, a puff profile from years ago when she had been involved in charity work. Nothing about her seemed unusual — she had been described as a socialite, someone with the means and connections to move fluidly through high socicty, a benefactor of several causes. But as he read on, he noticed the careful omissions. Her family was never mentioned, nor was there any detail about her past. She appeared in photographs, always at the center of attention, surrounded by people of influence and power, but there was never a direct reference to what she did. It was as if she existed in the periphery, controlling events from the shadows, yet remaining invisible.

The more David dug, the more he realized that Alexandra was not just a passive participant in this web of chaos. She was the one pulling the strings. The revelation hit him with a strange clarity — Alexandra wasn't merely connected to the case; she was the linchpin. Everything that had happened, every crime, every piece of corruption, led back to her in one way or another.

But who was she really? And how had she managed to stay hidden for so long?

David's next step was to track down anyone who had been close to Alexandra. It wasn't easy. Most people clammed up when her name was mentioned. Even those who had spoken about her in the past seemed to grow nervous, their words carefully measured. It became increasingly clear that Alexandra had more power than he had initially realized. She was more than just a mysterious figure in the background; she was a force to be reckoned with.

One evening, after another long day of investigation, David found himself in a bar, nursing a drink and contemplating his next move. That's when he heard it — two men in the corner, speaking in hushed tones, mentioned her name. His ears pricked up, and he listened closely. They were talking about some recent development, something big. One of them looked around nervously before saying, "Alexandra's not going to let this go. She's in too deep now."

David's heart raced. It was confirmation of what he had suspected. Alexandra wasn't just involved; she was in control. But how far did her reach extend? And what was she trying to protect?

He couldn't shake the feeling that he was standing on the edge of something much larger than he had anticipated. The deeper he delved into Alexandra's world, the more dangerous it became. Friends turned into enemies, and people he once trusted began to disappear or turn against him. Whispers of bribery, blackmail, and even murder started to surface, all tied back to her influence.

David began to feel the pressure closing in on him. Every step he took was fraught with peril, but he couldn't stop now. He was too close to the truth, and he knew that unraveling this conspiracy would either make or break him.

But the more he pulled at the threads, the tighter the knot became. Alexandra seemed to anticipate his every move. She was always one step ahead, leaving him chasing ghosts while she continued to operate from the shadows. It was as if she had orchestrated everything from the beginning, knowing that eventually, someone like him would come looking for answers.

As David continued his pursuit, he realized that the real danger wasn't just in exposing Alexandra's crimes — it was in understanding her motivations. She wasn't doing this for money or power alone. There was something deeper, something personal driving her actions. She had a vision, a plan that extended far beyond the chaos she had created.

The turning point came when David found a journal, hidden deep within the files of one of Alexandra's former associates. It contained cryptic notes and plans, all pointing to something much larger than anyone had imagined. Alexandra wasn't just manipulating a few corrupt officials or laundering money through shell companies. She was building an empire, one that stretched across continents and industries, all designed to consolidate her control over key figures in politics, finance, and media.

And yet, despite everything, David couldn't help but feel a strange admiration for her. She had done the impossible — created a system so intricate, so foolproof, that it took years for anyone to even suspect its existence. She had built a fortress of lies, one that few dared to challenge.

But now, with the pieces finally coming together, David knew that it was time to bring the whole thing crashing down. The unraveling had begun, and there was no going back.

As he prepared for the final confrontation, David couldn't shake the feeling that he was about to face something far more dangerous than he had ever anticipated. Alexandra was no ordinary criminal; she was a master manipulator, someone who had spent years perfecting her craft. And if he wasn't careful, he would become just another pawn in her game.

The unraveling was only the beginning. The real challenge lay ahead.

2. Confronting the Puppeteer

It had been weeks since the first clue had surfaced, a small slip of information buried deep within an otherwise mundane financial report. The numbers didn't add up. Transactions that should have been insignificant appeared to weave together in a pattern so subtle that it had almost gone unnoticed. Almost. For Ethan, that small inconsistency set off a chain reaction. What began as an ordinary investigation into money laundering now spiraled into something far larger, more dangerous, than he could have anticipated. He had sensed from the beginning that something—or someone—was pulling the strings behind it all. The elusive puppeteer.

The search had taken him across borders, through countless layers of deception. Each time he got close to an answer, the trail shifted, as if mocking him. Yet now, after everything, Ethan stood at the precipice of discovery. The man behind it all was not a myth. He existed, and Ethan was closing in.

The abandoned mansion loomed in front of him, shrouded in mist and decay. This was it, the place where his journey had led him, a relic of the past left to rot, much like the empire of secrets he had been chasing. Ethan had received an anonymous tip—just like many others before—but this time, it felt different. The message had been cryptic, yet unmistakable: "Meet me where it all began."

He stood still for a moment, his breath steadying as he surveyed the grounds. There was no turning back. He had sacrificed too much already—his career, his friends, his sense of safety. Now, it was time for answers. Ethan walked toward the grand entrance, the sound of his footsteps swallowed by the fog. The heavy oak door creaked as he pushed it open. Inside, the air was thick with dust and memories. Long-forgotten chandeliers hung from the ceiling, casting eerie shadows across the cracked marble floors. Silence greeted him, but it was a silence laden with anticipation, as though the very walls knew that something was about to break.

Ethan's heart raced as he moved deeper into the mansion. Every creak of the floorboards seemed to echo his thoughts, growing louder with every step. He had prepared for this moment for so long, imagining the confrontation, planning how he would corner the man who had manipulated so many lives from the shadows. Yet nothing could have fully prepared him for the weight of the truth he was about to uncover.

In the drawing room, a single lamp flickered dimly. At the far end of the room sat a figure in the shadows, his back turned to Ethan. The scent of cigar smoke filled the air, lingering like an unspoken accusation. Ethan stopped in the doorway, his pulse quickening. This was him. The puppeteer. The man whose name was whispered in dark alleys, whose reach extended into the highest echelons of power and finance.

"I see you found me," the voice called out, smooth and controlled. There was no surprise, no urgency in his tone. He had been expecting this.

Ethan stepped forward, his gaze locked on the figure. "It was only a matter of time," he replied, his voice steadier than he felt.

The man chuckled softly, setting down his cigar. "You've been persistent, I'll give you that. Most would have given up long ago."

"I'm not most people." Ethan's eyes narrowed, scanning the room for any signs of a trap. "And I'm not here for your games. I'm here for the truth."

The figure shifted slightly in his chair, the dim light finally revealing part of his face. He was older than Ethan had imagined, his silver hair neatly combed, his face lined with age and wisdom. He didn't look like a man capable of orchestrating the chaos Ethan had uncovered. But looks were deceiving. This was a man who thrived on deception, who had built his empire on lies and manipulation.

"And what truth do you seek, Ethan?" the man asked, his voice calm, almost patronizing. "Do you think uncovering my identity will change anything? The world doesn't work that way."

Ethan clenched his fists. "You've destroyed lives. Entire families have been torn apart because of you. You've hidden in the shadows for too long. It ends now."

The man rose from his chair with an air of casual authority, as though he held all the cards. "Ah, you see, that's where you're wrong." He began to pace slowly, his hands clasped behind his back. "You've spent all this time chasing me, hunting down every lead, every shadow, and yet... you still don't understand. This isn't about me. It's about power. Control. You take me down, another will rise in my place. The game doesn't end because one player is removed."

Ethan's mind raced, but he refused to be drawn into the man's philosophical musings. "You've laundered billions, funded wars, fueled corruption. You're not some necessary cog in a machine. You're the disease rotting it from the inside."

The man turned to face him fully now, his eyes sharp, piercing. "And yet, here we are. You, the righteous prosecutor, willing to do whatever it takes for justice. And me, the villain, content to let you play your role in this little drama." He paused, watching Ethan closely. "But have you ever asked yourself why you care so much? Why you've sacrificed everything to find me? Could it be because you, too, are part of this system? Just another pawn in the same game?"

Ethan stiffened, his mind flashing back to the moments of doubt, the sleepless nights when he questioned if any of this was worth it. But he had made his choice long ago, and he wasn't about to let this man twist the narrative.

"I'm nothing like you," Ethan spat, stepping closer. "You manipulate. You destroy. I'm here to stop you."

The man smiled, a cold, calculating expression. "You think you can stop me? You think your moral compass will save you? Let me tell you something, Ethan. In this world, the only thing that matters is leverage. Money, influence, secrets. I hold the keys to all of them. And that's why I'll always be one step ahead of people like you."

Ethan felt a wave of anger rise in his chest, but he forced himself to stay calm. "You think you're untouchable, don't you? That no one can bring you down?"

The man's smile faded slightly. "Not untouchable. Just... necessary. People like me exist because the world allows it. Because the powerful need us to do their dirty work while they keep their hands clean. You take me down, you take down the very system you claim to serve."

For a moment, silence hung between them, thick with unspoken truths. Ethan stared at the man, his mind racing with the weight of the words. Could it really be true? Was this man so deeply embedded in the fabric of society that removing him would only cause more chaos?

But then he remembered the faces of the victims. The innocent lives destroyed by this man's greed and hunger for control. No, this wasn't about the system. This was about stopping a monster who had taken advantage of it.

"You're wrong," Ethan said quietly, but firmly. "There's always a choice. And today, I'm choosing to end this."

The man tilted his head, a flicker of something—maybe curiosity, maybe admiration—crossing his face. "We'll see," he said softly. "But I promise you this, Ethan. You might stop me today, but the game will go on. And one day, you'll realize that everything you've done... was for nothing."

Ethan's jaw tightened. He wasn't about to let this man plant seeds of doubt in his mind. He had come too far for that. With a final glance at the man who had haunted his every step, Ethan turned and walked toward the door.

This wasn't the end. But it was the beginning of the reckoning.

3. Choices Made

He sat in the dimly lit office, his hands resting on the cold, polished surface of the desk. The clock on the wall ticked with a slow, deliberate rhythm, marking time in a way that felt oppressive. Outside, the city hummed with life, oblivious to the decisions being weighed in this silent room. To anyone looking in, it would seem like a man deep in thought, perhaps considering mundane matters. But the choices laid before him were far from ordinary—they were the kind that changed lives, destroyed futures, and altered destinies.

Michael never imagined that his life would come to this. As a prosecutor, he had always believed in right and wrong, in the clear line that separated justice from corruption. He'd dedicated years to serving the law, to upholding the principles that he had once thought were unshakeable. But in the underworld, those principles were malleable, twisted by those with enough power and money to reshape them to their will. Now, he found himself entangled in a web that was far more intricate—and far more dangerous—than anything he'd ever encountered in his career.

The file on his desk contained everything. The names, the numbers, the locations—all of it laid out in a carefully constructed case that could bring down an empire. It was the culmination of months of painstaking work, countless sleepless nights, and more than a few close calls. But it wasn't enough to simply possess the evidence. The real challenge lay in what he was willing to do with it.

In another world, in another version of himself, Michael might have acted without hesitation. He might have handed the file over to the authorities, ensuring that justice would be served. But the world he lived in now was not so simple. His every move was being watched, his every decision scrutinized by forces much larger than himself. And then there was the woman.

Her face came to mind, unbidden but persistent. Sophia. The enigmatic woman who had become the centerpiece of his investigation—and the source of his turmoil. From the moment they met, Michael knew there was something different about her. She wasn't just another player in this game of deceit and corruption; she was its architect, or at least one of the key pieces. Yet, for all her involvement, there was something about her that unsettled him, something that made him question everything he thought he knew about right and wrong.

Sophia had come to him with an offer. One that was as seductive as it was dangerous. He could use the information he had gathered to his advantage, she had said. He could make a deal, secure his future, and walk away from the mess unscathed. The only cost was his integrity, the very thing that had defined him for so long. It was a choice between the safety of the path laid out before him, or the uncertain, dangerous road of doing what he once believed was right.

But what was right anymore? That was the question that plagued him. Could he really trust the system to do the right thing? Every step of this case had shown him that corruption ran deeper than he had ever imagined. The hands that held the reins of power were stained, and if he wasn't careful, he could be dragged down with them. And then there was the personal cost—the people he cared about, the life he had built. Was it worth risking everything for a chance at justice?

The choices were laid out clearly before him, yet none of them felt like the right one.

He stood up, pacing the room, trying to shake off the weight that clung to him. His mind raced with possibilities, each one fraught with its own set of risks and rewards. There were moments, brief flashes, where he considered walking away. Closing the case, leaving the city, starting fresh somewhere far from the tangled mess of lies and deceit. But every time that thought crossed his mind, something held him back. A deep, gnawing sense of unfinished business, of a duty not yet fulfilled.

Michael reached for his phone, his fingers trembling slightly as they hovered over the screen. One call. That's all it would take. He could tip the scales in any direction with a simple conversation. On one end of the line was his contact in the FBI, someone he knew he could trust—or at least, he hoped he could. On the other was Sophia. The one who had woven herself into the fabric of this entire operation. One word from her, and everything could change.

His thumb hovered over the screen for what felt like an eternity before he placed the phone down. Not yet. He needed more time. More information. The choices, as clear as they seemed, were muddled by the countless variables swirling in his mind. He couldn't afford to rush this. Not when so much was at stake.

But as he sat back down, Michael knew that time wasn't on his side. The clock continued to tick, its steady rhythm a reminder that every moment he delayed was another moment for the forces arrayed against him to gain the upper hand. He had to make a decision, and soon. But for now, all he could do was think, plan, and hope that when the time came, he would know what to do.

The room felt smaller, as though the walls were closing in on him. He loosened his tie and leaned back in his chair, staring up at the ceiling. Was this what it all came down to? After everything he had been through, all the sacrifices he had made, was this the moment where it would all unravel? Or was it the moment where he would finally take control?

Sophia's words echoed in his mind. "We all have choices, Michael. It's just a matter of what we're willing to live with."

But what if he couldn't live with any of them?

The rain started to fall outside, tapping lightly against the window, a soft reminder of the world moving on, indifferent to the storm brewing inside him. He closed his eyes, letting the sound soothe his racing thoughts, if only for a moment. Tomorrow, he told himself. Tomorrow, he would make his choice.

But deep down, he knew that the decision was already made.

4. A Betrayal Uncovered

The room was quiet, too quiet for the weight of what had just been revealed. The faint hum of the city outside seemed distant, muffled by the walls of the small apartment where secrets had been whispered and truths had been kept hidden for too long. Dominic sat in his usual chair, eyes fixed on the documents spread out before him on the old wooden table. The world had shifted in the last few moments, the foundation of everything he believed shaken, and yet there he sat, as if the calm exterior could keep him from crumbling inside.

The words on the paper, though black and white, blurred together in a haze. It couldn't be true. He reached out, fingers trembling slightly, and picked up the letter again, reading the words that had ripped through him like a dagger. The neat, practiced handwriting seemed almost mocking, the words laced with the cruel truth he had been too blind to see. "You were never meant to find out, but I guess secrets have a way of surfacing, don't they? I warned you about trusting the wrong people. Now you know."

It wasn't just any letter. It was a confession, though one without regret. A betrayal so deep that it would leave scars long after this moment had passed. It wasn't the nameless criminals or shadowy figures that had turned on him. No, this was personal. This was someone close, someone who had woven themselves into the very fabric of his life, only to rip it apart at the seams.

Dominic had spent years chasing criminals, exposing their schemes, tearing apart the webs of deceit they spun to control the world. He had seen betrayal in all its forms, had witnessed the darkness people were capable of. But this? This was different. This was closer to home. He had trusted them, relied on them. Every decision he had made, every lead he had followed, had been with their counsel, their voice guiding him in the shadows. Now, that voice was the one that had deceived him all along.

The realization came crashing down like a tidal wave—his partner, the person he had shared countless sleepless nights with, piecing together the tangled web of this criminal organization, was the very one who had been feeding him misinformation. Mark.

Mark had been with Dominic from the beginning. They had met at the academy, both hungry for justice, both determined to make a difference in a world where corruption was the currency of power. Mark had always been the one to see things clearly, to point out the flaws in Dominic's thinking, to offer solutions when the path ahead seemed blocked. And Dominic had trusted him implicitly, never questioning the advice, never doubting the friendship.

It had been easy to follow Mark's lead, to lean on his insight. Together, they had been unstoppable, cutting through the layers of deceit that shrouded the powerful criminal organization known only as The Hand. They had uncovered financial transactions that spanned continents, tracked down offshore accounts, and connected the dots between seemingly unrelated events. Dominic had believed they were making progress, that they were close to bringing down the empire that had eluded justice for decades.

But now, looking at the evidence in front of him, Dominic saw it for what it was—a carefully constructed ruse. Mark had played him, feeding him just enough truth to keep him on the trail but steering him away from the heart of the conspiracy. Every time they had gotten close to the leaders of The Hand, Mark had found a reason to pull back, to shift focus elsewhere. Dominic had chalked it up to caution, a need for more evidence, but now he saw the truth. Mark had been protecting them all along.

Dominic felt a surge of anger rise up within him, but beneath it was something far worse—betrayal. He had trusted Mark with his life, had let him in on every aspect of the investigation, and now it was clear that trust had been misplaced. The magnitude of the deception was overwhelming. Mark hadn't just been protecting criminals; he had been working for them.

The signs had been there, Dominic realized, but he had ignored them, blinded by loyalty and the belief that they were on the same side. The late-night meetings Mark had insisted on holding in secret, away from the prying eyes of the office; the phone calls that were always just out of earshot; the subtle ways Mark had deflected certain lines of questioning. It had all been there, and Dominic had been too close to see it.

He stood abruptly, the chair scraping against the floor as he pushed it back. He needed air, space, anything to clear the fog of rage clouding his mind. He paced the small apartment, each step feeling heavier than the last, the weight of the betrayal pressing down on him.

How long had it been going on? How deep did Mark's involvement run? The questions swirled in his mind, but there were no answers yet, just more uncertainty. Dominic knew one thing, though—he had to act, and he had to act fast. If Mark was working for The Hand, then everything they had uncovered was compromised. Every step they had taken was part of a larger plan, one that he hadn't seen coming.

Dominic grabbed his phone from the table and dialed a number he hadn't used in years. Agent Kelly. She was someone he had worked with before, back when things had been simpler, back when the lines between right and wrong hadn't been so blurred. She picked up on the third ring, her voice crisp and professional, just as he remembered.

"Dominic?" she said, a hint of surprise in her voice. "It's been a while."

"I need your help," Dominic replied, his voice steady but laced with urgency. "It's Mark. He's been playing us all along."

There was a pause on the other end, the weight of his words sinking in. "Tell me everything," Kelly said, and Dominic did, recounting the events of the last few hours, the letter, the realization, the years of deceit.

When he finished, there was silence again, but this time it was a calculating silence. Kelly was processing, thinking, and Dominic knew she would have questions.

"Do you have proof?" she asked finally.

"I have enough to know he's been compromised," Dominic replied. "But I don't know how deep it goes. That's where you come in."

Kelly didn't hesitate. "Meet me at the old safe house in an hour. We'll figure this out."

Dominic hung up and took a deep breath. The safe house had been their headquarters back in the day, a rundown building on the edge of town that no one paid attention to. It was perfect for clandestine meetings, and it had served them well during their previous operations. Now, it would be the starting point for what would undoubtedly be the most dangerous mission of Dominic's life.

He didn't have time to pack. He grabbed his coat, shoved the letter into his pocket, and left the apartment without looking back. The streets outside were bustling, but Dominic barely noticed. His mind was racing, calculating his next move, trying to stay one step ahead of Mark and whoever else might be involved.

As he drove toward the safe house, the weight of the betrayal settled deeper into his bones. It wasn't just about Mark—it was about everything they had built, everything they had fought for. The trust that had been shattered would never be repaired, but Dominic couldn't afford to dwell on that now. There were bigger things at stake, and he had to stay focused.

The city blurred past him as he drove, and for a moment, Dominic felt like he was chasing ghosts, shadows of a past that had slipped through his fingers. He had always believed in the system, in justice, but now that belief felt fragile, like a thread that could snap at any moment.

He pulled up to the safe house and killed the engine. The building looked the same as it had years ago, abandoned, forgotten by time. He stepped out of the car and approached the door, his senses on high alert. He didn't know who he could trust anymore, but for now, Kelly was his best bet.

The door creaked open as he stepped inside, the familiar smell of dust and old wood greeting him. The memories flooded back, but Dominic pushed them aside. He didn't have time for nostalgia.

Kelly was already there, seated at the small table in the center of the room. She looked up as he entered, her expression unreadable. "You look like hell," she said, not unkindly.

"Feels like it," Dominic replied, sitting across from her. He pulled out the letter and handed it to her without a word.

She read it quickly, her eyes narrowing as she took in the damning words. "This is bad," she said finally, setting the letter down. "But it's not enough. We need more."

Dominic nodded. "I know. That's why I called you."

Kelly leaned back in her chair, her fingers tapping lightly on the table as she thought. "We'll need to dig deeper, find out who Mark's been working with. This goes beyond just him."

Dominic agreed. Mark was just the tip of the iceberg. There were others involved, and they needed to be exposed.

5. The Cost of Justice

Justice, in its purest form, is an ideal. It's the delicate balance between right and wrong, the force that should protect the innocent and punish the guilty. But in reality, justice is rarely so straightforward. It's complex, messy, and often comes at a cost that few are prepared to pay. For those who seek it, the pursuit of justice can consume them—physically, mentally, and emotionally—leaving behind scars that may never heal.

The pursuit of justice isn't just about facts and evidence. It's about power. Those in control shape the narrative, and in many cases, justice is not defined by the truth but by the ability to bend the system in one's favor. This is the first lesson for anyone who steps into the world of high-stakes litigation or criminal prosecution. The law is supposed to be blind, but more often than not, it favors those with the deepest pockets and the most influential connections. For the idealists, this is a bitter pill to swallow.

The prosecutor in this case knew this all too well. As he sat in his dimly lit office, pouring over the mountains of documents and files that had become his life, he couldn't help but feel the weight of his decisions. The case had started as just another routine investigation into financial crimes—money laundering, offshore accounts, bribery. But as he dug deeper, it became clear that what he was dealing with was something far more insidious.

The organization he was investigating wasn't just laundering money. It was orchestrating chaos, manipulating governments, and destabilizing economies. Billions of dollars moved in the shadows, fueling criminal enterprises and, in some cases, even terrorism. And yet, no one seemed to care. Or perhaps, they were too afraid to care.

The cost of justice, he realized, wasn't just about the personal toll it took on him, though that was significant. His relationships had suffered—his wife had grown distant, his children barely recognized him anymore, and his friends had stopped calling. But worse than the personal sacrifices were the ethical compromises he had to make.

Every day, he had to decide what lines he was willing to cross in order to get closer to the truth. Was it worth bending the rules, fabricating evidence, or cutting deals with criminals in order to bring down the larger target? Where did the pursuit of justice end, and his own ambition begin? These were the questions that kept him up at night.

And then there were the threats. They started as whispers—anonymous emails, veiled comments in court. But as the case gained momentum, the threats became more personal. His car was keyed one night while he was working late. Another time, he found a note under his door warning him to back off. But the worst came when he arrived home one evening to find his daughter's favorite stuffed animal, ripped and mangled, sitting on the front porch.

That was when he truly understood the cost of justice. It wasn't just his life on the line. It was his family's. But even then, turning back wasn't an option. He was in too deep. The web of corruption he had uncovered was too vast, too intertwined with the highest levels of power. Walking away would mean allowing those responsible to continue their reign of terror, unchecked.

The closer he got to the heart of the conspiracy, the more isolated he became. Colleagues who had once supported him now kept their distance. His superiors, too, seemed less interested in the truth and more concerned with the potential fallout of exposing such powerful figures. It was becoming clear that even if he won the case, he would lose something far greater—his career, his reputation, maybe even his life.

But justice, true justice, was never supposed to be easy. It required sacrifice. The prosecutor remembered the stories his father used to tell him about the great legal minds of history—those who had fought against oppression, corruption, and tyranny. They had all paid a heavy price, but their names were remembered because they had stood for something greater than themselves.

That was the legacy he wanted to leave behind, even if it meant losing everything in the process.

The trial, when it finally began, was a media circus. Reporters from every major outlet crowded the courtroom, eager for the spectacle that was about to unfold. The defendants were powerful men—business tycoons, politicians, and even law enforcement officials. Their lawyers were the best money could buy, and they had no intention of going down without a fight.

The prosecutor stood tall as he delivered his opening statement. He spoke of justice, of the need to hold those in power accountable for their actions. He laid out the evidence in painstaking detail, piece by piece, weaving a narrative that exposed the full extent of the conspiracy. But even as he spoke, he could feel the tension in the room. The defendants' lawyers smirked, knowing they had tricks up their sleeves. They had the resources to drag this trial out for months, maybe even years. And the longer it went on, the more likely it was that public interest would fade, witnesses would disappear, or the prosecutor himself would be discredited.

It was a game of endurance, and the prosecutor wasn't sure how much longer he could last.

The defense came at him with everything they had. They questioned his motives, his integrity, even his mental health. They painted him as a rogue prosecutor, obsessed with bringing down powerful men for his own gain. They discredited witnesses, destroyed evidence, and manipulated the media to sway public opinion in their favor.

For every step forward he made, they pushed him two steps back. And yet, he couldn't give up. The truth was on his side, and he believed that, in the end, justice would prevail.

But belief, he realized, wasn't enough. The system wasn't designed for people like him. It was designed to protect those with power, to uphold the status quo. And as the trial dragged on, he began to see the cracks in his own resolve. He had always believed in the law, in its ability to bring about change. But now, standing on the edge of defeat, he wondered if it had all been for nothing.

One night, after a particularly grueling day in court, he found himself alone in his office, staring at a bottle of whiskey on his desk. He hadn't touched alcohol in years—his father had been an alcoholic, and he had sworn never to follow in his footsteps. But now, as the weight of the case pressed down on him, he couldn't help but reach for the bottle.

As he poured himself a drink, he thought about all the lives that had been destroyed in the pursuit of justice—his own included. Was it worth it? Could he live with the consequences of his actions, knowing that even if he won, the victory would be hollow?

He took a sip, the burn of the alcohol sharp and bitter on his tongue. The cost of justice, he realized, wasn't just measured in legal fees or lost sleep. It was measured in lives—lives that were torn apart, piece by piece, in the relentless pursuit of truth.

And as he sat there, staring into the depths of his glass, he wondered if he was willing to pay that price.

6. A Reckoning

The room was thick with the silence of unfinished business. Dark mahogany shelves lined the walls, filled with books that no one had touched in years, relics of a mind that preferred to play in the shadows rather than in the open. The heavy velvet curtains blocked out any trace of sunlight, leaving the room in a dim, suffocating gloom. It was a place built for secrets, and it was here, in this very room, that the reckoning would begin.

Alexei stood at the center, his back to the door, gazing at the worn leather chair behind the old oak desk. His fingers drummed lightly on its surface, but his mind was anything but calm. His breath came in shallow bursts, his heart racing as he tried to gather his thoughts. There was no turning back now. Everything had led to this moment. He had played the long game, collected the pieces, and finally, the web of deceit he had been caught in was about to unravel. But the cost of truth was heavy, and deep down, Alexei knew that no one would emerge from this unscathed.

The door creaked open, and in walked a man who seemed too composed for the storm that was about to break. Viktor Petrov was a man who thrived on control. He had built an empire from the ground up, a web of power, money, and influence that extended far beyond what anyone could imagine. His every move was calculated, his every word carefully chosen. To the outside world, he was a pillar of society, a businessman with an untouchable reputation. But Alexei knew better. He had seen the other side of Petrov's empire—the side that lived in the shadows, the side that destroyed lives with a whisper.

"I see you've made yourself comfortable," Viktor said, his voice cool and measured as he closed the door behind him. His eyes flicked to the chair, then back to Alexei. "Though I suppose comfort is not what you're here for."

Alexei didn't move. His eyes remained on the desk, tracing the faint scars on the wood, remnants of another time, another conflict. "It's not about comfort," he replied softly. "It's about closure."

Viktor raised an eyebrow, a slight smile tugging at the corners of his mouth. "Closure? Is that what you think this is?" He walked slowly to the opposite side of the desk, his hands casually in his pockets, the picture of relaxed authority. "There's no such thing as closure in this world, Alexei. Only more questions. More consequences."

"I'm tired of the questions," Alexei shot back, his voice tightening. "I'm tired of playing your games."

Viktor's eyes hardened, but the smile remained. "Careful," he said, his tone dripping with warning. "You may not like the answers."

There was a long pause, the tension between them almost palpable. Alexei clenched his fists, trying to hold back the anger bubbling inside him. He had waited too long for this moment, fought too hard to let it slip away. Every memory, every betrayal came rushing back—the friends he had lost, the lies he had been forced to tell, the lives destroyed by Petrov's cold, calculated greed. It was all too much.

"You destroyed everything," Alexei whispered, his voice shaking with barely restrained fury. "For what? For money? For power?"

Viktor's smile vanished. "For survival," he said sharply. "This world isn't kind to those who play by the rules. You know that as well as I do."

"Survival?" Alexei's laugh was bitter. "You call this survival? You built an empire on the backs of broken people. You tore apart families, manipulated the system, buried the truth under piles of cash. And for what? To sit in this room and pretend you're some kind of king?"

Viktor's eyes narrowed, and for a moment, a flash of something darker crossed his face. "You think you understand?" he hissed, leaning forward across the desk. "You think you know what it takes to build something in this world? You don't. You've been playing at rebellion, trying to bring down something you could never hope to control."

"I never wanted control," Alexei said, his voice steadying. "I just wanted to stop you."

"Stop me?" Viktor laughed, a harsh, mocking sound. "You can't stop what you don't understand. You think you're the first one to come here, to challenge me? You think you're the first to try and bring me down? You're nothing, Alexei. Just another piece in a game you don't even know you're playing."

Alexei's jaw tightened. "That's where you're wrong."

Viktor's eyes flicked with curiosity. "Oh? Enlighten me."

Alexei reached into his coat pocket, pulling out a small USB drive and placing it on the desk between them. Viktor's eyes followed the movement, and for the first time, a hint of uncertainty crossed his face.

"What's that?" Viktor asked, his voice losing some of its earlier confidence.

"Everything," Alexei said simply. "Everything you've tried to hide. Every deal, every bribe, every dirty little secret. I've been collecting it for years, piece by piece. And now, it's all here. Ready to bring your empire crashing down."

Viktor's face was unreadable, but his eyes burned with barely concealed rage. "You think this will change anything?" he asked, his voice low and dangerous. "You think this will end me?"

Alexei met his gaze, unwavering. "It's not just about ending you. It's about justice. For everyone you've hurt. For everyone you've destroyed."

"Justice?" Viktor spat, his composure slipping for the first time. "There's no such thing as justice, Alexei. Not in this world. There's only power. And I have it. You're just a fool chasing a fantasy."

"We'll see," Alexei said, turning his back on Viktor and walking toward the door.

As his hand reached for the doorknob, Viktor's voice stopped him.

"You walk out that door," Viktor warned, "and you'll never be safe. Not you, not anyone you care about. You think you can destroy me? I'll tear apart everything you've ever loved."

Alexei paused, the weight of Viktor's threat hanging in the air. He knew the risk. He had known it from the beginning. But he also knew there was no turning back now.

Without another word, he opened the door and stepped into the hallway. The reckoning had begun.

• • • •

THE NIGHT AIR WAS COLD, biting at Alexei's skin as he stepped out onto the street. The USB drive in his pocket felt heavier than ever, a symbol of everything he had fought for—and everything he stood to lose. He glanced up at the darkened windows of the building, knowing that somewhere behind them, Viktor was already planning his next move.

But Alexei wasn't afraid. Not anymore.

He walked briskly, his breath visible in the chill of the night, his mind racing with what needed to be done. There were still steps to take, still people to contact. But he had the evidence. And now, for the first time in years, he had the upper hand.

The streets were mostly empty at this late hour, but Alexei's senses were on high alert. Every passing car, every shadow in the alley, felt like a potential threat. Viktor's reach extended far, and Alexei knew that he wouldn't hesitate to use it. But Alexei was ready. He had spent years preparing for this, and he wouldn't let fear stop him now.

As he reached the corner of the street, he pulled out his phone and dialed a number. It rang twice before a voice answered.

"It's done," Alexei said, his voice low but firm. "We're going to bring him down."

There was a pause on the other end before the voice responded. "You know this is just the beginning, right? He won't go down without a fight."

"I know," Alexei replied, glancing back at the building one last time. "But this time, we're ready."

He hung up and slid the phone back into his pocket, his mind already focused on the next step. The reckoning wasn't over yet. It had only just begun.

Chapter 10: Redemption and Closure

1. The Aftermath

The city was quiet in the way only a place ravaged by chaos can be. There was an eerie stillness in the air, as if the world itself was holding its breath. The events of the past few days had left an indelible mark on every corner, every shadow, and every soul that had been caught in the storm. For those who had witnessed the unraveling of everything they thought they knew, "normal" seemed like a distant memory, almost a myth.

The skyline, once a symbol of power and wealth, was now a stark reminder of how fragile everything truly was. Glass windows shattered, buildings scarred with evidence of the violence that had swept through the streets, and the scent of smoke still lingered, refusing to be washed away by the light drizzle that had started to fall. It was as though the city itself was grieving, mourning the loss of something intangible — a sense of order, of control.

For James Moreau, standing at the edge of the city square, the scene felt almost surreal. His clothes were disheveled, his shirt untucked, and a thick layer of dust clung to his skin. He hadn't slept in what felt like days, but time had become meaningless in the chaos. His mind was a haze of jumbled thoughts, fragments of the past few weeks flashing before his eyes: the faces of those he'd trusted, now twisted by betrayal; the secrets unearthed that should have stayed buried; and, worst of all, the look in her eyes.

The woman at the center of it all — Sofia. She had been an enigma from the start, a shadow moving in the background, orchestrating events with a precision that left even the most seasoned players in awe. James had thought he understood her, thought he could predict her next move, but Sofia had always been two steps ahead. Now, standing in the aftermath of the storm she had helped create, he wasn't sure he'd ever really known her at all.

The sound of footsteps behind him broke through his thoughts. James turned slowly, expecting to see another ghost from the past, but instead, it was Detective Carla Hayes. Her face was drawn, her eyes weary, but she moved with the same determination that had carried her through this entire ordeal.

"James," she said, her voice low but steady. "It's over."

He let out a bitter laugh. "Is it?"

Carla's expression didn't change. "The arrests have been made. The accounts frozen. The people responsible... they'll pay for what they've done."

James shook his head. "People like them don't pay, Carla. Not really. They slip through the cracks, rebuild in the shadows, and come back stronger. This... this was just one battle."

Carla crossed her arms and looked out over the wreckage. "Maybe. But we made a dent. That's more than most ever manage."

For a long moment, they stood in silence, side by side, each lost in their own thoughts. James knew she was right, in a way. The web of corruption they had untangled over the past months had been more intricate and widespread than either of them could have anticipated. It had started with whispers, small leads that seemed insignificant at first. But each thread they pulled had revealed another, and another, until the entire city's elite had been exposed as players in a game that stretched far beyond the borders of their world.

It was Sofia who had orchestrated it all, who had known where to pull the strings to make the powerful bend to her will. She was the puppeteer, and James had been one of her pawns — willingly, at first. He had been drawn to her, captivated by her intelligence, her charm, her ability to see through the façades people wore like armor. But as the layers had peeled away, the truth of her nature had come to light.

He thought back to their last conversation, the moment when he'd finally realized just how deep her deception ran.

"You never really cared about the cause, did you?" he had asked her, his voice hoarse with disbelief.

She had smiled, that same enigmatic smile that had once made him weak. "Care? James, caring is a luxury for those who have the time for it. I did what I had to do."

"For what?" he had demanded. "Money? Power? What was it all for?"

Her smile had faded then, replaced by a cold, distant look. "For survival."

That was Sofia, in a single word. A survivor. She had been playing the long game from the start, and James had been too blinded by his own ambition to see it.

Now, as he looked around at the ruins of their world, he couldn't help but wonder if she had been right all along. Maybe, in the end, survival was the only thing that mattered. Morality, justice, those were ideals for people who had the privilege of living in a world that made sense. But their world had never made sense. It had always been chaotic, ruthless, driven by the desires of the few at the expense of the many.

James felt a weight settle on his chest as he thought about the people who had been caught in the crossfire. The innocents who had been hurt, the lives destroyed by the greed and ambition of a select few. He had tried to protect them, tried to be the one who brought justice to the forefront, but in the end, all he had managed to do was survive.

"We did what we could," Carla said, as if reading his thoughts.

James sighed. "Maybe. But it doesn't feel like enough."

Carla's eyes softened. "It never does. But you can't carry the weight of the world on your shoulders, James. No one can."

He didn't respond, but her words lingered with him as they walked through the streets together, surveying the damage. The city would rebuild — it always did. The scars would fade, new buildings would rise, and the people would move on, just as they always had. But the memory of what had happened here, the secrets that had been revealed, would never truly disappear.

As they rounded a corner, they came to a small café, one of the few places that hadn't been touched by the chaos. Inside, the lights were dim, and the tables were nearly empty. James and Carla took a seat near the window, both too exhausted to speak.

The waitress came over, her smile tired but genuine. "What can I get you?"

"Just coffee," Carla said, her voice barely above a whisper.

James nodded in agreement. "Same."

As the waitress left, James found himself staring out the window, watching the rain fall in slow, steady drops. It felt cleansing, in a way, like the city was trying to wash away the blood and dirt of the past few days. But no amount of rain could wash away the memories.

He turned to Carla. "What happens now?"

She took a deep breath, as if the question itself was heavy. "Now? Now we pick up the pieces. We start over."

James raised an eyebrow. "Just like that?"

Carla gave him a small, sad smile. "Just like that. It's what we do, James. We move forward, even when it feels like we can't."

He looked down at his hands, the lines of his palms etched with dirt and sweat. "And Sofia?"

Carla's smile faded. "She's gone. We'll find her, eventually. But for now... she's out there. And we just have to live with that."

James nodded, though it didn't bring him any comfort. Sofia had always been elusive, always one step ahead. He knew she wouldn't disappear for long. She'd surface again, somewhere, somehow. And when she did, the game would begin anew.

But for now, in the aftermath of everything, all he could do was sit in the quiet of the moment and wait for the storm to pass.

2. Healing Old Wounds

The air was thick with the scent of rain, though the sky had yet to break. It hung there, a weight over the city, pressing down as if nature itself knew the tension winding through its streets. Daniel stood on the edge of the park, his hands shoved deep into his pockets, eyes scanning the horizon. He had spent years trying to escape this place, running from the ghosts of his past. But now, he was back. And there was no more running.

Healing. That was what they called it. The professionals, the therapists, even well-meaning friends. "You need to heal," they'd say. "You can't move forward until you've faced your past." But no one seemed to understand that the past wasn't just a series of memories you could confront and resolve. It was alive, breathing—interwoven into the present in ways that made it impossible to separate the two.

As Daniel took a seat on one of the park benches, he let his mind wander to the events that had led him here. He had thought he had put the worst behind him, had buried it deep enough that it couldn't claw its way back to the surface. But old wounds had a way of reopening at the most unexpected times, and now, as he stared into the misty distance, he felt the pull of a pain that refused to be ignored.

It wasn't just about what had been done to him—it was about what he had done, too. The decisions, the betrayals, the lies. They sat heavy in his chest, as real and tangible as the day they had been made. He had spent so much time trying to atone, trying to make things right, but how could you ever truly make amends for things that had changed the very fabric of who you were?

A crack of thunder echoed in the distance, and Daniel's thoughts shifted. He had agreed to meet Julia here, though every instinct in his body told him not to. She was part of the past he had tried so hard to forget, a reminder of everything that had gone wrong. They had been inseparable once, closer than family, bound not by blood but by experience. The scars they shared ran deep, both physical and emotional, and for years, they had leaned on each other to survive. But then, like all things that grow under pressure, their bond had fractured.

The rain began to fall, a soft patter at first, then heavier as the wind picked up. Daniel didn't move. He didn't care about getting wet—there was something cathartic about it, as if the rain could wash away everything that had come before. But he knew it wasn't that simple. Healing didn't happen in a single moment; it wasn't a grand gesture or a dramatic confrontation. It was a process, a slow, painstaking one, and there were no guarantees.

When he saw her walking toward him, the rain beading off her umbrella, his chest tightened. She looked older, of course—they both did. But there was something else in her eyes, a weariness that hadn't been there before. He wondered if she saw the same in him. As she approached, neither of them spoke at first. They just stood there, the rain filling the silence between them, the weight of years pressing down.

Finally, it was Julia who broke the tension.

"You came," she said softly, her voice barely audible over the rain.

Daniel nodded, not trusting himself to speak just yet. He had rehearsed this moment in his head countless times, but now that it was here, words failed him. How do you begin to mend something that's been broken for so long?

Julia sat down on the bench beside him, careful to keep the umbrella positioned so it covered both of them. They sat in silence for a few more moments, the only sound the steady rhythm of raindrops against the concrete.

"I wasn't sure if you would," she continued, her tone more resigned now.

"I wasn't sure either," Daniel admitted, his voice rougher than he intended. "But I'm here."

Another stretch of silence. It wasn't awkward, exactly, but it was heavy—laden with everything unsaid between them. Years of guilt, anger, loss. All the things they hadn't been able to put into words back then, still hovering, waiting to be dealt with.

Julia let out a long breath, her shoulders sagging under the weight of it. "I've been thinking a lot lately," she said, her voice barely a whisper. "About what happened. About us. About how we just... let it all fall apart."

Daniel swallowed, feeling the familiar knot of regret tighten in his throat. "We didn't let it fall apart, Julia," he said softly, but with an edge of bitterness. "It was already broken. We were just too blind to see it."

She nodded, though she didn't seem entirely convinced. "Maybe," she said. "But that doesn't mean we didn't play a part in it. We both made choices. And I've been living with the consequences of mine for a long time."

The rain continued to fall, and for a moment, Daniel thought about getting up and walking away, letting the past stay buried where it belonged. But something in her voice stopped him. There was a vulnerability there that hadn't been present before, a crack in the armor she had always worn so tightly around herself. He knew that if he walked away now, he'd be carrying this wound with him for the rest of his life.

"I'm not looking for forgiveness," Julia said, turning to look at him for the first time since she'd sat down. "I know I can't ask for that. But I needed to see you. I needed to say... I'm sorry."

The words hung in the air between them, fragile and raw. Daniel stared at her, searching her face for any sign of insincerity, but all he saw was the truth. The same pain he had carried for years was etched into her features, and in that moment, he realized that they had both been running from the same ghosts.

He let out a long breath, leaning back against the bench, feeling the weight of everything settle over him. "I'm sorry too," he said quietly. "For a lot of things."

Julia looked down at her hands, the raindrops collecting on her skin. "I didn't know how to fix it," she said after a moment. "I didn't know how to fix us. So I just... ran. And I hated myself for it."

Daniel shook his head. "You're not the only one who ran," he said, his voice low. "We both did."

They sat there for what felt like hours, just letting the rain fall around them, the cold seeping into their bones. But there was something cleansing about it, too. Something that made the old wounds feel less raw, less immediate. Maybe they weren't healed, not completely, but there was a sense that they had finally begun to close.

Eventually, Julia spoke again, her voice quieter now, more subdued. "Do you think... it's possible to fix things? Not just between us, but with everything? Do you think we can ever really heal?"

Daniel thought about it for a long moment. He wanted to believe that healing was possible, that the scars they carried could someday fade into the background. But he knew that the process wouldn't be easy. It would take time, and effort, and maybe even more pain along the way.

"I don't know," he said honestly. "But I think we can try."

She looked at him, her eyes searching his for any sign of hope. And for the first time in a long while, Daniel felt like maybe—just maybe—they could find a way forward. Not by forgetting the past, but by facing it together, one step at a time.

The rain had slowed to a light drizzle by the time they stood up, and as they walked away from the park, side by side, Daniel felt a strange sense of peace settle over him. Healing wasn't a straight path, and there would be days when the pain resurfaced, as sharp as ever.

But now, for the first time, it didn't feel like he was walking that path alone.

And maybe that was enough.

3. A New Beginning

It was a brisk autumn morning, the kind that carried a chill sharp enough to cut through your coat, yet not cold enough to bite your skin. The sun hung low in the sky, casting long, stretching shadows across the streets. The air smelled of fresh rain and distant woodsmoke, the sort of scent that always felt oddly comforting, even in the midst of uncertainty. For Michael Carrington, today was supposed to mark a new beginning, though the knot in his stomach suggested anything but.

He stood at the edge of the bustling city square, watching the people as they moved with purpose, eyes focused, strides confident. They were part of the rhythm, part of the pulse of a world that seemed to hum with a frenetic energy he hadn't felt in a long time. Yet, here he was, an outsider, watching from the periphery, waiting for something — anything — to make him feel connected again.

His hands were buried deep in his pockets, fingers unconsciously curling into fists as he replayed the events of the past few months in his mind. The fallout from his last case still lingered like a bad taste in his mouth. It had been messy — too messy. The kind of mess that made you question everything you thought you knew about yourself, your morals, and the system you were meant to uphold.

But today was different. Today was supposed to be the first day of the rest of his life, or so he told himself. He had left the prosecutor's office, walked away from the job that had consumed him for over a decade, and now stood at the precipice of something new. A chance, perhaps, to start fresh. But could you ever really start fresh when the past clung to you like an invisible shroud?

Michael had always been good at compartmentalizing. It was a skill honed through years of navigating the complexities of the legal system, of dealing with people who lied as easily as they breathed, of watching the innocent suffer and the guilty walk free. You had to learn how to put things in boxes, to close the lids tightly, and never look back. But some boxes, he had discovered, refused to stay closed.

His phone buzzed in his pocket, pulling him out of his thoughts. He fumbled for it, squinting at the screen. It was a message from an unknown number. He almost ignored it, but something — perhaps curiosity, perhaps instinct — made him open it.

"We need to talk. Meet me at the usual place. It's important."

No name, no signature. Just that. For a moment, Michael felt the familiar flicker of suspicion flare in his chest. He hadn't heard from anyone from the old life since he'd walked away. He had made it clear he didn't want to be found, didn't want to be dragged back into the labyrinth of power plays and deceit that had defined his career for too long. Yet, here it was, like a ghost from the past, knocking at his door.

He thought about deleting the message, about ignoring it and going about his day. He had plans. Small ones, but plans nonetheless. He was going to find a quiet café, sit by the window, and read a book he had no real interest in, just to remind himself what it felt like to not care. To not have the weight of the world on his shoulders. But even as he considered it, he knew he couldn't. There was something about the message — the urgency in its simplicity — that gnawed at him.

The usual place. He knew exactly where that was.

The café on Mulberry Street, a small, nondescript spot that had served as a neutral ground for many clandestine meetings over the years. It was the kind of place that didn't ask questions, didn't care who you were, so long as you paid in cash and didn't cause trouble.

Michael hesitated for only a moment before turning and heading in that direction. His feet moved automatically, as if they had a memory of their own. The streets were familiar, yet they felt different today, as if the city itself was holding its breath, waiting for something to happen.

As he approached the café, his heart began to race, though he couldn't say why. He pushed open the door, and the small bell above it chimed softly, announcing his arrival. The place was mostly empty, save for an elderly couple in the corner and the barista behind the counter, who barely glanced up from her phone.

He scanned the room quickly, his eyes landing on a figure sitting at the far table, their back to him. The figure was wearing a dark coat, the collar turned up against the cold, a hat pulled low over their face. Michael felt a twinge of recognition, though he couldn't place why. He approached slowly, his footsteps soft on the worn wooden floor.

As he reached the table, the figure turned, and Michael's breath caught in his throat. It was Claire. He hadn't seen her in years, not since the case that had torn them apart. She looked older, though the same fire burned in her eyes, a fire he had once admired and feared in equal measure.

"Claire," he said, his voice low, uncertain. "What are you doing here?"

She looked up at him, her lips curling into a faint smile, though it didn't reach her eyes. "We need to talk, Michael. There's something you need to know."

He didn't sit down right away. Instead, he stood there, staring at her, trying to reconcile the woman in front of him with the memories he had carefully locked away. He had thought he was done with this, done with her. But here she was, as if no time had passed at all, as if they could just pick up where they left off.

"What could you possibly have to say that I'd want to hear?" he asked, though he already knew the answer. Claire had always been one step ahead of him, always knew more than she let on. If she was here, if she had reached out to him after all this time, it meant only one thing — she was involved in something big. Something dangerous.

She gestured to the seat across from her. "Sit down, Michael. Please. This isn't about us. It's about something much bigger."

Reluctantly, he pulled out the chair and sat down, his body tense, ready to spring into action at a moment's notice. "Talk," he said. "I don't have all day."

She took a deep breath, her fingers tracing the edge of the coffee cup in front of her. "You walked away, and I get that. But things didn't stop just because you did. The people we were after... they didn't disappear. In fact, they've only gotten stronger."

Michael narrowed his eyes. "What are you talking about?"

"The network," she said, her voice barely above a whisper. "The one we thought we dismantled. It's still alive, Michael. And it's bigger than we ever imagined."

He felt a chill run down his spine. The network. It was a name he hadn't heard in years, a ghost from his past that he had buried deep. They had been involved in everything — money laundering, human trafficking, arms deals. It had taken years of his life to bring them down, and even then, he had never been sure if they had truly succeeded.

"I don't do this anymore, Claire," he said, shaking his head. "I'm out. I left that life behind for a reason."

She leaned forward, her eyes locking onto his with an intensity that made his skin prickle. "I know. But you're the only one who can help. They trust you. They think you're still on the inside."

Michael clenched his fists under the table, his mind racing. "What do you want from me?"

"I want you to go back in," she said, her voice steady, unwavering. "I want you to find out what they're planning, and I want you to stop it."

He stared at her, incredulous. "You're insane. I barely made it out alive the first time. You really think I'm going to throw myself back into that fire?"

Claire didn't flinch. "I wouldn't be asking if I didn't think you could do it. If I didn't think you had to do it. They're planning something, Michael. Something big. And if we don't stop them, a lot of innocent people are going to get hurt."

For a long moment, neither of them spoke. Michael's mind was a whirlwind of conflicting emotions. Anger, fear, regret, and, beneath it all, a sense of duty that he had tried so hard to ignore.

Finally, he sighed, running a hand through his hair. "This is a mistake."

Claire smiled, but it was a sad, knowing smile. "Maybe. But it's one we don't have a choice in."

Michael stared down at the table, his heart pounding in his chest. He had promised himself he was done with this, that he would never go back. But deep down, he had always known that the past had a way of catching up with you, no matter how fast you ran.

A new beginning, he had called it. But maybe there was no such thing. Maybe, in the end, there were only new endings.

And this one, he feared, was going to be darker than any he had faced before.

4. The Legacy of Chaos

The distant hum of the city blended with the fading daylight, casting long shadows over the skyline. From the rooftop where he stood, Michael Navarro could see the city sprawling beneath him, unaware of the storm brewing within its veins. The skyline was impressive, a mixture of old-world charm and modern glass towers reaching for the clouds, but to him, it was just a façade, a glittering mask hiding the rot beneath. Michael had spent years uncovering that rot, digging deeper and deeper until he found himself standing on the precipice of something much bigger than he'd ever imagined.

It had all started with a single case—a routine investigation into money laundering that should have ended quickly, wrapped up with a few arrests, a couple of confessions, and a pile of paperwork. But as the investigation progressed, the threads unraveled faster than Michael could keep up. Every lead took him further from the surface and closer to the underworld that quietly ran the city, the world where money wasn't just power—it was chaos.

What had seemed like a simple operation grew into something monstrous. The deeper he dug, the more he realized that this was no ordinary crime syndicate. It was an intricate web, spun over decades, with roots so deep that entire governments, corporations, and law enforcement agencies had been compromised. And at the center of it all was a name whispered in the shadows: the Hand.

The Hand, as Michael soon discovered, wasn't just one person, nor was it a typical criminal organization. It was a legacy, passed down from one generation to the next, a ghostly presence that controlled everything without ever being seen. No one could say for sure who the original members were, but the group's influence stretched back more than half a century. Whispers of the Hand first emerged after World War II, when entire economies were being rebuilt, and the foundations of modern financial systems were being laid. It was in this chaotic post-war landscape that the Hand first found its grip.

The Hand thrived on disorder, on the chaos that followed every war, every financial crash, every political upheaval. They were the unseen architects, the ones who pulled strings from the shadows, ensuring that their wealth grew with every disaster. War, famine, political instability—these were not tragedies to them. They were opportunities.

Michael had come across the Hand almost by accident. His investigation had led him to an offshore account in the Caymans, which in turn had pointed to a series of shell companies. Each company seemed legitimate on the surface, but a closer look revealed the same pattern—a subtle flow of money from one to the next, a delicate dance that ended in the same place: the Hand's pocket.

But no one could touch them. The Hand's fingerprints were everywhere, but they were never caught. Whenever someone came close to exposing them, they disappeared, either through ruin or death. Michael had seen the pattern, read the reports. Journalists who had uncovered too much, politicians who had tried to pass laws that threatened their operations, even law enforcement officials who had gotten too close—none of them survived for long. Their lives ended in accidents, or their careers were destroyed by sudden, inexplicable scandals.

Michael knew he was next. He had already felt the cold breath of the Hand on his neck. Anonymous threats had begun arriving at his office. His phone calls were tapped. He had noticed the same black sedan following him for weeks now, always keeping its distance, but never letting him out of its sight. His colleagues had started distancing themselves, no doubt sensing the danger he was bringing closer with every step. But he couldn't stop now. He was too far in, too deep to turn back.

It wasn't just about the investigation anymore. It was about exposing the truth, about breaking the cycle of chaos the Hand had perpetuated for so long. Michael had grown up in this city, had seen firsthand the devastation that corruption brought to the streets, to the lives of ordinary people. He remembered the night his father lost everything—his business, his home, his dignity. It had all been wiped away in a financial collapse orchestrated by men who never showed their faces, men who profited while the rest of the world burned.

As a young boy, Michael had sworn he would bring those men to justice. That vow had driven him through law school, through his years as a prosecutor. And now, standing on this rooftop, he realized just how close he was to fulfilling that promise. The Hand was within his grasp, but it was also slipping away.

The Hand thrived on chaos, and now they were creating it around him. The more he pressed, the more the world seemed to spin out of control. A high-profile politician was assassinated just days after Michael interviewed him about possible connections to the Hand. A building that housed crucial financial records was torched in an apparent arson. People close to Michael were suddenly finding themselves in legal trouble, scandals erupting from nowhere.

They were tightening the noose around him, one strand at a time. But Michael had anticipated this. He had prepared. Years of chasing ghosts had taught him to be cautious, to think several moves ahead. He had allies—people in high places who believed in justice as much as he did. They had warned him about the dangers, about the risks of going after the Hand, but Michael had been undeterred. Now, as the chaos swirled around him, he knew he was walking a razor's edge. One wrong move, and he would be just another name on the list of those who had tried and failed to bring the Hand to light.

But there was one thing the Hand hadn't anticipated—Michael had uncovered their greatest secret. It wasn't just about money. It was about control. The Hand didn't simply thrive on chaos; they orchestrated it. Every war, every financial crisis, every political scandal—they were all part of the Hand's grand design. The chaos wasn't just a byproduct of their greed. It was their weapon.

Michael's investigation had led him to a series of documents—hidden in plain sight among legal papers, tax filings, and corporate records. At first, they seemed like meaningless jargon, the kind of bureaucratic nonsense that lawyers and accountants dealt with every day. But as Michael dug deeper, he realized what he was looking at. These were plans—detailed blueprints for the world's next disasters. Political coups, economic collapses, civil wars—each one meticulously planned, with the Hand waiting in the shadows to profit from the fallout.

They had no loyalty, no ideology, no goal other than to sow chaos and reap the rewards. Governments meant nothing to them; borders were irrelevant. They were above it all, moving pawns on a global chessboard, watching as the world tore itself apart.

The weight of this realization hit Michael like a freight train. He wasn't just up against a crime syndicate or a cartel. He was fighting an enemy that thrived on the very disorder it created. And now, he was their next target.

Michael stared out at the city, his mind racing. He had the evidence, the proof of the Hand's existence, but what could he do with it? Who could he trust? If he went public, they would destroy him before the truth ever saw the light of day. If he tried to fight them quietly, he would be swallowed by the chaos they were already beginning to create around him.

As he weighed his options, his phone buzzed in his pocket. A single text message lit up the screen: "We're watching."

Michael's pulse quickened. He knew it wasn't a threat; it was a promise. The Hand was always watching. They always knew. And now, as the legacy of chaos loomed over him, Michael realized he had only one choice. He couldn't destroy the Hand. But maybe, just maybe, he could outplay them.

Turning away from the cityscape, Michael descended the stairs into the shadows below. He had one last move to make. And this time, he would create the chaos.

• • • •

IT STARTED SMALL. A leaked document here, a whisper in the right ear there. Michael began playing the game the Hand had perfected, planting seeds of doubt, setting traps for those who thought they controlled the chaos. He knew he couldn't fight them head-on. But if he could turn their own weapon against them, if he could create just enough disorder in their ranks, maybe, just maybe, he could expose them for what they were.

It wasn't long before the cracks began to show. Rival factions within the Hand started turning on each other, their carefully crafted plans unraveling as Michael fed them disinformation. The chaos was spreading, but for once, it wasn't under the Hand's control. Michael had become a ghost in their machine, an unseen force manipulating the manipulators.

But with every move he made, the danger grew. The Hand's reach was vast, their power nearly limitless. Every time Michael thought he was one step ahead, they reminded him just how deep their roots went. Yet he kept going, driven by the knowledge that if he stopped, if he hesitated for even a moment, the Hand would swallow him whole.

The world around him was changing. Protests erupted in major cities, economies faltered, governments toppled. It was chaos on a global scale, the kind the Hand had always thrived on. But this time, Michael wasn't just a victim of their game. He was a player.

As the storm raged around him, Michael knew there was no going back. The legacy of chaos was all-consuming, and he was caught in its center. But for the first time in his life, he felt a strange sense of control. He had become part of the very chaos he had spent his life fighting.

5. Lessons Learned

The fallout from the case had left deep scars, not just on those directly involved, but on everyone who had watched it unfold. As the dust settled, the city was left with an eerie sense of quiet, a silence that could only come after a storm of chaos. The prosecutor, now far removed from the events that had changed the course of his life, sat in the dim light of his office, reflecting on all that had transpired. The world, as he once knew it, had been permanently altered, and with that change came hard lessons—some that he wished he had learned earlier, others that still felt too painful to fully accept.

For all the accolades, for all the praise that had followed the exposure of one of the most insidious criminal networks, the victories tasted hollow. The headlines proclaimed justice had been served, but the prosecutor knew better. The truth was far more complicated than the black-and-white narratives the public clung to. Justice, as it turned out, was more of an illusion than a reality—a fleeting concept that bent and shifted based on power, influence, and, most of all, money.

He had spent months unraveling the web, tracing the flow of billions through offshore accounts, uncovering layers of deceit so intricately woven that it was hard to believe anyone could have built such an empire without being caught earlier. And yet, they had. The organization had thrived for years, its tentacles reaching into every facet of society—politics, business, even law enforcement. There were moments when he had questioned if he was part of the very system he was trying to bring down. The lines blurred more than once, making him wonder if the pursuit of justice was worth the price he was paying.

In the beginning, the case had felt like a beacon of hope. There was a sense of righteousness that fueled him, that made every sleepless night and every close call feel like it was part of something larger, something meaningful. But as he dug deeper, he began to see the cracks. Not just in the system, but in himself. How many rules had he bent to get here? How many times had he compromised his own ethics, telling himself it was for the greater good?

The lesson that stung the most was that corruption was not just external. It wasn't confined to the criminals he had spent years hunting down. It lived inside every person who justified a wrong decision with the promise of a future good. He had seen it in colleagues, in the people he once trusted implicitly. Some had been seduced by the power that came with proximity to wealth, others by the simple human need to belong to something larger than themselves, no matter how dark that thing was.

One of the earliest lessons he had learned in law school was that the law was designed to protect the innocent, to maintain order. But in reality, it often became a weapon for the rich and powerful, a tool to bend the world to their will. In his naïveté, he had believed that if you worked hard enough, if you played by the rules, you could expose the truth and bring about change. That belief had been shattered.

The case had brought to light not just the crimes of the organization, but the deep flaws within the very institutions that were supposed to uphold justice. The trial had been a spectacle, filled with drama, twists, and betrayals. Witnesses who had once sworn to tell the truth turned out to be on the payroll of the very criminals they were testifying against. Evidence that should have sealed convictions disappeared, buried by bureaucratic red tape or, worse, bribes that no one could trace. And through it all, the prosecutor found himself becoming more cynical, more hardened to the idea that the truth alone could save anyone.

He had seen the faces of victims—people whose lives had been torn apart by the greed and corruption of a few powerful individuals.

But even they were not untouched by the poison that ran through the veins of the system. Some had tried to fight back, others had accepted their fate, believing that no one could truly stand up to the machine. And in moments of weakness, the prosecutor wondered if they were right.

The lessons he had learned were not the ones he had expected when he first stepped into the courtroom. He had thought it would be a straightforward battle of good versus evil. Instead, it had been a maze of gray areas, where morality was a shifting target and where justice was not a clear outcome, but a compromise. In the end, the organization had fallen, but at what cost? There were casualties on both sides, and not all of them were counted in the final tally.

Some of the most painful lessons came from the personal relationships he had lost along the way. People he had once considered allies had turned against him when the stakes grew too high. The pressure to make deals, to compromise, to let certain things slide in exchange for bigger wins became overwhelming. There were moments when he almost gave in. Almost. But in the end, he had stuck to his principles, even when it meant standing alone.

The aftermath of the case left him questioning everything—his career, his choices, his future. He had won, technically. The criminals had been exposed, their operations dismantled. But it didn't feel like a victory. Too many loose ends remained, too many questions unanswered. The system he had believed in so fervently had shown itself to be flawed, and the world of black-and-white had been replaced with shades of gray that he struggled to navigate.

One of the hardest lessons he learned was about trust. Trust in people, trust in institutions, and, ultimately, trust in himself. He had believed in his own moral compass, but the case had shown him how easily it could be swayed by external forces. The temptation to take shortcuts, to cut deals, to look the other way had been real and ever-present. And while he had managed to resist, he had seen what those choices had done to others. Good people, people with the best of intentions, had been corrupted by the very thing they sought to fight.

The prosecutor sat in silence, staring out the window at the city below. It looked peaceful now, but he knew better. Beneath the surface, the same forces that had fueled the chaos were still at work, waiting for their moment to rise again. He had learned that no matter how many heads of the hydra you cut off, another would grow in its place. The battle wasn't over; it never would be. But at least now, he knew what he was fighting.

In the end, the lessons were simple but profound. The world was not a fair place. Justice was not always served. And sometimes, doing the right thing meant making sacrifices you never thought you'd have to make. The prosecutor had paid the price for those lessons, but he had emerged stronger, more resilient. He had learned that the fight for justice was not about winning or losing—it was about enduring, about standing firm in the face of overwhelming odds, even when the outcome seemed uncertain.

As he closed the file on the case, he knew one thing for certain: he was changed. He had come out the other side a different person—wiser, perhaps, but also more wary. The lessons he had learned would stay with him for the rest of his life, shaping every decision, every move he made. And while the chaos may have subsided for now, the hand that fueled it was still out there, hidden in the shadows, waiting to strike again.

6. A Hand in the Shadows

The air in the dimly lit room was thick with the scent of cigar smoke and the weight of secrets. No one would have guessed that behind the lavish facade of this opulent, old-world mansion, shadowy deals were being forged that could shake the very foundations of the global economy. It was a place where power didn't just reside, it thrived—quietly, insidiously, and always in the shadows.

On the surface, the room seemed like any other study belonging to a man of wealth. Heavy oak bookshelves lined the walls, brimming with leather-bound volumes that no one had read in years. A polished mahogany desk sat proudly at the center, its surface reflecting the glow of a single brass lamp. But beyond the books, beyond the gold-leaf paintings, lay an invisible world. One where every whispered conversation was worth billions, where silence could cost lives, and where loyalty was as fleeting as the flicker of a flame.

The man sitting behind the desk had a face that was as forgettable as his demeanor was calculated. He had mastered the art of blending into the background, of becoming invisible while manipulating the most visible levers of power. He was simply known as "The Broker," though few had ever met him in person, and fewer still knew his real name. His influence reached into boardrooms, political offices, and criminal networks alike. For years, he had been the unseen hand guiding events from behind the curtain. No one ever saw him coming. They only felt his presence when it was too late.

Tonight, The Broker was awaiting a visitor—a young prosecutor who had been digging too deep into things better left buried. For months, whispers of this prosecutor's name had begun to circulate in the circles that mattered, and while The Broker normally didn't concern himself with low-level lawmen, this one was different. He was persistent. He was smart. And more worryingly, he had come closer to unraveling the web of offshore accounts, shell companies, and money laundering schemes than anyone else ever had.

The knock on the door came, low and deliberate. The Broker smiled faintly. "Enter," he said, his voice smooth, almost soothing.

The door creaked open, revealing a man in his mid-thirties, tall, with an air of determination about him. His eyes were sharp, filled with suspicion and a flicker of unease. He was not used to being in places like this—places where the rules of the world seemed to bend and shift.

"Mr. Larkin, I presume?" The Broker leaned back in his chair, his fingers steepled in front of him.

"Prosecutor Larkin," the man corrected, stepping into the room. He let the door close behind him with a heavy thud, though the silence that followed felt even heavier.

The Broker smiled, as though amused by the formality. "Ah, yes. Prosecutor. My apologies." He gestured to the chair across from him. "Please, have a seat."

Larkin hesitated for a moment before taking the offered seat. His eyes scanned the room, taking in every detail, but he found nothing overtly sinister. Just wealth. And power. And a sense of something much darker lurking beneath.

"I understand you've been asking a lot of questions, Prosecutor," The Broker began, his tone conversational, but with an undercurrent of something far more dangerous. "Questions that might lead you into places you don't want to go."

Larkin met his gaze, unwavering. "I'm just doing my job."

"Are you?" The Broker's smile didn't reach his eyes. "You see, there's a difference between doing one's job and overstepping. And from what I've gathered, you're dangerously close to the latter."

"I'm not afraid of threats," Larkin shot back, his voice steady. "If you think you can intimidate me—"

"Oh, I don't deal in threats, Mr. Larkin," The Broker interrupted smoothly. "Threats are crude. Inefficient. No, I much prefer... persuasion. A nudge here, a favor there. It's remarkable what people are willing to do when properly incentivized."

Larkin's jaw tightened. He had expected intimidation, but this was something else. Something far more subtle—and far more dangerous.

"And what do you want from me?" Larkin asked, leaning forward slightly, his hands resting on the edge of the desk.

The Broker's smile widened ever so slightly. "What I want, Prosecutor, is for you to stop. To walk away from this case, from the questions, from the people you've been investigating. In return, I can offer you a future far more... prosperous than the one you've imagined."

Larkin didn't flinch. He had heard these kinds of offers before, though never quite this directly. Still, there was a part of him that was tempted. A part that had been worn down by the months of dead ends, by the late nights, by the gnawing doubt that he was making any difference at all.

But he had come too far. "I can't do that."

The Broker's expression didn't change, but there was a shift in the air, a subtle tension that seemed to settle over the room. "Can't, or won't?"

"Both," Larkin said firmly.

For a long moment, neither man spoke. The silence stretched between them, thick and oppressive. Finally, The Broker leaned forward, his eyes locking onto Larkin's with a cold, calculating intensity.

"Do you know what happens to people who say no to me, Mr. Larkin?"

Larkin held his gaze, though he could feel his pulse quickening. “I’m sure you’re about to tell me.”

The Broker chuckled softly. “They disappear, Prosecutor. They vanish into the ether, their names erased from every ledger, their faces forgotten by the world. And yet... their influence remains. Quietly, persistently. Because you see, the world doesn’t need to know who’s pulling the strings. It only needs to feel the pull.”

Larkin leaned back, his mind racing. He had heard rumors of people disappearing—whistleblowers, journalists, even politicians—but he had always assumed it was just that: rumors. Now, sitting across from the man responsible for it all, the weight of the reality began to sink in.

But he couldn’t let fear guide him. Not now.

“I’m not going anywhere,” Larkin said, his voice steady despite the turmoil swirling inside him. “You can try to make me disappear, but I’ll fight you every step of the way.”

The Broker’s smile faded, his eyes narrowing slightly. “I was hoping you’d be more... reasonable.”

Larkin stood, his heart pounding in his chest. “Reasonable? You think I’m going to let you keep controlling everything from behind the scenes? That I’m going to let you manipulate lives, destroy families, and walk away clean? Not a chance.”

For the first time, The Broker’s composure cracked ever so slightly. His smile tightened, and the air around him seemed to darken.

“You’ve made your choice, Prosecutor,” he said, his voice low and dangerous. “I hope you understand the consequences.”

Larkin didn’t reply. He turned and walked toward the door, his footsteps echoing in the oppressive silence of the room.

As he reached for the handle, The Broker’s voice cut through the quiet. “One last thing, Mr. Larkin.”

Larkin paused, his hand hovering over the door.

"If you continue down this path, you won't just be fighting me. You'll be fighting an entire system. One that has existed long before you were born and will continue long after you're gone. You're just one man, Prosecutor. And men like you... you don't win."

Larkin didn't turn around. "We'll see about that."

With that, he opened the door and stepped out into the night, leaving the shadows of the room behind him. But he knew, deep down, that the real shadows had only just begun to close in.

Milton Keynes UK
Ingram Content Group UK Ltd.
UKHW042338121024
449589UK00001B/62

9 798227 299116